Sally.

The Host

Book Two of The Virus Series

Damien Lee

Prologue

"Come on, sleepyhead. Time to get up!"

Kara recoiled as sunlight burst into the room, shielding her eyes as Abigail tied back the curtains, her jet-black hair swaying as she spun around. Kara pulled the duvet over her head with an indignant grunt.

"Come *on*," Abigail sang, sustaining the last syllable as she threw herself on top of her girlfriend.

"Hey!" she called, struggling under the pressure. As she fought to free herself from her quilted embrace, she could hear Abigail giggling.

"Stop!"

She managed to escape, eyes filled with fury. They locked stares, each showcasing their most venomous scowl. Seconds passed, with Kara gradually succumbing to the allure of her girlfriend's deep azure gaze. She could feel the tension in her face easing, and when Abigail started to smirk, she knew she had lost.

They both laughed, falling back into the mattress, a tangle of arms, legs, and bedsheets.

"What time is it?"

"I told you: time to get up!" Abigail smiled, tenderly brushing the long brown hair behind Kara's ear. "The boys have been out and got the rest of the food from the corner shop."

"Really?"

"Yup, there's *so* much. We won't need to go back out for at least a week."

Kara propped herself up. "Really?"

"Enough to feed all five of us. Leanne is making breakfast as we speak."

Kara squeaked in excitement. She leapt out of bed and pulled on the long-sleeved top she had draped over the chair the night before. Then, grabbing the jeans that lay nearby, she hopped on one foot as she struggled to pull them up. Abigail laughed at her feverish efforts.

"Oh, so you'll get up when there's food involved?"

"You know it. I'm *starving*. Did they have any trouble?" Kara fastened her jeans and turned back to Abigail. Her smile had faded, her eyes lowered. "What's wrong?"

"They—uh—they saw Jo out there."

Kara sat down beside her and took her hand, interlocking fingers.

"I just wish she'd leave, y'know?"

"I know." She ran her thumb over Abigail's cheek, catching a solitary tear that escaped her eye. "There's nothing we could've done. She *wanted* to go out there."

Abigail closed her eyes, breathing deep.

"Hey." Kara placed both hands on her girlfriend's face, tilting her head. She waited for her eyes to flutter open, for the shimmering azure pools to stare back. "What's wrong?"

"I just don't want that to happen to you."

"It won't."

"How can you be sure?"

Kara took a deep breath, trying to find the right words. "Because Jo left to find supplies on her own. I'm never going to leave your side. Everything we do, we do it together. I'm not going to die."

"Promise?"

Kara smiled, lightly kissing her girlfriend's lips. "I promise."

She felt Abigail's fingers run along her arm, down to her hand, then intertwining with her own.

"C'mon." Abigail smiled. "Let's go and eat."

Kara allowed herself to be pulled up from the bed and led out into the dark corridor. Whilst her eyes had not welcomed the harsh sunlight, she still preferred the upper quarters. Downstairs, with every window boarded, they relied solely on candlelight.

They reached the top of the stairs, where the clink of cutlery and plates drifted up from the floor below. Kara ran a hand along the banister to guide her through the gloom. As they headed downstairs, she could hear Dan and Leanne's voices rising up to meet them.

"There were only one or two left in the street. Most had moved on towards the park area," Dan said.

"And they didn't spot you?"

"Nope. Made it there and back without issue."

"Is the shop empty now?"

"Pretty much. Sam thinks we can do another run, but I think we're going to have to start looking further afield."

"Where is Sam?"

"Went to check the radio again."

Leanne sighed. "I don't know why he bothers. It's a waste of time."

Kara followed Abigail into the kitchen and saw the pair standing beside the table. Both turned as they entered the room.

"Morning," Leanne chimed, her usual smile radiant in the candlelight. "Who's up for pancakes?"

"Pancakes?" Kara cocked an eyebrow, glancing around the room in anticipation of a punchline.

"Yep. The boys found a load of that ready-made pancake mix. Only needs water."

Leanne retrieved a plate piled high with pancakes.

"Holy shit!" Kara hurried to the table, hand-in-hand with Abigail. They sat in their usual places, while Leanne set five paper plates. Just past her, Dan turned off the small hexi-stove they used to cook their meals. He busied himself washing the pan while Leanne placed the pancakes down.

"There's no fruit left, but we've got syrup if you—"

The pair were already devouring their portion. The pancakes were dry and absorbed all the moisture in her mouth, but Kara didn't care, putting extra effort into swallowing before cramming in more. It had been almost twenty-four hours since her last meal, and she wasn't going to let superficial things like choking get in her way.

Dan laughed as she raised the plate to her mouth, catching the few crumbs that had escaped.

"Bloody hell, you really like pancakes," he chuckled. He sat down opposite her, with Leanne at his side.

"I really like *food*," Kara said, speaking through a mouthful. She grabbed a water bottle and took a hefty swig. "Thank you," she said, wiping her mouth.

"Don't thank me, Leanne is the super-chef." He placed an arm around his wife, planting a kiss on top of her head.

"You're the one risking your life for us." Leanne shoved him playfully, only to be pulled back into a tighter embrace.

"It wasn't just me. Sam came as well. I'd better let him know his breakfast is waiting."

Dan made to rise from the table, but stopped when Leanne placed a hand on his shoulder.

"I'll go. You eat—you deserve it."

She took one of the candles and stepped cautiously into the gloomy corridor. The trio watched the darkness envelop her and the flame as she made her way towards the stairs and disappeared from sight.

"So what's it like out there?" asked Kara, motioning towards the boarded windows.

Dan wiped his mouth, almost hesitant to answer.

"Not as bad as it was," he eventually replied. "Most of them have moved on. There are a few still loitering, but we managed to get there and back without being noticed."

"Abi said Jo's still out there?"

Dan's gaze flicked to Abigail, who stared forlornly at the table. "Yeah, she's there."

"Any sign of her leaving?"

"No. She's still right outside. It's almost as if she remembers, you know?"

It had been nearly three days since Abigail's cousin had ventured out on her own. Two since she had returned.

They had heard the snarling first. Then came the assault on the front door. When she looked out of the upper floor window, Kara had seen Jo, covered in blood, the flesh on the left side of her face stripped back to reveal a dripping, skeletal grin. She had persisted for hours, slamming against the door before trying to prise the boards from the windows.

Whilst the rest of the undead roamed aimlessly, Jo seemed driven, eager, desperate to get back into the house they had sought refuge in almost a week ago. Even now, despite the rest of the undead moving on, she remained outside.

"Where is she now?"

"Last I checked, she had moved down the side of the house. If she makes it into the back yard, we're going to have to find another way out to do supply runs."

Kara reached for Abigail's hand. She looked up, her eyes glazed with tears.

"Are you okay?"

"Yeah," she said, and ran the back of her hand across her eyes. "We've just eaten pancakes! I can't remember the last time we had them."

"Probably last year when we stayed at that little bed-and-breakfast in the Lake District."

A flicker of recognition illuminated Abigail's face. "Oh yeah! The one that had that cute little tree swing overlooking the lake?"

"The very same."

"That was beautiful."

"Reminds me of that one we stayed in when we visited the Highlands."

"Oh, and that place on the Isle of Wight."

"Jesus Christ," Dan laughed. They both glanced at him across the table. "You two are barely out of your teens, and you've already been further afield than me and Leanne."

"We're twenty-four!" Kara retorted. "Hardly teenagers."

"You're still well below us forty-somethings."

"Speak for yourself, Daniel." Leanne returned to the kitchen, her eyes narrowed and her lips pursed. "*I* haven't hit forty yet."

"And even when you do, you won't look a day over twenty-one, love."

"Hmm." She looked away as Dan planted a kiss on her cheek.

"Where's Sam?" Kara asked.

"He said he'll be down in a bit. He's still checking that bloody radio."

"Well, I hope he comes down soon." Dan spoke slowly, his voice deliberately raised. "I'd hate for someone to eat his pancakes because he took too long."

"Shh!" Leanne hissed, slapping him on the shoulder. "Jo might—"

An abrupt thud caused them all to jolt.

"There, you see," Dan beamed as footsteps echoed above them, "he's coming down."

Thunderous footfalls came down the stairs and Sam raced into the kitchen.

"Guys, we've got a problem!"

"Whoa, what's up?" Dan asked.

A response came in the form of cracking, splintering wood from the next room. Kara jumped to her feet. Visions of Jo prising away the window boards filled her mind.

"They're survivors," Sam gasped. "I saw them outside and motioned for them to come over."

"You what?" Dan ran to the cupboard and retrieved his baseball bat. The snapping wood ceased, replaced by the sound of smashing glass.

"They're getting in!" Leanne cried. She clung to Dan for support, but he shrugged past her as he rushed toward the noise and disappeared into the darkness. Sam and Leanne scrambled after him.

"They've got guns, Dan!" Sam's voice sounded from the next room.

Kara grabbed Abigail and pulled her towards the cupboard.

"C'mon!"

The dwindling candlelight from the kitchen all but vanished as they jumped inside and slammed the door. The smashing glass became muffled, but still competed with their frantic breaths as thin slivers of light flickered through the slats in the cupboard door. Kara peered through, only able to see the kitchen table and the pair of candles atop it. She listened to the clamour in the next room.

A scuffle.

Metal striking metal, and dull thuds.

Leanne screamed.

The commotion continued, escalating in pitch as it spilled into the hallway.

"Get them out of here," a gruff voice called. Kara readjusted her position, trying to see more of the kitchen.

"Dan!" Leanne wailed, her sobs piercing the stillness.

"Get them out!"

Her cries faded, but the sense of grief remained. Tears welled in Kara's eyes; she was certain of Dan's fate. Only one outcome could've prompted such heartbreak from Leanne. But what about Sam?

When footsteps sounded in the kitchen, Kara froze, praying the assailant hadn't heard her moving, or her frenetic breathing. She felt Abigail's hand clamp over her mouth, clearly sharing her concern.

The figure stepped through the kitchen as two others appeared behind him. They all wore the same dark clothing, one carrying what looked like an assault rifle, another carrying Dan's baseball bat, which was now slick with blood. The leader turned to his companions.

"There are five plates here. There must be others."

The words floored Kara. She could feel Abigail trembling, her hand still clamped over her mouth.

"Let's spread out and find them. We can't go back with just two."

A silent agreement amongst the trio prompted them to disperse.

One approached the back door while another stepped out into the hallway.

The man wielding the rifle approached their hiding place.

Kara squeezed her eyes shut, resigned to her fate. She heard a door swing wide, but it didn't belong to the cupboard. An almighty roar sounded.

"Fuck!" The man at the back door stumbled as Jo darted into the house and lunged for him, saliva spilling from her mouth as she sunk her teeth into his arm. His screams reverberated around the room, as Kara watched from her limited vantage point. The grappling pair disappeared behind the table, the man's pained shrieks pitched high above Jo's voracious moans.

The gunman dashed away from the cupboard and around the table, just as the third man re-entered the kitchen.

"What the fuck's going on?"

The gunman answered by firing three shots.

Jo's savage growls cut short, replaced by the whimpering of her victim.

"She got me," the man cried, "Timo, she got me!"

"I know," the gunman replied. He raised the rifle and fired again.

Silence enveloped the kitchen, the shot still ringing in Kara's ears. She looked to the side as more black-clad men stepped into the room.

"What happened?" one of them asked.

"Grayson got bit." The gunman turned and motioned for the door. "Let's go before more of them turn up."

The procession withdrew from the kitchen, their footsteps fading to silence as they left the house. Kara remained still, listening as an engine roared outside. She turned to face Abigail as the vehicle sped away, colliding with what she suspected were walking corpses as a diminuendo of thuds sounded.

Although she couldn't see her, she felt Abigail's arms wrap around her neck.

"Please don't ever leave me. Please don't die," Abigail said, in a whisper racked with sobs.

"I won't. I promise."

1

Lisa's footsteps echoed around the military base as she strode through the hallway. Narrow beams of light shone through the barricaded windows—the first rays of the morning sun. The pressing silence had become almost bearable after a week of coming to terms with it. Yet, she still longed for the soundtrack of her former life: birdsong, music, television, traffic… anything. The vacant army base was too big for the four of them, and it was easy to forget that others lived there. But now that their supplies were dwindling, she knew it was time to venture out.

She approached one of the rooms, where a dull *thwack* sounded on the other side of the door. It came again just as she stepped inside.

"Blondie!" beamed Gus Razor, flicking a knife between his fingers. "What brings you to my domain? I'd offer you a seat, but Action Man here is a dead weight."

Lisa glanced at the decomposing soldier on the other side of the room. It had been almost a week since he had shot himself in the head, yet Gus refused to have him removed, despite the growing smell. She pushed her nose into the nook of her arm as Gus hurled the knife. It struck the soldier's abdomen, joining two other knife handles jutting out side-by-side

"What the hell are you doing?"

"Target practice." Gus leaned back in his chair and retrieved another blade, twirling it between his fingers. "You didn't answer my question. What brings you to my domain on this fine day?"

"We need to talk. Our supplies are running out."

"It was going to happen eventually."

"Yeah, but it wouldn't have been this quick if you hadn't been eating like a king every night."

Gus patted his stomach, sending ripples beneath the tight-fitting shirt he had recovered from the barracks. "How else am I going to maintain this majestic form? You'd have a bit more meat on you, too, if it wasn't for your night-time activities with Frankie."

"What are you talking about?"

"You're inseparable. I'm surprised he's not hanging onto your arse right now. Where is he, anyway?"

"He's still asleep."

"All shagged out, eh?" He offered a wry smile and flicked the knife into the air. Lisa watched its spinning trajectory until he caught it by the tip.

"It's not like that."

"You what? I hear you every night: *Oh, Frank, yes, yes, more, Frank, more.*" He clasped his hands together, his voice two octaves higher than usual.

"You're full of shit, Gus. We haven't even—" Lisa trailed off. She knew it was only adding fuel to Razor's fire of ridicule.

A knowing smile spread across his face. "Ah, I see. So *that's* why Frankie's been in such a grump these past few days; you're blue-balling the poor bastard."

"This isn't a fairy tale, Gus. We haven't run off into the sunset together, spending each night fucking and living happily ever after. This is survival."

"True, but I bet he wouldn't be as snappy if you gave him a bit."

"He's snappy because we're stuck here with *you*. But that's not what I came to talk to you about."

"No. You came to ask me to accompany you both on a supply run, right?"

Lisa stared, words evading her.

"I thought so. Well, the answer is no, Blondie. Drag Zielinski along if you need numbers. God knows he needs the experience."

He threw the knife at the corpse, striking parallel to its counterparts. The linear formation gave Lisa an idea.

"Wow, you really *are* incredible with those things."

Gus cocked an eyebrow. "No point gushing over me, sweetheart. I like my clunge clean and STD-free."

Lisa ignored the remark. Resisting the urge to lash out, she breathed deeply. "I'm not flirting with you, dickhead. I'm genuinely impressed."

"Ha! If you think that's impressive, you should see me with a gun." He jumped to his feet and retrieved a handgun from the table. "Be a sport and go and lift his head up for me."

"What?"

"Pull his head back. I want to see what's left of his pretty face."

Still confused, she made her way toward the dead soldier. The blood spatter on the wall from his self-inflicted gunshot had faded to a dark brown. Bits of skull and brain matter still flecked the paintwork. His body leaned up against the powerless vending machine, his head bowed, offering a glimpse into the gaping exit wound.

Lisa gripped his forehead and pulled it back towards the wall. She had expected resistance from rigor mortis, but the head moved freely. Her surprise must have been evident to Gus.

"You've not been around many stiffs, have you?" he sneered. "Rigor mortis wears off after a couple of days. Makes it a lot easier to dispose of the body."

"Oh, I'm sure you have plenty of experience with that." She released the soldier and made to step away, but his head flopped back down to his chest.

"Jesus, you're no Debbie McGee, are you? Hold it in place!"

Lisa exhaled and pulled the man's head back. "Now what?"

"Now witness some *real* skill."

Before she could react, Gus aimed the gun and fired three shots. She jumped aside, clasping her ears to stem the ringing.

"What the fuck?"

"Ta-da!" He strode towards Lisa and lifted the soldier's head in triumph, showcasing the bullet holes in both eyes and the void where his nose used to be. The grisly sight reminded Lisa of a half-melted snowman. She released her ears, shaking her head.

"You're a sick bastard, Gus."

"And you're a manipulative slag. Now fuck off."

The remark caught Lisa off-guard, and she instinctively swung a fist, connecting with Razor's jaw.

He remained unmoved.

A second or two of uncomfortable silence passed, then his fist smashed against the side of her head, sending her crashing into the table.

The ringing sound returned, this time accompanied by blurred vision, the room swaying as if she were at sea. She could vaguely see him approach her as her senses gradually returned.

"Remember your place, Blondie." Razor's words seemed to come from afar, despite his standing directly above her. "Step out of line again and I'll rip you apart—"

The door burst open. Frank stormed into the room, handgun raised, his head darting back and forth. His eyes met Lisa's.

"What the—Razor?" Frank pointed the gun at Gus, who began to chuckle.

"You said this isn't a fairy tale, Blondie. Yet here's your white knight rushing to rescue the damsel in distress. Are you here to slay the dragon, Frankie?"

Gus cackled as Lisa staggered to her feet.

"You've gone too far, Gus," Frank snarled. Gus laughed harder, arching his back, his face contorted into unequivocal glee.

Lisa pushed the gun aside. "No. It's not worth it."

"Not worth it? What the fuck did he do?"

"An eye for an eye, Frankie!" Gus chortled. "Remember that."

Lisa blinked hard, focusing on the room as it regained clarity. "Come on, let's get out of here. I need to clear my head."

"But he—"

"I said it's fine."

She ushered Frank out of the room, leaving Razor laughing in the company of the newly decorated corpse.

When they were in the hallway, Frank stopped to examine her face.

"I'm gonna kill that bastard."

"No, you're gonna come with me to find some transport."

"Transport? For what?"

"We need supplies. The food is practically gone, and we only have a handful of water bottles left."

Frank sighed, scratching his stubbled chin.

"I just need my gun and we're good to go."

"No need." Frank removed another handgun from the holster at his hip. One perk of discovering the army base was the extensive equipment it housed. Not only did it offer them tactical equipment such as belts and holsters, but it also afforded them regular changes of clothing. The matching camo and boots they both wore was one such example.

"How considerate." Lisa smiled as she took the gun, but the gesture sent shards of pain up the side of her face. She tried not to show it as Zielinski came down the stairs.

"I heard gunshots. What's up?"

"Nothing," Frank replied. "Just Gus being a prick, as usual."

"Yeah, that sounds about right. Where are you two going?"

"To get another van, we're doing a supply run today."

"What's wrong with the van you guys came in?"

"A bit cramped for four of us," Lisa replied. "Besides, if we split into groups, we can cover more ground."

"I guess I'm stuck with Razor?"

Lisa shrugged.

"Shit."

"Go and see if we're clear," said Frank. "I haven't heard anything, but with Razor firing early-morning potshots, there could be hundreds on their way."

Zielinski nodded and strode back up the stairs as the pair moved the barrels fortifying the door. The only other time they had ventured outside was to unload the guns and ammunition they had brought. Since then, they had stayed within the confines of the base. *No wonder Razor is losing his shit,* Lisa thought.

Once the barrels were clear, they pressed themselves against the door, waiting for Zielinski's confirmation.

"Okay, you're good."

They swung the doors wide and stepped outside. The air was warm, despite the sun barely having risen. *It's going to be another hot day*. The notion didn't appeal to Lisa. The smell of stale sweat was one she thought she had grown accustomed to, but as Frank stepped past her, it made her nose twitch.

While the base had an abundance of practical equipment, it lacked any basic amenities for personal hygiene. Deodorant, soap, and running water were all things she had taken for granted before the outbreak, but now she longed for them more than ever.

She followed Frank over to their LGV, conveniently positioned below the windows on the first floor: their getaway plan if things turned south. Fortunately, living with the other criminals had been relatively innocuous. Until today. She massaged her cheek as she climbed into the van.

"That's going to bruise," Frank said.

"Probably."

"That fucking prick. What's he playing at?"

"It was self-defence. I punched him first."

"Why?"

"He called me a manipulative slag."

"Then you had every right to punch him."

Lisa leaned back in her chair as the LGV rumbled to life. She propped her feet on the dashboard as they trundled down the dirt path towards the main road.

"He's getting worse," Frank murmured. "He's flipping his lid at the slightest things. I've never seen him like this before."

"Really? I had him pegged as a lunatic from the moment we got here."

"Well, yeah, but he's circling the drain. He threw that bottle at Zielinski yesterday, just because he was breathing too loud."

Lisa nodded, her gaze flitting from tree to tree as the road meandered through dense woodland.

"I think we need to find somewhere else," Frank continued.

"Really?"

"Yeah, it's not safe there. Besides, it'll be a lot easier just the two of us."

Lisa considered the option. Whilst it would be nice to get away from the two criminals, the army base offered a great deal of security. "Where would we go?"

"I don't know. Somewhere else. Find our own place, secure it, and—"

"Live happily ever after?"

"Precisely."

"Pfft."

"What?" Frank asked.

"I think we need to be realistic. All of our weapons are there. It's also a lot more secure than anywhere out here." She gestured towards the endless fields which had displaced the woodland. Aside from a distant barn, there were no structures, buildings, or any sign of habitation.

"It's our safety *inside* I'm worried about."

"Well, how about we find a car, get back to the base, and see how our supply run goes? You never know, Gus might not make it back."

"That's if he goes."

"If he refuses, shoot him. Problem solved."

They veered onto another road that led towards Doxley. The small town loomed ahead, with a procession of cars abandoned along the way. Lisa sat up as Frank pulled over at the side of the road.

She looked ahead, straining her eyes, trying to make out the figures in the distance. Their movement was slow and gradual. The undead had clearly not seen them as Frank leapt down from the driver's seat.

"Shall we?" He closed the door and waited for Lisa to meet him at the front. The weight of the handgun against her palm was reassuring, but did little to alleviate her racing pulse as she stepped beside him, her gaze still fixed ahead.

"Let's hope one of these has keys." Frank strode towards the nearest vehicle. "Oh nice, first time lucky."

He dangled the keys before sliding into the driver's seat. Lisa felt a flicker of relief. She turned away from the hostile town and approached the car, where Frank sat perplexed.

"What is it?" she asked.

"No fuel."

"What?"

She stepped back as Frank pushed open the car door and approached the next one. "Come on, we might have some luck with the others."

Lisa strode past him and approached a bright orange SUV. The tinted windows offered no indication of zombies within, but the prospect of peering inside wasn't appealing. Images of the undead slamming against the glass were certainly a viable premise. Instead, Lisa pulled the door wide and took a step back. The seats were unoccupied, and, after leaning inside, she saw the keys were left in the ignition.

"Yes," she whispered. She reached over and tried to start the engine, but it whined in protest. She tried again until she noticed the fuel gauge; it was empty.

"Same with that one, too."

She looked up as Frank approached, motioning to the car behind him.

"Someone has siphoned the fuel," she muttered.

"It looks that way." Frank gestured to the other vehicles parked nearby. All the fuel covers were open, some with the fuel caps lying idly next to them.

"They've done them all? Who needs that much diesel?"

"That's not what worries me." Frank stooped down beside the SUV and dipped his finger in a dark circle beneath the fuel tank. "This is still wet. They've only done it recently."

"How recently?"

Realisation dawned as Lisa turned back towards the town. The slight movement she had seen earlier had ceased. Now, a sizeable pickup truck moved instead. It was getting closer, coming towards them.

2

A gentle knock roused Amy from her slumber. She hurriedly patted her hair into an acceptable state as she sat up in bed.

"Come in."

The bedroom door creaked open, pushed aside by a laden breakfast tray. Ben stepped into the room, wearing a sheepish expression and the clothes he had recovered from the previous occupants of the cottage they were taking refuge in.

"I brought you breakfast in bed." He raised the tray, placing it at the foot of the bed. A steaming mug of coffee stood beside an apple and a couple of crackers. Amy felt her heart melt.

"Oh, you're so sweet." She scooted up, careful not to spill the coffee beside her feet. She leaned over and picked the mug up carefully.

"Did you sleep well?"

She nodded as she took a sip, and looked away. In truth, she had barely slept for more than a couple of hours since they had found the abandoned cottage over a week earlier. If it wasn't every miniscule noise keeping her awake, it was the floods of tears she regularly shed. Losing her mother was a pain like no other, and even now, it still felt as raw as the day she saw her die.

She set the mug on the bedside table and reached for the crackers. "Did you?"

Ben shrugged. "I barely sleep anyway, to be honest. But with my room being east-facing, I get the sun streaming in at the crack of dawn."

An awkward silence formed. Amy's initial reaction was to suggest he sleep in her room. But would that be crossing a boundary? They had been inseparable for over a week now, and despite the odd flirtatious comment, Ben hadn't really shown much of an interest in her. Maybe he wasn't a forward guy. Maybe he was as nervous as she was. Maybe he didn't feel the same, and she'd risk pushing him away. The prospect was enough to keep her from mentioning it, and instead she focused on the second cracker.

"These are really good," she mumbled through her mouthful, horrified as a spray of crumbs covered Ben. "Oh my god, I'm sorry." She clasped a hand to her mouth as Ben laughed.

"Don't worry," he said, brushing down his trousers. "And make sure you enjoy them—they're the last ones."

"Have we run out already?" she gasped, wiping the excess crumbs from her mouth.

"Yeah, we knew it would happen eventually, right?"

"What do we have left?"

"A tin of sardines and a couple of biscuits—oh, and the apples, of course."

Amy looked down at the solitary apple on her tray. When they had found the cottage with a freshwater well in the back garden, she had been overjoyed. It was the perfect setup. After discovering the apple trees in the adjacent field, she figured they would never have to leave. But now the harsh truth was starting to sink in.

"We're going to have to go into town, aren't we?"

Ben chewed his bottom lip, as if trying to find an alternative solution, but after a few seconds, his eyes met hers. "I think so."

"Which one?"

"I don't know. But we'll have to—"

A clattering outside prompted Ben to his feet. Amy scrambled out of her sheets, dashing after him as he approached the window. They peered down into the garden, where an undead couple staggered on broken limbs. The male shuffled closer to the house, dragging a foot that was bent at a right-angle. His female counterpart walked slower, hunched to the side—an effect of the gaping hole in her ribcage which had caused her body to crumble.

Whether it was due to lack of sleep, Ben's kind gesture, or the news that they would have to venture out, Amy was unsure, but tears welled in her eyes. The undead couple appeared around the same age as she and Ben. Aside from a few minor variations, their physicality was the same, too. Is that how they were going to end up? Was it only a matter of time?

"They haven't seen us," Ben muttered. "We're going to have to wait for them to pass before we can leave."

"Good." Amy wiped her eyes. "It'll give us time to plan our next move."

"Yeah." Ben turned towards her and froze. His eyes moved down her body before darting back up to her face. "I—uh…" He cleared his throat, directing his gaze skyward, his face adopting a crimson hue. "Sorry, I'll let you get dressed."

Amy felt her heart lurch with the sudden realisation she was wearing only a t-shirt and underwear. She longed for the security of the duvet, but felt reluctant to show her embarrassment. Whilst she wrestled with her thoughts, Ben took a step back, looking in any direction but hers.

"I—I'll wait for you downstairs."

With that, he turned and stepped out of the room. Any other day, his awkwardness would have made her laugh, had she not been so mortified herself. Once he had left, she scooped up her black leggings from the floor and quickly dressed. Whilst Ben had sourced a change of clothes from the previous occupants, she had not been so lucky. The lady of the house had been a robust woman, ten sizes bigger than Amy, and with only a multitude of summer dresses, trousers, and oversized blouses on offer, she had no option but to keep wearing the same blood-spattered clothes she had arrived in.

She stared at her reflection in the floor-to-ceiling mirror, dismayed by the haggard, puffy-eyed woman looking back. She tried to fix her hair, but the thick tangle was going nowhere other than a messy bun. Retrieving the apple from the bed, she picked up her coffee cup and made her way downstairs.

The rustic staircase creaked with each step, a fitting composition given the old-fashioned aesthetic of the cottage. An oak coffee table stood in the centre of a large living room, surrounded by a three-piece leather suite. Overhead beams, stained the same colour as the furniture, added to the rustic appeal of the cottage.

Amy turned into the kitchen to find Ben sitting at the table. He looked up as she approached, his eyes flitting nervously as she took a seat opposite.

"This coffee is great, thank you." She smiled as she took another sip, watching him relax again.

"Yeah, shame there's no milk."

"You don't like black coffee?"

"Nah, not really. I'm more of a tea man, anyway." He raised his cup, taking a hefty swig.

"Oh no, tea without milk is gross."

Ben scrunched his nose as he placed the cup back on the table. "Yeah, you're right."

They shared a laugh before the clatter outside came again. Amy winced, putting a finger to her lips as the sound drew closer. Despite having boarded all the windows (using some floorboards from the third bedroom), she was uncertain how secure the house was. If a zombie really wanted to get in, there was a good chance it'd be able to.

"So where shall we go?" she whispered, sinking down in her chair as if a smaller posture would make her less detectable.

"I don't know. I think the closest town is probably Newchurch. Either that or Bealsdon."

Neither option sounded appealing. Newchurch was the first town they had approached after leaving Gordon Chesterfield's slaughterhouse. The ongoing carnage was the worst they had encountered. Before they had even made it past the outskirts, they had opted to leave in search of an alternative. Bealsdon, on the other hand, was less populated. Yet, they had already ventured there in search of supplies for Frank and his band of misfits.

Amy wondered if the group were still alive. Whilst she felt an unrelenting guilt for leaving them behind, she knew it had been the only option. She couldn't imagine any of them had survived. The number of zombies that had crowded their lorry, bringing it to a halt—there was no surviving that. She thought back to her time in the supermarket with Elaine and Glen and felt an instant pang of sorrow. Glen was dead. She knew that much. How he'd come to be infected, she wasn't sure. He'd still managed to drive the lorry into her grandparents' house. *The lorry full of food.*

"I've got it," she said, louder than intended. She flinched as one of the zombies growled outside, earning a snarling exchange from its counterpart.

"What?" Ben whispered.

"The lorry that Glen crashed. It was full of food. That would keep us going for months."

Ben narrowed his eyes. "Hmm, it's a good idea. Bit of a trek, though."

"True, but it's less likely to present a threat."

Ben nodded. "Only…"

"What?" She watched him for a response.

"What if it's already been ransacked?"

Amy's gaze dropped as she ran her fingers over the cup. "The only other people who knew it was there were the others, and they…"

"They might not have died. For all we know, they might still be out there and have already taken the supplies."

"I guess. Can you think of anywhere else, though?"

"Well, Newchurch is closer. We could swing by there first?"

"Okay, and if we don't get any joy, we can head back to my grandparents' house."

"Right…" Ben offered a smile, which faded when one of the zombies approached the window. It moaned against the boards, leaning in close, almost as if it were trying to see through the windows: an unsettling notion that made Amy glad she had shut all the curtains.

"…Just as soon as these guys move on."

***

"Kara, please. We need to come up with a plan."

"It's a bit late now. We need to keep moving."

Kara looked down the desolate street, relieved to see it was empty. She held Abigail's hand as they dashed to the end of the road, their bodies hugging the row of terraced houses as they passed.

"We don't even know where we're going. We're sitting ducks out here."

Kara slowed as they reached the last house. With a kitchen knife held in front of her, she peered around the corner.

It was empty. A further row of houses greeted them, along with a series of abandoned cars. She looked back up the street and saw they were still the only ones there.

"Okay." She turned to face Abigail, running a hand through her dark hair. "This way will take us out of Doxley."

"I don't know *why* we're leaving Doxley. Why did we leave the house?"

"It was insecure. And you heard that guy, the zombies would've heard the gunshots. We were lucky to get out when we did."

"But why are we leaving? Why not find another house?"

"What if those guys come back? What if they search *every* house? You saw what they did to their own guy. What they did to Dan."

Kara fought to suppress her grief. The dead man's body resurfaced in her mind's eye. After they had left the refuge of their cupboard, they had discovered Dan's corpse in the living room. A bulbous swelling covered the right side of his head, with his vacant eyes staring blankly at the ceiling. She guessed an impact from a blunt object had caused the enormous bump, possibly his own baseball bat, when the men had disarmed him. The thought of it happening to her or Abigail made her feel sick. She squeezed her girlfriend's hand, more for reassurance that she was still there and had not succumbed to a similar fate.

"Why did they do that?" Abigail's voice trembled.

"I don't know."

"They were looking for people. Trying to round us all up. Where do you think they took Leanne and Sam?"

Kara shrugged, longing for an answer herself. She glanced around, ensuring they were still alone.

Abigail took a deep breath, composing herself. "So what do we do?"

"We need to find more people. We can't survive on our own, and I'm not going to lose you." She pressed her forehead against her girlfriend's, desperate for her to see sense.

"Okay," Abigail whispered. "But we can't escape on foot."

"Do you have a better idea?"

Abigail motioned to one of the cars. "Why don't we look for keys? We could drive out of here."

"Do you suddenly know how to drive, like? Because I don't." She forced a laugh, trying to conceal her fear, but she was sure the trembling knife gave her away.

"I mean… Do you think it's that hard?"

"I don't know. But I don't really want to hang around to find out. I wouldn't know where to begin."

Abigail's eyes were still fixed on the car.

"Come on, we're not crash test dummies." Kara pulled her around the corner, and together, they rushed further down the road.

"Well, how do you hope to find people if we leave Doxley?" Abigail asked.

"I don't know. I just want us to get somewhere safe. We can come up with something then."

"But there's nothing out there, only a few old farms and—"

"The army base!" Kara interrupted, turning to face Abigail once more. "We can go there! I bet it's full of soldiers. They can protect us."

The hesitant look on Abigail's face told her she needed to try harder. "Just think: it's secure, it'll be well-stocked, and those guys back there wouldn't dream of attacking an army base! The soldiers will have guns."

"Do you think it'll be safe?"

"A hell of a lot safer than being out here."

Kara looked past Abigail and felt her stomach lurch.

"We need to move. Now!"

She yanked Abigail's hand, dragging her further down the street. She didn't look back, but she heard the chorus of shrieks and roars as the crowd of zombies began their pursuit.

3

Frank lay motionless on the back seat of the SUV. He aimed his gun at the window, watching as the pickup stopped beside them, its rumbling engine growing louder as it slowed to a crawl. As soon as a face appeared, he would fire. It was their only chance. He tilted his head slightly until he could see Lisa crouched in the footwell, aiming her gun towards the opposite window. They had both sides covered.

"Where the hell did this come from?" The male voice sounded close as the pickup door slammed shut.

"Are you sure it wasn't here before?" answered a female voice.

Frank listened to their diminishing footsteps as they approached the lorry.

"Are you kidding? If I had seen it, I would've suggested putting the barrels in here. This can hold way more than that shitty pickup." The sound of the lorry's door opening and closing came in quick succession. "There's no keys."

Frank slowly twisted his head back towards Lisa. She presented the key chain in her free hand, and he could see the flicker of a smirk on her face.

Master thief. He focused back on the pickup that filled his window. A collection of oil drums was secured to the back, filled with what he surmised was fuel. Lisa's previous query played on his mind. *Who needs that much diesel?*

Before he could ponder the question, the footsteps grew closer. He tightened his grip on the gun, eye over the sight, visualising one of the newcomers stepping into his line of fire. A single trickle of sweat ran down the bridge of his nose. Despite it being early morning, the heat in the car was overpowering. He tried to remain focused as the droplet tickled its way down his cheek.

"What are you doing?" the woman asked.

"The engine is still warm."

The man was right behind the SUV.

"They have to be here."

Frank could see a shadow looming beyond the window.

Come on, you bastard. Just a little more.

"We're not on a scouting mission," the woman pressed. "Let's just get this stuff back."

The man's shadow disappeared as he crouched beneath the SUV.

"Oh, I don't intend to bring them with us." He rose to his feet again, this time directly in front of Frank's window, reaching for the door handle. "I'm going to kill th—"

Bang!

Frank's shot shattered the window and a section of the man's face. The tinted shards exploded out, granting the

34

sun's blinding rays access to the car. Frank recoiled from the light as Lisa leapt out of the other door.

"Billy!" the woman screamed.

A series of gunshots pierced holes in the car. Frank dropped into the footwell, shuffling to Lisa's open door as bullets whizzed overhead. The woman's gun clicked empty, offering him the chance he needed. He darted outside, joining Lisa near the front of the SUV.

"You shot Billy," she muttered.

"Yep, and now I'm going to shoot her."

Frank chanced a look over the top: the woman stood beside the pickup, her eyes fixed on him, along with her handgun. He dropped to the ground as a bullet ricocheted off the roof.

"Shit," he hissed. "She reloads quick."

"Or she's just grabbed Billy's gun. Why do you think I haven't moved yet?"

"Because you need my help?"

"Pfft, in your dreams, pal."

Frank smiled as he lowered himself to the ground. He peered beneath the SUV, checking for any sign of movement.

Nobody was there.

He listened, but no sound came.

A sudden wave of paranoia struck him as he envisaged the woman standing over him. He rolled onto his back, but saw only the clear blue sky.

"I don't see her," he whispered.

Lisa reached up and yanked the wing mirror from the car. She eased it above the engine block, changing the angle ever so slightly. Another series of gunshots came, blasting the mirror to pieces. Lisa recoiled, hissing in pain as she cradled her hand.

"Are you okay?"

"Yeah," she said through gritted teeth. "She's behind the pickup."

Frank lowered himself to the ground once more and scanned the area beneath the other vehicle.

"I still can't see her."

"I've got an idea. Go to the back of the car and wait for my signal."

Frank wanted to query her, but the urgency in Lisa's voice told him to remain quiet. He shuffled to the back of the SUV.

"Shoot the barrels," called Lisa, louder than necessary. "We'll blow the bitch to kingdom come!"

She raised her hand, signalling Frank to wait. It only lasted a second before she gave a thumbs-up. He jumped up, immediately spotting the woman sprinting away from the pickup. He raised his gun, but Lisa beat him to it. She fired three successive shots, causing the woman to poleaxe the ground.

"Nice one," Frank praised. "Let's get their guns and get out of here."

"Hold on, she's still alive."

The woman was writhing in the distance. "So what? She's zombie food. And we'll be next if we don't get out of here." He studied Lisa's torn expression. "What is it?"

"Something she said."

Lisa looked back and forth, checking for threats as she jogged towards the downed woman. Frank followed suit, noticing a small gathering in the distant town.

"We need to be quick; those guys will be here in a minute or two."

Lisa dragged the woman onto her back. Her eyes rolled as she fell in and out of consciousness, blood trickling from her mouth.

"Hey!" Lisa shook her, waiting for her eyes to focus. "What did you mean 'scouting mission'?"

The woman coughed. A gurgling sound spilled from her throat.

"He... He'll..."

"What?"

Frank looked away from the exchange as the erratic shrieks and wails grew closer. The congregation of corpses was sprinting towards them.

"Lise, we gotta go." He nudged her with his leg, but she ignored him, shaking the woman, whose eyes were beginning to glaze over.

"Tell me!" she snapped.

A coughing fit came in response. The woman wheezed, "He'll... kill... you."

Her head lolled back, hitting the ground as Lisa released her lifeless form. Lisa looked pensive for a second until she jumped to her feet.

"Okay, let's get out of here. You want the pickup?"

Frank shrugged. With a parting glance at the encroaching crowd, he jumped into the driver's seat and started the engine. He waited for Lisa to perform a U-turn in their LGV, his gaze fixed on his mirrors. The zombies were close; close enough for him to make out the wild, hungry look on their faces, close enough for him to match the roars with each gaping mouth.

Once Lisa had set off, he followed, cursing the slow progress of the pickup. He watched the horde in his mirrors as they engulfed the woman's corpse. Her final words played through his mind. *He? Who's 'he'? and what does he want with all this fuel?*

Frank looked over his shoulder at the numerous oil drums. There was no way that many had been filled in one morning. It had to have been gathered over a number of days. Either that, or it had been a collective effort. The prospect of more people posing a threat was one he didn't want to consider. What if this guy had even more people working for him? It was bad enough having to spend every day cooped up with Gus, but what if more people stumbled across the base? What if they attacked? It was one thing having to fight off an undead army, but how would they fare against a human one?

Back at the base, Frank pulled up alongside the LGV, where Lisa was waiting.

"I've been thinking," she said as he hopped down, "what if there are more out there?"

"I know, that's what I'm thinking, too. This place isn't safe." He motioned back towards the smashed barrier.

"Yeah. We need to secure it."

"Secure it? We need to get the hell out of here."

"And go where? Those guys had guns, too. We don't know what else they've got or how many there are. If we leave now, we're sitting ducks. I think we should secure this place, to keep out the dead *and* the living."

"How? There's nothing here to secure it with."

Lisa massaged the bridge of her nose, her eyes closed. "I don't know."

"We could broach it with Gus, see if he and Zielinski want to get stuff to secure this place while we look for food?"

"It couldn't hurt."

"Let's just hope he's in a talkative mood. If he lays hands on you again, he's dead."

"Don't worry, I always get what I want. He'll realise that soon enough." Lisa squeezed his arm as they stepped through the double-doors, where Gus and Zielinski greeted them.

"Well, if it's not Bonnie and Clyde. What the fuck have you two been doing?"

"Getting shot at," Frank replied. "You?"

"*We've* been checking our supplies. Did you know we've got fuck all left?"

Lisa scowled. "We talked about this earlier."

Gus stared at her, as if searching for a response. Or a memory. After a prolonged silence, he looked back at Frank. "Who's been shooting you?"

"A couple just outside of Doxley."

"They seemed to be working for someone," Lisa added. "They syphoned all the fuel from the cars. There's barrel-loads of the stuff. We've brought them all back."

"Fuel? What do they want fuel for?"

"Farming equipment, generators, a jumbo fucking jet. How are we supposed to know?"

Zielinski chuckled, earning a glare from all three of them. His eyes appeared bloodshot below his heavy lids.

"What happened to you?" Frank asked.

"Don't even start," Gus snapped. "He's been on the Jamaican woodbines, hasn't he. Found a stash yesterday in the barracks and been puffing away in secret."

Zielinski's glazed eyes and relaxed stature offered credence to the account.

"Anyway," Gus muttered. "We'll bring those barrels in after we've had breakfast. Come on, I'm starving." Not waiting for a response, he turned and walked towards the bar area.

"So, did you kill them both?" Zielinski asked as Frank and Lisa followed.

"We came away with their truck full of fuel. What do you think?"

"I think you're lucky to get out of there."

Frank scoffed. "Yeah, no thanks to you. You can go out next time."

They entered the bar where Gus was perched on a stool up against the pool table. A single bottle of beer stood before him, along with the remaining rations.

"Quit harping on and get over here." He waved a sealed pack at them. "We need to talk."

"Agreed." Lisa approached the table, choosing the furthest stool away from Razor.

"Fucking hell, Blondie, I don't bite." Gus busied himself tearing the corner of the packet.

"No, but you can certainly pack a punch."

He looked up with furrowed brows, his eyes flitting between her developing bruise and Frank as he sat down opposite.

"Here," Gus muttered, shoving the remaining bags across the table. He eyed Zielinski, who sat next to the pair. "What are you doing? You're not on a fucking parole board. Get your arse on this side, Zielinski."

The man chuckled, obeying the command. Frank grabbed the ration packs and handed one to Lisa.

"So, where are you taking us for food?" Gus mumbled, still working at ripping open the packet.

"We need to split up," said Frank.

"You can fuck right off. I'm not babysitting this wet wipe on my own." He motioned to Zielinski, who closed his eyes, clearly trying to compose himself.

"We don't have a choice, Gus. We need food and we need stuff to secure this place."

"What are you talking about? This place is secure."

"There isn't even a barrier. All we've got is a few metal drums holding the door in place, and wooden boards covering the windows."

"It's worked so far."

"Yeah, against zombies. The *wooden* boards won't do shit against bullets."

Gus growled as he slapped the ration pack down. He retrieved his knife and sliced open the top, squeezing the contents onto his plate. The maroon gloop landed with an unappetising splat.

"That's got to be the worst chilli con carne I've ever seen," he grumbled. "Blondie, why don't *you* cook? I bet there's an apron in that kitchen with your name on it."

"Why me? Because I'm a woman?"

"Precisely. I bet you can knock up a good egg-and-chips if you put your mind to it. Show Frankie here that you're housewife material."

Frank clenched his fist, fixing Gus with an acid glare. It went unnoticed as Gus toyed with the contents of his plate.

"Well, sorry to inform you, but I can't cook," Lisa replied. "I tell you what I can do—I can shoot." She placed her handgun on the surface of the pool table. Gus sneered, still fixed on his meal.

"Nobody is gonna be cooking shit if we don't have any food," Frank said, changing the subject to alleviate the tension. "We're splitting up. Lisa and I will get food. You two will get things we can use to barricade this place."

Gus shovelled a forkful into his mouth, smacking his lips, his face contorted into a grimace.

"I'm not convinced," he managed after swallowing the morsel. "As far as I'm concerned, we need food more than anything. Those water bottles won't last forever either. You two get food, me and Zielinski will get water. This place is secure enough."

Frank caught Lisa's eye. The look on her face told him she was thinking the same as him: when they left, they wouldn't be coming back.

Zielinski suddenly held a hand to his mouth, suppressing a giggle.

"Are you sure he's not taken anything else?" Lisa asked, eyeing him warily.

"Fuck knows," Gus muttered. "Zielinski, shape up, or you'll be spending the night outside."

This prompted a further giggling fit.

"I'll fucking chin you in a minute!" Gus snapped.

Zielinski snorted and held a hand up in apology. "Sorry."

The room fell quiet, filled only with slurping and lip-smacking as they ate the last of the rations.

"This stuff tastes like zombie shit," Gus groaned, eyeing the food in disgust.

"That's an idea," Zielinski said thoughtfully. "Do zombies actually shit?"

The trio exchanged a confused glance.

"No, think about it," he continued. "They're all munching on flesh, yeah?"

Frank nodded half-heartedly.

"So where does it go? If they don't shit it out, they'd burst, wouldn't they?"

Gus shoved his plate aside with a nauseated grunt. He eyed Zielinski with contempt as he took a swig of beer.

"Well, their organs still work, according to those documents we found," Lisa offered. "Their heart still pumps blood, lungs still work. It means they don't decompose as fast as normal corpses."

Gus cleared his throat, clearly not enjoying the conversation. It was then Frank realised Lisa was deliberately winding him up. He could see the mischievous glimmer in her eyes, just above the bruise that had started to form. *If he goes for her again, he's dead.* Frank subtly gripped his handgun as Lisa continued.

"I can't remember reading about their digestive system, but I guess it still works."

"So, they shit out the rotten flesh?" Zielinski sniggered.

"Yeah, I guess they do."

"Oh, fuck that!" Gus bellowed. He jumped to his feet, the bar stool clattering to the floor. "I'm not having zombies shitting in my yard! Zielinski, sort your fucking head out. We're going to find a way of keeping them out."

With that, he stormed out of the room, chuntering obscenities under his breath.

Frank turned to Lisa, who grinned back at him. "I told you, I always get what I want."

4

Amy grabbed her rifle once the shambling couple had disappeared into the distance. She picked up a box of bullets, but without pockets, she wouldn't be able to carry them.

"Okay, they're long gone," she announced as she left her room and made her way downstairs. Ben was waiting for her next to the front door, his rifle slung over his shoulder, a handgun pointed downward.

"Can you carry these?" she asked, offering the box of bullets. "I need some new clothes. Something clean, with pockets!"

Ben smiled and took the bullets. "We'll do some retail therapy while we're there."

"Oh, ha ha. It's okay for you, you've got a change of clothes."

"Yeah, and I look like my grandad," Ben countered, holding his arms out to offer a better look at his attire. "All I'm missing is a flat cap and pipe."

Amy chuckled as he pushed the makeshift blockade from the door. Not convinced a lock would keep out the undead, he had opted for additional security in the form of a chest of drawers topped with a vase ("So we can hear it break if the zombies try to get in."). Once the door was clear, he turned back to her.

"You ready?"

"Yeah, let's get it over with. The sooner we're out, the sooner we're back, right?"

"Don't want to come up with plans A-Z?"

"Wow, you really are a comedian today, aren't you?" Amy rolled her eyes. "I think I broke a rib, I'm laughing so much."

Ben cast her a parting grin before prising open the door and stepping outside. Amy glanced back and forth, eyeing both sides of the road as they made their way towards their vehicle. The red sports car had saved them on more than one occasion, but while it excelled in speed, it failed miserably in air con. The suffocating heat billowed out as Amy opened the door.

"Oh god," she muttered, turning her head away.

"Windows down," Ben said, climbing into the car. Reluctantly, she fell into the seat, the electric windows gradually falling.

"What I'd give for some rain."

"You and me both, I'm surprised that well hasn't dried up yet."

Amy's heart quickened. She hadn't even considered how the heatwave could affect their water supply. As they turned onto the main road and picked up speed, she made a mental note to collect some water bottles.

They raced along the country lane, indifferent to the occasional ravaged corpses of human and animal alike. It dawned on Amy how detached she had become since the start of the pandemic. Where once she would have found herself upset at the sight of standard roadkill, now she felt nothing, despite the horrific deaths the corpses surrounding them must have met. After accepting the death of her mother, her grandparents, and presumably the rest of her family and friends, she was left with no feeling at all.

She turned to Ben. "How are you holding up?"

"Huh?"

"With this… with everything. Your dad… and Fran."

Ben's eyes darkened. He gripped the wheel tighter, pushing the car harder. "I'm fine."

"Really? We can talk about it if you like?"

His mouth twisted, and she couldn't tell if he was trying to conceal anger or sorrow. After a few seconds, he exhaled and glanced back at her with a faux smile. "Nah, I'm good. How about you? You've lost everyone, too."

Amy looked ahead at the approaching treeline. "It's hard. I have good days and bad days, y'know? I don't think it's going to get easier, but I'm hoping it'll be more manageable." She side-eyed Ben, hoping that if she opened up, he would too. "I can't stop thinking about them."

Ben nodded, his gaze flitting back and forth, almost as if he were searching for answers. Either that, or contemplating his own loss. "Yeah, I know what you mean."

"I just miss them so much." Amy's voice broke. Tears rolled down her cheeks, her sudden grief astounding her.

Ben looked across, equally surprised. "Hey, hey."

He pulled over at the side of the road. "I'm here for you. Always." Reaching across, he placed an arm around her shoulder.

Amy hurriedly wiped her eyes. "I know, sorry. I don't know what came over me."

"It's perfectly natural. Honestly, how *couldn't* you cry after everything you've been through?"

Amy inhaled a shaky breath, trying to regain her composure. "You seem to manage fine." It came out with much more of an accusatory tone than she'd intended.

Ben slid back in his seat. "Are you kidding? I've cried almost every night."

Amy blinked, taken aback by his confession. She had wanted him to open up, but she hadn't anticipated he would. After a moment of silence, she finally asked, "Is my company really that bad?"

She cursed herself the minute the words escaped her lips, but humour had always been her go-to resource in awkward situations. She looked at Ben, relieved to see a smile on his face.

"Ha! It's your company that's getting me through this. If I didn't have you… I don't know what I'd do."

Amy smiled, the feeling of unease replaced by a nervous excitement. He needed her just as much as she did him. They were on the same page, or at least she hoped they were—

A loud rustling beside the car halted her train of thought. The foliage parted, and out sprung a bloodied deer, emitting a ravenous cry as it darted towards them.

Ben started the car and swerved into the road, narrowly escaping impact from the undead animal. Amy looked back as other beasts joined the pursuit. She counted two deer, a stag, and what looked like a fox. While the animals were fast, the sports car proved faster, and with a roar of the engine, they turned onto another road and escaped their pursuers.

"It's like Noah's Ark back there," Ben muttered, his eyes flitting between the windscreen and the rear-view mirror. "I just hope Newchurch isn't as eager to see us."

As it turned out, Newchurch had become a ghost town. Each house they passed either had broken windows, doors left ajar, or both. The congregation of abandoned cars stood in a similar state, with many sporting additional bloody smears on the paintwork. Yet, there was nobody in sight.

"It's deserted," Amy muttered, as the rumbling engine permeated the pressing silence. "Where is everyone?"

Ben shook his head. They turned onto the main high street, where a gigantic shopping centre stood. The looming white building sported a multi-storey car park to its side, with a cumulation of abandoned cars rammed into the exit ramp. The entrance of the building had once sported floor-to-ceiling windows, which had been reduced to a carpet of glass. The car pulled up alongside the entrance, which offered a clear view of the unoccupied space within.

"Looks like every shop has been ransacked," Amy muttered.

"Yeah, let's see what's left." Ben grabbed the rifle and jumped out of the car. Amy joined him near the front, the sound of crunching glass beneath her feet heightened by the sheer silence of the town. They remained still, listening for any noise.

"Come on," Ben whispered, striding through the smashed entrance and into the derelict shopping centre. Despite the lack of electricity, the interior was well-lit, courtesy of the huge skylight running across the entire roof. Sections had been broken, with blood spatter evident amongst the remaining shards. The source of the damage became clear once they rounded the escalators.

"Shit." Amy held a hand to her mouth. Corpses were scattered around the food court as far as she could see. Some had smashed through tables, others were impaled on upturned chairs, with one corpse floating in a large water feature that had subsequently turned a rusty brown.

"The zombies must be on the roof. Or were, at least," she said, looking up at the colossal skylight. "They must've walked onto the glass."

"Maybe. I just hope they *were* zombies."

Amy looked back at Ben with wide eyes. The prospect of living people falling through the glass had not dawned on her. But now, it was all she could think of. She glanced around the rest of the complex. The large, open area allowed for an unobstructed view to most of the stores and the upper floors. More importantly, it gave them a good vantage point, should any zombies still be present.

"Reminds me of Dawn of the Dead," Ben muttered.

"Huh?"

"You know, the film?"

"I've never seen it."

Ben's eyes widened. "You've never seen it? It's a classic."

"I'm not really a horror fan." Amy shrugged. "I mean, I'd watch them, but I'm the type who hides behind a pillow whenever anything jumps out."

Ben grinned. "And look at you now: a total badass surviving a zombie apocalypse without a pillow in sight."

"Sometimes we're forced to change. It's not always for the better." Amy replayed her mother's death. The loss of her family, her friends, and humanity weighed heavily once more. She fought back the grief that threatened to overpower her, and swallowed hard. Slinging his rifle over his shoulder, Ben wrapped his arms around her, pulling her in close.

"You're still alive," he said, resting his chin on top of her head. "That's all that matters."

Amy nodded. She reduced her breaths to steady, rhythmic inhalations as he stroked her back.

"We're in this together, and we're going to get through this."

She nodded again, her face rubbing against the buttons of his shirt. The strong musty smell of the fabric caused her to suppress a laugh.

"What is it?" Ben asked, leaning back to look at her.

She met his eyes, trying to maintain a stoic expression. "You smell like an old man."

It was no use. As soon as Ben's eyes narrowed, she couldn't help but smirk.

"Oh, hilarious," he said, trying to suppress his own amusement.

Amy wiped her eyes. "Sorry."

"Come on, then," he chuckled, "let's go and find some new clothes so I don't have to put up with any more abuse."

They left the fast-food plaza behind. But then it dawned on Amy that while there were no obvious signs of the undead within the shopping centre, that didn't negate the need for caution. She looked into each store as they passed. Most were in darkness, the natural light of the skylight not reaching the confines of the windowless shops.

"So where do you normally shop?" Ben asked.

"I'm a Primarni girl, through and through."

He laughed. "Well, imagine I've given you a credit card with no spending limit. Where are we heading?"

Amy stopped in her tracks and seized his arm. "There."

Not waiting for a response, she hurried over to the high-end fashion store set over two floors. Whilst it was as gloomy as the others, it appeared relatively untouched. A few discarded items and baskets littered the aisles, but aside from that, it looked relatively normal.

"Shall we?"

"After you." Ben swung his arm majestically towards the store, bowing as Amy passed.

"Such a gentleman. I bet you wouldn't be like this if it was full of people."

"No. I'd be shooting them all," Ben quipped.

"I meant *before* all this, you div. I bet you were one of those men who sat there looking all depressed while their girlfriend tried on clothes."

"Well, we'll soon find out."

Amy's heart quickened, trying to decide whether Ben was aware of what he had implied. She stepped cautiously down the aisle of clothes, casting a wary glance toward each open space. There was nobody there. Yet, she couldn't shrug off the feeling she was being watched. She turned back to Ben, who stood admiring a dark *Ralph Lauren* t-shirt.

He's got good taste, she mused. Yet, the feeling of being monitored by a sinister voyeur still made her feel uneasy. She grabbed a few items, balancing them carefully, before heading over to the stack of folded leggings.

"Hold up," Ben hissed. He dashed towards her, a number of shirts in one hand, and a gun in the other. "Don't stray too far. We need to stick together."

"Well, I'm going to try these on. Are you coming into the changing rooms with me?"

Despite the gloom in the shop, Amy could see Ben's cheeks flush red. She laughed, swatting his arm as she grabbed a handful of leggings. "I'm joking. I'm sure they'll fit. Come on, let's get these bagged up and get out of here."

"Right."

Amy led the way over to the sales counter, cautiously meandering through the racks of clothes. Whilst it had already occurred to her they may not be alone, the lack of sound proved reassuring. The undead had so far shown no inclination towards stealth attacks. In fact, the only quiet zombies she had seen were the dead ones.

They rounded the counter, finding every till smashed open. Loose coins littered the floor, with the rest of the cash gone.

"It's hard to understand the mentality," Ben said as he grabbed a large bag. He shook it wide, filled it with his chosen items, and offered it to Amy.

"It's the end of the world; if you're gonna die, you may as well die rich," she mocked, placing her clothes in the bag. She turned, but before she could walk away, Ben grabbed her wrist.

"Whoa, hold on. We said this was retail therapy. There's nothing therapeutic about having to carry your bags around. Allow me."

"And they say chivalry is dead."

"Nah, just everything else."

Amy handed over the bag and led the way out of the store.

It was then she noticed that the dull clunk of her shoes had merged with another new sound.

She stood still, trying to interpret the rhythmic scraping that continued even after she had stopped moving. It sounded close, and it was getting louder and louder.

"What's that noise?"

The words had barely escaped her lips before movement to the right caught her eye. The scraping stopped as she locked stares with the undead corpse that shambled around the corner. The dead man was one they had passed in the food court; the one who had taken a nosedive through the skylight and landed amongst the tables and chairs. The metal chair impaling his torso scraped the floor again as he rushed toward them.

"Move!"

They sprinted away as the previously dormant shopping centre suddenly stirred. The shattered glass crunched under countless feet, the echoic area reverberating growls and cries as the undead rushed them from all angles.

"Shit."

They stopped short when a group appeared at the end of the precinct, rushing towards them at varying speeds. Amy looked back and saw more racing behind them. *We're trapped.*

"C'mon!" Ben grabbed her hand and pulled her towards the powerless escalators. They ascended the steps two-at-a-time as the surge of zombies broke behind them and spilled onto the confined walkway, fighting to ascend as Ben and Amy reached the top.

"Now what?" Amy gasped, searching for an escape route. Some of the scrambling zombies broke free of their counterparts and ran up after them. Screeches from the nearby shops told her there were zombies up here, too.

"This way," Ben urged. He kept hold of her hand as they ran towards a fire escape. Amy looked back as the zombies rounded the escalators and sprinted after them, accompanied by others appearing out of the dilapidated storefronts.

"We gotta go up."

Ben's words brought Amy's attention back. Ahead of them was a sign pointing to roof access. Her stomach lurched. They were running towards a dead end.

***

"Are you sure they've gone?" Abigail asked, approaching the window beside Kara.

"Yeah." She stepped back to grant her girlfriend a better look at the street beyond.

She had no idea how long they had been hiding. It felt as though hours had passed since she had last seen a corpse wandering outside. The mob pursuing them had been fast, and Kara knew it would be risky to try to outrun them. After rounding the street corner, she had instinctively dragged Abigail into a nearby butcher's shop. The pursuing zombies had all raced past. All except one or two who shambled along on broken limbs.

While the butcher's shop had provided sanctuary, it came at a price. The gagging smell of rotten meat had engulfed them as soon as they entered. Even after the amount of time they had spent in the store, Kara had still not become accustomed to the cloying stench. It left a sour taste in the back of her throat. She pulled her shirt up over her nose as Abigail turned back to her.

"What should we do?"

"We can't stay here," Kara replied, her voice muffled by her t-shirt. "I think we should keep going."

"But we can't see much from this window. What if they're only halfway down the street?"

Kara turned to the door leading into the rear of the store. Curiosity had driven her closer to it when they had first entered, but the pungent smell of decaying flesh pushed her back like identical poles on a magnet. She guessed it housed the majority of the meat, but the possibility of it concealing an undead butcher did not go unconsidered.

"We could head through there," she suggested, hiding her trepidation. "It might lead up to the next floor. Maybe give us a better vantage point?"

Abigail looked at the door, her unease plain to see. "I don't know. We don't know what else is in here."

Kara nodded, searching Abigail's face for a solution.

"We need to think of something," she managed. "All it takes is for a zombie to see us through that window and we're dead."

They both stared at the glass, lowering themselves in unison behind the counter to better avoid detection.

"Okay, we'll go for the door." Kara spoke positively, more to convince herself than Abigail. "Let's see if we can get upstairs."

She stepped away from the counter and towards the closed door. The luminosity outside only stretched so far within the shop. The door itself was shrouded in gloom, doing nothing to ease her growing anxiety as she reached for the handle. In the back of her mind, she wondered whether the door would open. If it was locked, they'd have no choice but to venture outside and leave the rest of the store unexplored. The notion was one she favoured.

The handle turned with ease, along with Kara's stomach. She took a deep breath and pulled the door wide, revealing nothing but a black void and an overwhelming stench. The large knife trembled in her grip. She remained rooted to the spot, eyes set on penetrating the vast darkness, stomach fighting back the vomit that threatened to surface. She felt Abigail's hands brush against her hips, ready to pull her back should anything come lunging out of the void.

Seconds passed, with no movement, no sound, no indication of life—or death—at all.

Kara placed one hand over Abigail's. "Let's go," she whispered.

She took a step forward, but felt resistance on her hip.

"No," Abigail said. "I don't think we should."

Kara turned to reassure her, but no sound came out. Instead, she spun back to the darkness as a soft clatter drifted out. Before she could process the sound, others came. Rhythmic thuds that were getting louder and faster.

By the time she realised it was footsteps, it was too late.

She shrieked when the zombie lunged out of the darkness, reaching out for her face. She recoiled, stumbling into Abigail and then into the meat counter, where she hit the floor. The undead butcher landed on top of her, his foaming mouth inches from her face. With her forearm beneath his chin, Kara kept him at bay, avoiding his thrashing hands and snapping teeth.

"Kara!"

Abigail's scream sounded distant, as if it had come from the end of the street and not within the confines of the shop. Kara couldn't see her beyond the butcher's huge frame, even if she wanted to. Her efforts were on keeping him away, a task that was becoming more arduous by the second. The man was heavy. And Kara's strength was quickly starting to wane.

Suddenly, the zombie's head lunged forward and his body went slack. His wide eyes looked through her, his mouth hung loose, and as she shoved him aside, she noticed the meat cleaver jutting from the back of his head.

"Are you okay?" Abigail cried, reaching down and pulling her to her feet. Kara blinked, dazed and in shock. Abigail wrapped her in an embrace, which gradually returned her senses.

"I—I think so."

Abigail leaned back, casting an appraising eye over her. "Are you sure?"

"Yeah."

Her hands shook as she pulled her girlfriend closer, peering over her shoulder at the motionless corpse. The meat cleaver had lodged deep in the zombie's skull. Abigail had to have used a huge amount of force.

"It's stuck," she said. "I tried to pull it back out, but I couldn't."

"I'm surprised you didn't split his head in two." Kara tried to offer a laugh, but the shock of the attack still had her nerves on edge, and what came out sounded like a hoarse cough.

"Here." Abigail gripped both of her hands and ushered her away from the corpse. "Let's get out of here. If we stay out of sight, hopefully we can reach the army base without anything else happening."

Kara nodded, trying to ignore the flicker of guilt, and instead focus on Abigail's soothing voice. Her steadfast approach had almost got them killed. Now she began to doubt if the army base *was* a good idea.

5

"You've got a couple of hours," Gus told them, leaning out of the pickup truck. "Any more than that and I'm sending Zielinski out for food, and you two aren't getting back in. Clear?"

"Crystal," Frank shouted back from the LGV. "Same goes for you; if we get back with food, and you two haven't returned, you're not getting back in either."

The rumble of the engine drowned Razor's response as Frank started the lorry. Without looking back, he drove toward the end of the road.

"I don't know how they plan on fixing that," Lisa muttered, motioning to the destroyed barrier. "Or how they plan on keeping the zombies out. Short of building a wall, they'll be able to climb over anything that's put in their way."

Frank shrugged as he turned onto the narrow lane. "I don't care what they do, as long as they take their time doing it. It's nice to get away."

"Aww, you want to spend some time with me?"

"Of course, why wouldn't I? Maybe we can find somewhere nice and secluded and pick up where we left off? You can show me more of your tattoos."

"You've got Bob Hope and no hope, pal."

Frank shot her his best wounded-puppy expression.

"You've been watching too many films," she laughed. "This is reality. We haven't washed in over a week! I can smell you before I see you."

"So?"

"So, you're not coming anywhere near me while you smell like sweaty sourdough."

"Didn't stop you in the cottage," Frank laughed.

"That was day one. I assumed you were clean."

Frank cast her a mischievous grin.

"Ugh, you're gross."

"You know what those prison showers are like. Get in, get out, don't drop the soap."

"No, I don't. I'm not a *convict,* unlike some."

"Not through lack of trying, I bet."

"Some of us are too good to get caught." She patted Frank's leg sardonically.

"Ah, of course, the master thief."

Frank made another turn, taking them out of the encompassing woodland and onto the open road. Roaming fields surrounded them for as far as he could see. Not a single building, except for a lone petrol station. Whilst no cars were present on the forecourt, display cases had been upturned, windows smashed, and the store's contents strewn in different directions.

"What are you doing?" Lisa asked, as Frank pulled up alongside the building. "There won't be anything worth eating in there."

"I think you'll find there's something *really* valuable in there."

Frank reached beneath his seat. He found his shotgun next to the bolt cutters which Lisa had insisted on bringing. Grabbing the gun, he leapt from the vehicle, waiting for Lisa to join him.

"Care to elaborate?" she asked.

"You'll see."

They stepped inside, the broken glass and discarded food packets crunching beneath their feet. Frank looked around. Practically every shelf was bare. A few packets of crisps and bars of chocolate lay on the floor, with the odd bottle left in the powerless chiller. Behind the counter, every packet of cigarettes had been taken, as well as the limited medicine supply.

"See, there's nothing here," Lisa said, kicking an empty bottle aside. "We can take the last packets of crisps, but we'd be able to find more than this in a town."

Frank didn't respond; he'd found what he was looking for. Countless packets of chewing gum remained untouched at the front of the store. He picked up the box and grinned.

"At least we can have fresh breath. I might be able to steal a kiss now."

Lisa smirked. She slung the rifle over her shoulder and took one of the packets.

"You came looking for chuddy so you can get a kiss?"

"Nah, I came in here looking for condoms, but chewing gum was next on my list."

Lisa snorted, swatting his arm as she turned to leave.

"You're a dick, Frank Lee."

"Whoa, hold on," Frank said, jogging to catch up as she strode outside. "How do you know my last name?"

"Gus mentioned it. He was taking the piss saying if we ever got married, I'd be Lisa Lee, and I'd make a good double-act with Lucy Liu."

Frank sighed, shaking his head as they got back into the LGV. "So, what's your surname?"

Lisa chewed her gum with a smug grin. "Knowledge is power, my friend. And right now, I'm more powerful than you."

"Is that right?" he laughed as he started the engine. They veered back onto the road, moving slowly as he unwrapped his own packet of chewing gum. He bit down on two pieces, immediately hit by the strong taste of menthol.

"Good to clear your airways in winter." Lisa smirked at Frank's expression.

"Yeah, if we live that long."

"Are you kidding? We've got these." She produced the packets of crisps and chocolate she had taken from the garage. "This'll keep us going for months."

"You know sarcasm is the lowest form of wit, right?"

"Pfft, whoever said that was the victim of one too many sarcastic retorts."

Frank laughed. "So, do I get that kiss now, then?"

"Sure."

Lisa pursed her lips, but as Frank moved in, she blew a large bubble that popped in his face.

"Oh, thanks," he muttered, picking the gum out of his stubble, listening to Lisa's howling laughter.

"I'm sorry," she wheezed. "But you were asking for it."

Frank shook his head, trying hard to suppress his smile.

"Here." She leaned over and pressed their lips together, completely blocking his view of the road. He eased off the accelerator as her hand caressed his face, her tongue mingling with his. He took his hands off the wheel to roam over her back before she pulled away.

"There, happy?"

"Very."

He frowned when he felt an addition to his mouth. He picked out an extra wad of gum, prompting another snort of laughter from Lisa.

"Looks like I'm not the only master thief." She took the gum and popped it back in her mouth. She sat back against the chair.

"Did you—?" She leaned forward, reaching behind her back. "You unhooked my bra. Nice work."

"Magic fingers," Frank replied, raising his hand off the wheel. "They can do all kinds of wonderful things."

"Oh yeah? Like what?"

Frank grinned. "Knowledge is power, remember? Maybe you'll find out one day."

"Oh, touché."

"Could've found out at the cottage, if it wasn't for all those cockblockers."

"True. I wonder if they're still alive. Blob and Blubber will be long gone by now, but I hope Tina made it."

"I couldn't give a shit. It would've been ten times better if it was just us two."

"Yeah, without a doubt."

"Still, it's probably for the best we got interrupted. I doubt unprotected sex is a good idea during a zombie apocalypse. And I doubt old Ronald had condoms kicking about. We would've ended up looking after real babies instead of those adult ones tagging along with us."

He glanced at Lisa, concerned by her sudden straight face. "Are you okay?"

"Yeah," she replied. "But you don't need to worry about kids. I can't have any."

"Huh?"

"I'm sterile."

"How come?"

"Cancer." She looked back out of the window, staring into space. "I got it in my late teens. Had a full hysterectomy, but I got the all-clear. So, I guess it worked out alright."

"Oh, I'm sorry."

"Sorry for what? I'm still alive, and more importantly, no risk of any crotch goblins!" She beamed. But despite the smile, Frank was sure he could see sorrow in her eyes.

"Win-win, I guess." He reached across and patted her leg.

"That still doesn't negate the fact you smell like a hobo's armpit." She pinched his wrist and flicked it away from her thigh. "But nice try."

"Should've looked for deodorant in there."

"You need some soap in your life," Lisa countered. "Although you did give me a good idea just now."

"I did?"

"Yeah, talking about the cottage."

"What about it?"

"Well, why aren't we there anymore?"

"Because that fucking zombie hippy drove a lorry into it," Frank growled, recalling Glen's face before he put a bullet in his head.

"And what was in that lorry?"

Frank's eyes widened. "Oh shit, of course. That lorry was *full* of food."

"Do you remember how to get there?"

"Maybe from the base, but I don't know my way from here. Hell, I don't even know *where* we are."

"Well, what does that sign say?" She pointed at a billboard as they approached.

"*Eden Spa Hotel,*" Frank read, slowing the vehicle to a halt. "*The UK's first eco hotel.*" He looked past the sign at the vast, isolated building in the distance. "Means nothing to me."

"*Natural spring, solar power, infinity pool, jacuzzi,*" Lisa continued reading, leaning across Frank to see more. "Stuff the cottage. Let's go there."

"There?" Frank looked back at the distant building. "How is that going to have enough food to tide us over?"

"I'm not thinking about food. I'm thinking about a place we can secure and call our own. This place has a natural spring. That's a constant water supply. It's got solar power.

Hell, that jacuzzi might even work. Oh my god, it'll have showers, and *hot* water!" Lisa smacked her thighs excitedly. "When was the last time you were in a jacuzzi?"

"Fuck knows."

"There you go. Let's check it out!"

Frank didn't need telling twice. He accelerated down the road, noting the rows of solar panels, stretching as far as he could see.

"Christ, how much energy does a hotel need? And look at those!" He pointed towards the looming wind-farm in the distance. "You could power an entire town on all this."

"It's England," Lisa said. "How often do we get sun? They'll probably need both to keep the place running."

They veered onto the track leading up to the building, glancing out of both side windows, assessing the isolation. The spa certainly boasted a secluded location, but that meant nothing if it was already crawling with the undead. The tall metal fencing—normally reserved for building sites—ran the perimeter of the hotel, but the gap allowing vehicles through offered ready access. However, as they pulled into the car park, he was surprised to see there were no other vehicles there.

"Can't have been very popular."

"That's because it's not due to open for another couple of weeks." Lisa pointed to a banner on the side of the hotel. "C'mon, let's check it out."

They jumped out of the LGV and approached the large glass doors. The foyer within was gloomy, but looked in pristine condition. Shiny gold letters spelled out *Eden Spa Hotel* above a polished reception desk, topped with a computer monitor and a single chair behind it. A staircase veered off to the right, with a plush red carpet leading up to the next floor. To the left, a sign pointed towards the changing rooms.

"Well, I'm not sure how we're going to get in," Frank said. He tugged the door to clarify his point and met resistance.

"We could break in," Lisa offered. "If we're gonna stay, we're going to have to block these glass doors, anyway."

"True, but smashing them would draw attention."

Lisa looked around. "There's nobody here."

"We don't know that. There could be some inside."

"Okay, then let's have a look around. We'll need to see the layout first, anyway."

Frank nodded and led the way around the side of the building. The hotel had at least three floors and offered panoramic views over the Yorkshire Moors. They would be able to see any incoming threats for miles around. They just needed to find a way in.

"Wouldn't it be nice if somebody had left a fire door propped open or something?" Lisa said.

"Ha, we're not that lucky."

"Are you sure?" She pointed up. Frank followed her direction, checking out the uniform windows until he saw one on the top floor that was ajar.

"Well, unless you're secretly Spider-Man, I don't know how we're supposed to get up there."

"Not there. *There*." Lisa turned his head to one of the lower windows, which was also ajar.

"Okay, but how are we going to get up *there?*" The window was at least twenty feet above them, with no way of climbing up.

"Pull the van alongside the wall. We can climb on top and get in that way."

"Do you think?"

"Sure. C'mon, chop-chop."

Frank did as requested. When he was directly underneath the window, he jumped out and joined Lisa at the front.

"I still don't think it's high enough."

"If we both stand on top and you give me a boost, we can get in."

"If you say so." He followed Lisa as she scrambled on to the front of the lorry before hoisting herself on top. Their position allowed them to see into an adjacent window, which revealed a lavish hotel bedroom. A large double bed occupied one side, with a wall-mounted TV opposite and a desk and fridge beneath. A wardrobe stood at the far end of the room beside a door which he guessed led into a bathroom, and another which probably led onto the corridor.

"Holy shit, an *actual* bed," Lisa gasped. "We won't have to sleep on those military bunks anymore."

"True." Frank looked up at the window above them. It was only open an inch, but the gap was enough to make his heart sink. "Shit, it's got a window restrictor."

"What?"

Frank pointed at the thick white wire connected to the window. "See? It's like a window lock to stop it from opening any further. Even if we *do* get up there, we won't be able to open it."

Lisa pondered for a second before she smiled. "That's why we brought the wire cutters, dear."

"Oh yeah, because you knew we'd be breaking into a hotel?"

"Not really. I just didn't want a repeat of the last time I went looting and had to smash a bunch of windows."

"Right." Frank jumped down from the lorry and retrieved the wire cutters from beneath his seat. He climbed back up, offering them to Lisa as he examined the distance once more.

"Are you ready?" she asked, placing her rifle next to his at their feet.

"Sure. Let's do it." He intertwined his fingers and bent down, allowing Lisa to step into his palms. With her foot clasped tight, he lifted her higher until she could reach the window. She manipulated the wire cutters through the gap and forced the two handles together. Frank could feel her body shaking beneath his hand, until finally, an audible snap sounded.

"Yes," she whispered. "Push me up."

Frank readjusted his grip so he could lift her above his head. He watched as she scrambled through the gap in the window, his mind whirring.

If the hotel is closed, why is the window open?

He stared, waiting for Lisa to reappear. Waiting for her smiling face, or a sarcastic remark. Waiting for something.

The space remained empty.

Seconds passed, with his anxiety gradually increasing. *Why would they leave windows open?*

He stepped to the other side of the van for a better look at the hotel room, but the height restricted most of his view.

They wouldn't. Not unless they were planning on staying...

Frank finally heard movement in the room beside him, as realisation hit.

...Not unless they were still inside.

6

"We need to barricade the door!"

Amy scanned the rooftop from her position against the heavy metal door. It was barren—a vast field of gravel topped by the occasional ventilation system, and of course the smashed skylight. To the right of the building stood the neighbouring cinema complex, and to the left, a hundred-foot drop.

"There's nothing here!"

The metal door clanged as the undead crashed against the other side. Their muffled shrieks and howls interspersed with the assault as the door shook in its frame. Ben pressed his shoulder against it, struggling to maintain his footing on the loose gravel. He fumbled with a loose padlock, swinging the latch over, before clicking it in place.

"We don't have enough bullets."

Amy eyed the neighbouring cinema, contemplating how far they would have to jump in order to reach it. She ran over to the side, careful not to venture too close to the edge.

"What are you doing?" Ben called.

She ignored the query as she appraised the gap. It was almost nine feet wide and stood over another hundred-foot drop. Her heart hammered against her chest as she weighed up the options. The cinema rooftop was lower than the shopping centre. If they built up enough speed, they could make it across no problem. But what if they didn't?

"Amy!"

She turned back to Ben. "We have to jump."

"What?"

"Come here, quick."

Ben eased away from the door, leaving the padlock to withstand the assault. It held up well, but shook violently with every strike.

"Look," she said, pointing to the cinema, "we can make it."

"Are you crazy? What if we fall? What if—"

"We haven't got time. Let's do the 'what if's' once we're over."

She unslung the rifle from her back and hurled it over the gap. The gun sailed high before skittering across the cinema rooftop. Ben followed suit, throwing his own rifle, and then swinging their bag of clothes like an Olympian competing in the hammer throw. The bag sailed through the air, landing beside their weapons.

"Okay, now it's us." Amy breathed rapidly, her body trembling as they strode towards the door. She tried to ignore the metallic bangs, tried to ignore the prospect of the zombies breaking through at any second.

I can do this. I can do this.

She stared at the ledge, trying to steady her nerves. She imagined it was the same feeling a sprinter had before a race. The roaring zombies were the crowd. The prospect of living was her gold medal. The clamour of the door swinging open was her starting pistol. Not looking back, she sprinted forward as the zombies spilled onto the rooftop. She ran towards the ledge. Towards her only hope of survival…

…And jumped.

As soon as her feet left the ledge, she regretted her decision. The gap suddenly seemed so wide, the drop so steep. Her momentum carried her high into the air, yet what took only a second felt like a lifetime. She hit the rooftop hard. Her legs buckled, and she rolled onto her back. A tide of relief washed over her until she realised she was alone.

"Ben?" She lurched upright, her head darting back and forth. She took it all in within a second. The pair of rifles. The bag of clothes. Nothing else.

The wave of zombies on the shopping centre roof flowed over the top. Some attempted to make the jump, others merely strode off the end, but all plummeted to their inevitable death. Amy felt grief overwhelm her as she dashed to the edge. *How could he have fallen? He's taller, faster. He was right behind me. Wasn't he? Maybe he mistimed the jump? Maybe he managed to grab the side?*

The thoughts soon dissipated as the final zombie fell. She looked over the edge at the carpet of bodies that littered the alleyway. There were no figures clinging to the side, nor was there anywhere to hold on to. It was a sheer drop, one Ben certainly would not have survived. She scanned the corpses, trying to locate him. She wiped her eyes. The teary shroud only merged the bodies into a colourful blur. Then she saw him.

"Ben?"

"Yeah." He walked towards her from the other rooftop, slamming the open door as he passed.

"How did you—I thought you were dead!"

"Yeah, so did I when they burst through; I was next to the door. I managed to duck to the side as they followed you over the top."

Amy exhaled, tilting her head back towards the sky.

"Sorry," Ben called.

"Don't be silly, you're alive! That's all that matters."

"Yeah, well, that remains to be seen." He peered over the edge of the roof at the colossal drop below.

"True. You only get one chance. Don't mess it up."

"That's easy for you to say. You're already over there."

He took a few steps back, breathing deeply.

"It's not all bad. You've got a squishy landing now if you do fall."

Her attempt at humour did nothing to alleviate Ben's nerves. He closed his eyes, psyching himself up to jump.

"You need to give yourself a good run-up. You won't make it from there."

Ben opened his eyes and reconsidered the distance. He started taking a few steps back until the door behind him swung open. Just as it had for Amy, the metallic clamour served as a jolt for Ben as he raced forward.

He's too close.

The thought barely registered in Amy's mind before she saw him jump. He cried out, clearly aware he wasn't going to make it. His midriff struck the edge of the rooftop, cutting his yell short. The air blasted out of him as he scrambled to establish a grip, quickly slipping over the side.

"Ben!"

Amy lunged forward and grabbed him by the wrists. She slowed his momentum, but could feel herself being dragged over the loose gravel.

"Hold on."

She kicked out, her foot finding a pipe jutting out of the rooftop. She hooked her leg around it just as Ben's shoulders reached the ledge.

"I've got you."

With her foot as an anchor, she dragged him back up. It was then she saw the movement behind him. The zombie that had burst through the door had now reached the edge. It let out an eager shriek, darting forward and soaring through the air. It didn't reach the side, but it reached Ben.

Amy felt the weight double. They slid further down, the sudden yank almost causing her to lose her grip on the pipe. She could feel Ben bucking in her grasp, trying to free himself from the zombie. But in doing so, he was also freeing himself from her. She gripped him tighter, his head now the only part above the precipice. The undead corpse shrieked below, dragging Ben further. She no longer held his wrists, but his hands, which were slipping from hers.

"I can't hold on!" she cried.

With a final lurch, Ben swung to the side. One arm slipped free, but, based on the diminishing roar and subsequent thud, he had also freed himself of the zombie. Amy clasped his hand with both of hers. When he brought his other arm up, she grabbed both hands and dragged him back. She felt her heart soar when he heaved himself up, getting a leg over the edge and rolling onto his back. He had barely made it to his knees before she swung her arms around him.

"I thought I'd lost you," she whispered, her face nestled against his neck.

Ben stroked her back. "It'll take more than that to get rid of me."

Another zombie growled from the shopping complex. They watched as it emerged onto the rooftop. It looked around until it spotted them on the opposing roof.

"Come on," Ben said, breaking their embrace to retrieve his rifle. They looked on as the zombie made a feeble attempt to clear the gap. A sickening crunch sounded as it struck the ground, its angry wails still apparent.

"Now all we need to do is find a way down from here."

***

Anthony reached across the table and lifted a candle from its holder.

"Where are you going?" Heidi whispered, looking up from her tin of cold beans.

"I gotta pee."

"Okay, but don't do it over the balcony again. They saw you last time."

"Relax, I'll use the bucket."

Anthony stepped into the gloomy hallway, his footsteps muffled in the plush carpet. He passed their makeshift barricade by the front door: a combination of chairs, tables, and the empty refrigerator. The dead had tried to gain access three times, and each attempt had proven futile. The front room was a lost cause. Having found no way of covering the windows, they had opted to secure the door instead. They had heard smashing glass on the first night, but no further sound. That door had a chest of drawers wedged up against it. It would take a battering ram to smash through.

Anthony climbed over the drawers and headed for the stairs. He passed a series of frames, showcasing what their life had been like before the apocalypse: his and Heidi's wedding day, their honeymoon, the time they visited the Grand Canyon, and their underwater diving experience. All memories. All fragments of a life that no longer existed. With a hefty sigh, he reached the top of the stairs and made for the bathroom.

They had emptied the water tank on the first day, filling the bath with as much liquid as it could hold. He looked at the bath again, noticing there were barely a couple of inches left. That, coupled with the dwindling supply of tinned goods, told him they needed to venture outside: something they had both agreed would not be ideal, but was always going to be inevitable.

He grabbed the bucket from atop the toilet seat and walked into the bedroom. Light shone through the balcony doors, or at least the parts it could penetrate. They had nailed heavy planks of wood—the remnants of their bedside cabinets—over the doors, concealing the shattered glass on the other side. Anthony had assumed they would need to barricade only the ground floor, and that the upper floor would be safe.

He had been wrong.

The first bang against the window had roused him from sleep. The second smash had caused Heidi to scream, which in turn dragged him out of bed. The pigeon that had smashed through the window lay on its side, flapping and grunting. Broken glass had sliced its wings to ribbons, but the bird didn't seem to notice. It squawked with rage, leaping across the ground, trying to attack. Anthony had thrown an old sweater over it before stomping down hard, again and again. When the bird finally stopped moving, he had scooped up the bundle and thrown it out of the window.

That had been almost a week ago, and since then there had been no further aerial assaults. But, with the incident still fresh in his mind, he cautiously opened the balcony doors. Sunlight filled the room, bringing with it an intense heat that almost made him recoil as he stepped outside. The sky was clear, with no demonic birds in sight.

He looked back at the bucket before unzipping. Despite all the drawbacks that came with a zombie apocalypse, there was one advantage he was quick to exploit: relieving himself over the top of the balcony.

The stream of urine flowed in an arc onto the street below, the dark orange colour and the strong smell of ammonia warning him of his dehydration. He looked further down the street and flinched when he saw a woman staring back at him. He guessed she was a zombie—she had to be—why else would she be standing there? But something seemed off. Whether it was the look in her eyes, the crowbar she was holding, or the fact that her limbs were all intact, Anthony knew she was alive.

The urine trailed off, and he quickly tucked himself back in his jeans. The woman beckoned him down, motioning towards the van parked next to her. *Who the hell is she? Does she need help?* He watched as a broad man appeared beside her. He held a machete, his eyes fixed on Anthony, his motions mimicking the woman's. *They want me to come down. Maybe they've found somewhere safe. Somewhere secure. With more survivors.*

Anthony hesitated. *Or maybe they want to kill me?* He shook the notion out of his head. Why would they want to kill him? Why would they risk their lives standing on the street only to hack him to death? *I need to get Heidi.*

He held up his index finger. 'One minute,' he mouthed, and headed back inside. He dashed down the stairs, vaulted over the chest of drawers, and ran into the kitchen.

"Heidi," he gasped, placing a hand on her shoulder. "There are survivors outside."

"Huh?"

"Survivors. Two of them, they've got a big van. They might have somewhere safe, with more people."

Heidi's face twisted in confusion as she tried to process what he was saying.

"Wait. You want us to go out there?"

"We're going to have to go anyway, eventually. This way, we'll have other people to help us. Hell, they might already have food and water."

"Or they might want *our* food and water."

"I'm not suggesting we let them in. Besides, they were telling us to come out. C'mon, Heids. I doubt they're going to hang around." Her blank expression offered no sign of conviction. "At least come up and look."

"Okay."

Anthony took her hand and led her out to the corridor. He quickly scrambled over the chest of drawers and retraced his steps back up to the bedroom. He approached the balcony, relieved to see the pair were still waiting.

"Look, see." He pulled Heidi beside him and waved. The woman on the ground waved back and motioned for them to come out.

"I don't know," Heidi stammered.

"Look, we need to go out there. This could be our only chance to do it with other people. Come on."

Not waiting for a response, Anthony climbed over the railing and lowered himself as close to the ground as possible. He let go, falling the remaining distance. He felt a jarring pain in his legs, but stayed on his feet. He looked back up at Heidi, who had also climbed the barrier.

"I can't," she hissed.

"Lower yourself down, I'll catch you," Anthony whispered. Aside from the pair on the other side of the road, they were alone. Heidi tentatively lowered herself down, slowly adjusting her grip on the bars until she reached the base of the balcony. Anthony reached up, guiding her legs. He clasped her waist as she dropped into his hands.

"See, wasn't so hard," he whispered. "Come on, let's head over."

He looked both ways before crossing the road. Whether it was down to the lack of noise, or merely an instinct developed since childhood, Anthony couldn't tell. But, as the couple pulled open the sliding door of the van, another childhood instinct reared its head. *Never get in a van with strangers.*

"So—uh. Who are you? Do you have somewhere you can take us?"

"Oh yeah, we've got somewhere," the man replied. "Get in."

Anthony felt Heidi's hand falter in his. He turned back, noticing the apprehension in her eyes.

"It's okay," he said.

He stepped into the back of the van, when he suddenly lost his grip on Heidi. He turned back, watching in horror as the woman dragged her to another van.

"What're you doing?"

He tried to get out, but the broad man with the machete shoved him back.

"Actually, you won't be going together."

"Heidi!"

"Anth! Help!" Heidi screamed. He tried to lunge outside again, but the man's bulk blocked his path. He watched as Heidi disappeared into the other van.

"Heidi!"

The door slid shut, plunging the interior of the van into darkness.

"Heidi!"

7

Frank lurched aside as the window swung open beside him. He aimed his shotgun, finger poised over the trigger, ready to destroy whatever came at him.

Lisa stuck her head outside. "Are you coming?"

"What the hell are you doing?" Frank gasped. He passed her rifle through the window before quickly clambering into the hotel bedroom. "How did you get down here?"

"I used the stairs," Lisa replied, matter-of-factly.

"You shouldn't have gone in alone. There could be loads of them in here."

"How else were you going to get in? I'm not dragging your arse up the side of a building. I am a *lady,* y'know?" Lisa flicked her hair in dramatic fashion.

"Yeah—but... Ugh."

Frank conceded and turned his attention back to the room. The door to the well-lit hallway stood ajar, revealing the same plush red carpet and magnolia walls.

"I take it you didn't get into any trouble?"

"Nope. Nobody here."

"Yeah, well, let's check the rest of the building first."

"Screw that. There's a jacuzzi downstairs calling out to me."

"Are you serious? This place could be swarming."

"After all the noise you've been making, surely they would've attacked by now?" Frank made to reply, but Lisa cut in. "—Besides, the floor above was empty, every door was shut, and the dead don't seem to have the ability to turn a handle, so we're good."

Frank couldn't argue with that logic. "Okay, but don't say I didn't warn you."

Lisa led the way to the corridor. The air smelled clean: a mixture of fresh paint and disinfectant. The vast window at the far end allowed sunlight to stream freely, illuminating the fixtures and fittings, which were polished to a mirror sheen. No expense had been spared on the décor.

They reached the stairwell. "Wanna take the lift?" Lisa motioned to the twin gold-plated doors that housed the lifts. With no LED screen to show which floor the carriage was on, it was unclear whether they had any power.

"I think I'll take the stairs."

"Don't be daft. This place is solar-powered. Let's see if they work."

Frank grabbed Lisa's wrist as she strode past him. "We still need to make sure this place is empty," he urged. "If that thing does work, the noise will give us away. We may as well have smashed a window."

Lisa shot him an exasperated look.

"There are other ways to check the power." Frank glanced around in search of a light switch, but there were none nearby. "Like your jacuzzi."

Lisa's eyes lit up. "Okay, let's go."

With a parting glance at the lifts, he followed Lisa down the staircase. In a previous life, he'd never have been able to afford to stay in such a luxurious hotel. Even before he went to prison, the costs of such an exclusive lifestyle had to have been astronomical. Yet, he struggled to understand why such a place had been built on the Yorkshire Moors in the first place. True, the panoramic views were stunning, and the area allowed for solar panels and wind turbines to create copious amounts of energy. But so could other places.

Then it hit him. *The spring.*

"Let's check out the water situation."

"I intend to."

"Not the jacuzzi," Frank muttered as they stepped into the foyer. "This place could have drinking water."

"It does." Lisa pointed to a row of bottles perched on a counter.

"You know what I mean."

"Yeah, I know," Lisa smiled, rubbing his arm. She picked up a leaflet from the reception desk and quickly skimmed through it while Frank listened for anything untoward. He heard nothing other than the rustling of the leaflet and Lisa's gasps of astonishment.

"Holy shit. Their signature spa treatments start at two hundred quid!"

"Yikes."

"And that's just a mud treatment."

"That's some expensive mud," Frank said, casting a wary glance out of the entrance windows. He thought he saw movement outside, was almost sure of it.

"They must've had healing hands."

"Probably dead hands now. Shall we move on?"

"Gladly."

Lisa stuffed the leaflet in her pocket and strolled into the changing rooms.

The aroma immediately changed from floral notes to a tinge of chlorine. Their footsteps echoed over the tiled flooring as they stepped into the changing rooms. Rows of lockers ran along one side of the wall, with a number of cubicles in the middle.

Frank stepped cautiously, glancing into each one as they passed, grateful that the doors were all wide open. At the end of the cubicles stood a long row of showers, which led into a huge glass atrium.

"Oh my god," Lisa gasped. They walked through the showers and entered the main spa area. The heat from the room was almost overpowering. It felt as though they had walked into a greenhouse. Frank looked up at the sun blazing through the overhead windows, wiping sweat from his brow.

A huge pool stood in the centre of the space, surrounded by wooden loungers. To the right was a large jacuzzi, and beyond that...

"A steam room!" Lisa grabbed Frank's arm. "This place is amazing."

"Not very secure, though."

"We're in the middle of nowhere. There's nobody here."

"No. But they could stumble across it, like us."

"Are you talking about the zombies or your convict pals?"

"Both."

Lisa turned away and walked back to the showers. "Well, they were heading to Doxley, which is nowhere near here, and we haven't seen a corpse for miles. Besides, that fence looks pretty sturdy," she said, pointing at the encompassing metal barrier. "I think we're safe for now."

She turned the handle and squeaked in excitement as the shower burst to life. The forceful spray against the tiles sent Frank's heart racing. He whirled around, anticipating an army of the undead.

Nobody approached.

The floor-to-ceiling windows offered a view across miles of open moorland. It was uninhabited, an open plain with rolling hills in the distance.

"Fuck me, it's *warm!*"

Lisa's outburst prompted him to turn, assisted by her tugging at his shirt.

"Look!"

Frank ran his hand under the spray. The warm water created a feeling of joy, as though somebody had given him a gift from a former life. Lisa pushed one of the wall-mounted soap dispensers and rubbed the gel into his palm.

"Look at all the dirt coming off you," she laughed as the water turned black at their feet. "I don't know who needs this more."

"It's been a hard week alright."

"Don't I know it. I call first dibs on the shower. Why don't you see if you can get that jacuzzi working?"

Lisa bent down to unfasten her boots, which oozed brown water underfoot as the shower washed away the mud and debris.

"I don't hear bubbles," she chided, clearly sensing Frank's gaze behind her.

With a jesting sigh, he made his way back into the atrium and strode over to the jacuzzi. The water was still and crystal-clear. He couldn't recall the last time he had even seen a jacuzzi. He looked around the top for any controls, but the encompassing mahogany surface was smooth.

Does it plug in to something? He circled it, looking for a power lead or control panel. Nothing. *There must be something.*

He stood for some time, his eyes flicking back and forth, trying to find a solution. He walked around it again until he found a break in the wooden surrounding. Digging his fingers into a groove, he flicked the mahogany panel aside. Beneath it were several controls. *There you are.*

He crouched down, listening to the patter of water from the shower. Images of Lisa lathering her body in soap filled his mind. He longed to return to her. To finish what they had started a week ago. *All in good time.*

He analysed the blank LED screen and its countless buttons. Some had icons above them, giving a vague hint as to their purpose. Frank pressed a couple, but nothing happened. *Maybe there's no power.* He pressed another. And then another. But still nothing. Discouraged, he tried one more. The jacuzzi burst to life. Motors whirred and the jets responded, creating a frenzy on the surface of the water. The LED display lit up, revealing the temperature.

"Yes!" He tapped a button to increase the temperature, but was reluctant to move it above twenty-five degrees, given the intense heat of the atrium. He stood back, watching the roaring water. The noise filled the area, drowning out the din of the shower. If there were any zombies in the building, they'd surely come running now. He looked out at the fields, ensuring there were no new additions, but they were as barren as before. He turned back to approach the showers.

"Jesus Christ," he gasped.

He stared in awe as Lisa approached him, her wet body glistening in the sunlight. She held the rifle close, concealing her left breast whilst her right jiggled in time with her movements. His gaze roamed down the floral tattoo adorning her side.

"My eyes are up here, pal."

Frank blinked, focusing on her eyes temporarily before roaming over her body once more.

Lisa sniggered as she reached him. "Are you just going to stand there catching flies?"

Frank closed his mouth. He blinked again, searching for a sarcastic remark, a witty retort, anything. But words failed him, his brain as dumbfounded as the rest of him. He looked on as she sauntered past, watching the droplets of water that trickled down her back, running over her arse.

"Stop ogling and start washing." She stepped into the jacuzzi, not looking back at Frank, who remained motionless. The floral, soapy aroma of shower gel and the allure of the warm water beckoned him, but he could not turn his back. He remained transfixed on her curvaceous figure, watching as the water wrapped around her legs until she disappeared into the centre of the jacuzzi. She turned back to Frank, only her head visible amongst the blanket of churning bubbles.

"Go on."

"Fine." Frank dashed over to the showers and pulled off his caked clothes. He stepped into the warm spray, eager to get back to Lisa. But once the pressure hit, he couldn't move. A wave of ecstasy spread throughout his body as the water massaged his head and upper back. The water swirled around the drain, forming a murky puddle at his feet. He washed quickly, conscious not to let his guard down completely. Whilst the building may be empty, it wouldn't take much for the undead to smash their way in.

Lisa's right. We're in the middle of nowhere. They won't be this far out.

Despite his attempt at reassurance, he kept an eye on the entrance to the changing rooms. His anxiety peaked when he washed his hair, and the soapy suds prevented him from monitoring his surroundings. He quickly scrubbed them away, his gaze snapping back to the atrium and the exit to his side.

After a couple of minutes, the water ran clear around his feet —a prompt that he was dirt-free. He felt clean for the first time in ages. He shut off the shower and made his way back into the spa area. Lisa was still in the jacuzzi, her back to him, taking in the stunning views. The jets roared as loud as ever, drowning out his footsteps as he drew close. He expected she would see him in the reflection of the windows, but she seemed in a daze as he silently lowered himself behind her. Shuffling forward, he reached around, his hands cupping her breasts.

"Shit!"

Lisa jerked round, swinging an elbow into his face.

"Ow! Fuck!"

He staggered away, cupping his nose as blood filled his palms.

"Oh, I'm so sorry," Lisa gasped, cupping her face, unintentionally mimicking Frank. "I didn't know it was you."

"Who else would it be?" His voice had adopted a nasal tone. He pinched his nostrils together, tears stinging his eyes.

"It was an automatic reaction." Lisa sniggered.

Frank tipped his head back, using his other hand to rub the bridge of his nose. Searing pain shot through his face, causing him to wince. "I think you've broken it."

"Well, it's a good job I didn't break anything else."

He felt her fingers wrap around his erection. She pulled him closer, squeezing it between her thighs, their bodies flush together. Lisa pushed her breasts against his chest as she moved his hand away. Before the blood could trickle down again, he pulled her face towards his, their lips mashing together, tongues exchanging saliva.

Finally, the apocalypse was looking up.

8

"Look at the state of this. There's claret everywhere."

Gus leaned out of the truck, investigating the dead body in the middle of the road. A large puddle of blood had oozed from the hole in his head, running into the crevices of the asphalt.

"Must've been where Frankie and his tart had a shootout," Gus continued. He pulled the truck over to the side of the road and shut off the engine. They could see Doxley in the distance. The road leading towards it was rife with abandoned cars blocking their path.

"What are you doing?" Zielinski asked.

"Coming up with a plan. Lord knows one of us needs to; you're about as much use as Anne Frank's trumpet."

Zielinski remained quiet, opting instead to gaze out of the window.

"Oy!" Gus snapped, slapping his face. "Keep your head in the game. And you keep off those funny fags 'n' all."

"It's helping me cope."

"You'll be coping with my boot up your arse if you're not careful. You're no use to me when you're high as a kite. You barely have much use as it is, anyway."

"Then why keep me around?"

"I'm currently wondering that myself. What *do* you bring to the table? You can't shoot, you can't cook, you've got no skills whatsoever."

"I muck in when I have to."

"Really?" Gus leaned back in his seat. "Well, now's your time to shine, mucker. Where are we going to find a barricade?"

Zielinski stared out towards town, his brow furrowed.

"What is it?" Gus asked, following his line of sight. He spotted movement in the distance. Two women, running along the side of the road. They were far off, but getting closer.

"Those lasses."

"You mean *lassies*."

"What?"

"They're both a couple of bow-wows. It's like the start of a Pedigree Chum advert."

"There's nothing wrong with them."

Gus side-eyed Zielinski. "Nothing wrong with them? You could hoy a bone and they'd be after it like Usain Bolt. Fuck me, you're like a horny teenager. You can't get your leg over with Frank's sort, so now you're wanting to crack open a couple of cold ones?"

"They don't look like zombies. And since when have I wanted to screw Frank's bird?"

"Oh, do me a favour. You'd hump anything that moves, you horny bastard. She's the only one with tits, and I've seen how you look at her."

Zielinski fell silent. Watching the two women get closer.

"But," Gus continued, "you know Frank would break your neck if you so much as blew her a kiss. So now you've got your sights on these poor tarts. They've gone through enough, Zielinski. They don't need your Polish pork desecrating their corpses."

"I told you, I don't think they're dead."

Gus looked back at the pair, who had now slowed to a walk. They kept coming, but appeared hesitant.

"Bollocks. They look dead to me."

The women peered inside an abandoned car before moving on to the next.

"I bet you'd go for her on the right."

"What?"

"The light-haired one. She looks more your type: she's small, skinny, and probably wouldn't put up a fight."

"I'm not a rapist, Gus."

"Yeah, not through lack of trying, I bet. That one with dark hair is a stronger build. She'd have you for breakfast."

Zielinski ignored the remark.

"Tenner says I can shoot one in the tit," Gus said after a while. He retrieved his handgun and aimed out of the window.

"What?"

"Eeny, meeny, miny, moe." The gun danced back and forth, pointing from one woman to the other as they reached the next car, no more than thirty feet from their truck.

"Wait, Gus. They're alive."

"Fuck off, they're as dead as a—oh."

The women spotted the occupied pickup truck and darted behind an upturned van. Gus swung open his door and jumped down, his handgun by his side. He walked around the front of the truck, where Zielinski caught up to him.

"Alright, girls, we saw you. Come on out."

He watched the van for movement, but the women remained hidden.

"We're not going to harm you," Gus called. "Are we, Zielinski?" he added under his breath.

"No."

"And remember that. If I see your midget gem swinging about, I'm cutting it off, son. You understand?"

"Why do you care?"

"I don't. But I want to find out if they're any use to us before you attempt to woo them. God knows they'll sharp do one once the Casanova of Kraków starts thrusting his hips at them."

Gus turned back to the van.

"Right, c'mon, girls. I'm losing my patience now. Come out and answer some questions or I'll come back there and put a bullet between your eyes. Your call."

He tapped his foot, counting down ten seconds before he would make good on his threat. He got to three before the pair made an appearance.

"Ah, there you are. Come on, we don't bite, unlike all those other fuckers out there."

Gus had a quick check there were no zombies nearby as the women approached.

"Fuck me," he gasped. "You look… familiar."

The woman with thick black hair and piercing blue eyes confusedly glanced at her companion. She barely looked older than twenty-one, but was a dead-ringer for his first wife, Miranda. A range of emotions tormented his mind—a concoction of grief, anger, and heartbreak.

"I don't know if that's good or bad," the woman replied.

"Oh… good." Gus could feel himself becoming flustered as the memories plagued him. He shook himself free of their torturous grasp and turned to the other woman.

"So, where are you two headed?"

"Away," the woman responded.

"Anywhere particular?"

"Nope."

"What's it like in Doxley?"

"Dead."

Gus sighed. "It's like getting blood out of a stone."

He met the piercing eyes of the dark-haired woman and felt his stomach lurch. "What's your name?"

"None of your business."

He brandished his handgun, causing the two women to recoil. "How about now?"

"Fuck you."

"Oh, how rebellious. Let's see if that lasts after I put a bullet in your friend's head."

"It's Abigail," she shrieked, shielding her partner with her body as Gus trained the gun on her. "Abigail."

"Well, Abigail. If you want my advice, get yourself a weapon, or be ready to answer the gunman when he asks you a question. Understand?"

The woman gave him a prompt nod, still concealing her companion.

"And what's your name?" Gus asked, looking past her.

"Kara."

"Kara, this is my Polish dog, Zielinski. He has something to ask you." Gus turned to the wide-eyed man.

"What? I—uh."

Gus sighed. "He wants to know if you'd stamp his card."

"What?"

"He wants to know if you'd give him a bit. He's only a one-minute wonder. It'd be over in no time."

The woman's face contorted into a mask of revulsion. "No!"

"Well, there you go, Zielinski. Looks like we'll have to find you a furry exhaust pipe." He chuckled to himself, turning away from the party and climbing back into the pickup. A mumbled apology came from Zielinski, who dashed after him.

"You can come with us, if you want," Gus called out the window. "I can't say you'd be safer, but it'll probably be a lot more fun."

Abigail clenched her fist. She made to step closer, but stopped when her partner seized her hand.

"We're good," Kara retorted. She pulled Abigail back, whispering in her ear before they turned and made their way past the van.

Gus watched them in his side mirror, concentrating on the dark-haired woman.

"What the fuck was that?" Zielinski spat.

"What?"

"You were treating me like a retard. Asking permission for me to fuck her."

"So?"

"So, if I want to have them, I will. I don't need *permission*. I'll fuck both of them if I want."

"So much for not being a rapist."

"I'm not! But I'm not a pussy either, Razor."

Gus dragged his gaze from the departing women and fixed on his passenger. "Oh, leave off. They *both* have bigger bollocks than you, Zielinski. They'd eat you alive."

The women were leaving the road and heading for the treeline. Kara stopped short, her hands to her face, before Abigail embraced her. There was something about her demeanour that suggested they were more than friends: a tenderness, an affectionate nature. Then they kissed.

"Oh, ho!" Gus laughed. "They're rug-munchers. You poor bastard," he added, looking back at Zielinski. "You never stood a chance."

He started the engine and set off towards Doxley, still chuckling to himself. He looked back in the mirror, noticing the pair had disappeared from view. He felt a pang of loss, which he quickly dismissed as he turned his attention back to the road.

"Right, Zielinski. We need supplies and… what the fuck are you doing?" He stared at his passenger, who had his head between his legs, reaching under the seat.

"There's something under here," came Zielinski's muffled response. "I heard it scraping."

He came back into view, pulling with him a hefty metal toolbox.

"Oh, that's great work. Our problems are solved now." Gus rolled his eyes. "As I was saying, we need something to make a barricade. What are your thoughts?"

"Why don't we pile a load of cars over the entrance?"

"What are you, The Incredible Hulk? How the fuck do you propose we pile a bunch of cars on top of each other?"

Zielinski shrugged. "What about a lorry? We can park that over the entrance and fill the gaps."

Gus swerved around a burnt-out car as they drove deeper into the town. Aside from a few distant cries, the area seemed relatively unoccupied. He had expected more zombies congregating, but if the two women had escaped, perhaps it was empty? His mind drifted back to the one called Abigail. She had to have been in her early twenties, the same age his wife had been when he first met her. They looked identical. If he hadn't buried her twenty years prior, he would be sure it was her. *But the dead don't come back to life. Do they?*

The irony of his internal monologue caused him to smile. He weaved into the path of an oncoming zombie, ensuring he struck the corpse dead-centre. The elderly woman collided with the grill and rolled beneath the huge tyres.

The dead have come back. Why couldn't it be her?
How could it be her? She called herself Abigail.
So? What if she's confused?

You're confused. We buried her over twenty years ago. She'd be nothing but a pile of bones now.

But what if it is her? We could finally make amends.

We have nothing to apologise for. Miranda knew what she was getting herself into. We tried our best to protect her. We ripped her murderer to pieces. Do you remember?

It wasn't enough.

It never is.

That's why we didn't stop. That's why we'll never stop.

"Razor!"

Gus blinked. He rubbed his forehead in an attempt to dispel the discord in his mind. "What?"

"I asked you a question."

"Oh? And you're entitled to an answer, are you?"

His passenger fell silent.

"Don't fuck with me, Zielinski. I'm not in the mood."

"I only asked if you were okay. You didn't seem all there."

"Like you with your hippy lettuce, then?" Gus snarled. He turned a corner and was about to lay into Zielinski again until he slammed on the brakes. The truck screeched to a halt, throwing them both forward.

"What the hell?" Zielinski snapped. "What are you doing?"

"Look who it is." Gus pointed to the prison van blocking the road ahead of them. "The gruesome twosome."

"Who?"

"Lurch and Morticia! They nicked my van, remember?"

Zielinski looked ahead, his brows furrowed. "So, what do we do?"

"You go pay them a visit." Gus said, offering his handgun. "You tell them Gus Razor sends his regards."

"Why don't you tell them yourself?"

"Why bark when you've got a dog?"

Zielinski begrudgingly took the gun and leapt from the vehicle.

"Aim for the gut," Gus ordered through his open window. "I want them to die slowly."

"Whatever you say."

Gus leaned back in his seat, a sense of satisfaction coursing through him as he watched Zielinski approach the prison van. He pulled the sun visor down, and a packet of cigarettes and a box of matches fell into his lap.

"Oh, thank you."

He picked them up, retrieved a cigarette, and lit the end. The clogging smoke burned his lungs as he took a deep drag. He sighed in ecstasy, pocketing the two boxes and watching as Zielinski reached the front of the van. It was then he felt cold steel pressed against his cheek.

"You move and you're dead, sweetheart."

He tried to glimpse the gunman, but the pressure from the shotgun barrel prevented him from turning his head.

"Take the keys out, put them on the dash, and put both hands on the wheel."

Gus obliged, feeling an all too familiar rage start to burn in his stomach.

Who the fuck is this?

How am I supposed to know?

Whoever he is, he's a dead man.

Not yet, he isn't. He's still holding a gun to our head.

For now. Once his guard's down, I'm having his life.
You're not doing shit. I'll deal with this.
Make him suffer. Make him scream.
Of course.
Don't forget the blood. It's been too long since we painted the town red.

The gun momentarily left his face while the door opened, offering him a glimpse of his captor, who looked vaguely familiar. Gus wasn't sure if it was the scar running diagonally across his face, or the large mole beneath his left eye, but something sparked a memory.

He turned his head when the shotgun pushed against his cheek once more. Ahead of him, Zielinski was being led to the side of the prison van.

Two men pressed shotguns against Zielinski's back, ushering him into the cells within.

"Right, lovely boy. I want you to put your hands up, jump down, and stand in front of me. We're going for a walk," the man announced.

Gus did as ordered, his body shaking from the copious amount of rage racing through it.

We need to kill this moley motherfucker. Now.
We don't have the drop on him.
I'm going to rip him to pieces with our bare hands.
Not yet. But soon.

"Is that a toolbox in there? We'll be having that as well," said the man. Gus reached back in to retrieve it until he felt the shotgun against the back of his head.

"Ah, ah. I'll get one of the lads to fetch it. You just follow your pal over there."

Gus marched to the prison van, assisted by the weapon pressed against his back. His vision danced as the red mist began to take over, but before he gave in to his rage, he found himself bundled into a cell; the door slammed shut behind him.

They're going to die. They're all going to die.
Yes. Soon.

9

"Damn, I broke my watch," Ben said, holding his wristwatch to his ear.

"Huh?"

"I must've caught it when I jumped the roof."

"It doesn't matter. It's not like you're going to be late for any appointments or anything."

Amy smiled as he joined her at the side of the building. Getting down from the cinema proved easier than she had anticipated, with a fire escape at the far end of the roof leading down to the alley they now stood in. With her rifle pointed forward, she gradually eased out into the street.

"It's clear," she said, moving into the open. While the crowd of zombies seemed to have materialised out of thin air in the shopping centre, Amy was sure they were alone. They walked side-by-side until they reached their car.

"I can't wait to get changed," Amy said, as Ben threw the bag of clothes onto the back seat.

"You and me both." He tugged the flannel shirt in disgust.

"So, where to now?"

"I think you're right," Ben replied. "This place is too dangerous. Let's head to your grandparents' house and see what's left in that lorry. If we're out of luck, we'll have to come back this way, anyway."

Amy nodded, a flicker of relief forming inside. She had seen enough of Newchurch to know they weren't safe. But then again, nowhere was. Yet, as the car roared down the deserted road leading out of town, she was sure her grandparents' house was the safest option.

Sudden movement in her peripheral vision caused her to flinch.

"Look out!" she shrieked, as a Great Dane bounded into the road.

Ben hit the brakes and swerved to avoid a collision, but the creature ran on, hellbent on reaching them. It struck the nearside bumper with an almighty thud as the car mounted the pavement.

"Shit," Ben snarled, as he fought to regain control.

They skidded left and then right, narrowly missing a building, before veering back onto the road. They lurched to a stop, a momentary reprieve before the animal was striking once again. Amy flinched as it leapt at her door, bloody foam spraying the window, claws scraping the paintwork.

"Move!"

The words spurred Ben into action and they were off again, tearing down the road and onto a dual carriageway, meandering through the abandoned cars.

"Are you alright?" he asked.

"Yeah." Amy massaged her neck, trying to rub away her suspected whiplash. "You?"

"Yeah."

The built-up area quickly changed to serene countryside. Buildings became trees, abandoned cars transformed into open field, and the dead vanished. The car raced on, its engine piercing the silence. Whilst all the fields had a degree of similarity, there was something familiar about her surroundings. She guessed they had passed through here on their way to finding their cottage, but the sense of déjà vu was growing stronger by the second. She glanced at Ben, concerned by his sudden descent into silence.

"Are you okay?"

"Yeah. I—uh. Just concentrating on driving."

"Oh."

Whilst his driving skills had proven impeccable on the number of occasions that had warranted their use, they had never removed his ability to speak before.

Yet Ben's steely gaze remained fixed on the road until a break in the neighbouring hills stole his attention. Amy followed his stare and felt her stomach drop.

It was his father's slaughterhouse. Or what was left of it.

Previously standing tall and mighty against the backdrop of the Yorkshire Moors, the factory was now a smouldering ruin, a wreckage of charred steel and debris. She reached out and squeezed his hand resting on the gearstick.

"I'm really sorry, Ben."

"Don't be. The old man wanted to go out in a blaze of glory. Looks like he got his wish."

Amy nodded, unsure what else she could say to help.

"I miss Fran more," Ben continued, tearing his eyes away from the ruins as they approached a bend in the road. "I grew up with her. She was my entire life. It's hard to explain that kind of bond."

"You don't have to. I know what it's like to lose a sibling."

"What?"

Amy took a deep breath, preparing to reopen the wound she had long kept protected. "I have an older brother. Or... had."

"Shit, really? I had no idea. I'm sorry."

Amy shook her head. "No, it's fine. He had... problems. In the end, he became estranged from the family."

"What happened?"

Amy took another composing breath. "He developed mental health issues. He changed. When we were growing up, he was always so caring and thoughtful. He was my older brother; he looked after me."

She fell silent as the memories threatened to overpower her. She felt Ben's hand turn beneath hers, their fingers intertwined.

"You don't have to tell me this," he reassured her.

"No, it's fine. It's something I've had to come to terms with. He ended up being admitted to Moorside hospital. He's been there for years."

"Did you have contact with him?"

"I only ever visited him once. I had a call from the hospital telling me he'd been making progress and wanted to see me. I agreed to go."

Ben released her hand as another sharp turn loomed ahead. He dropped a gear, veering around the corner until the road straightened out once more. After regaining speed, he repositioned his hand in hers.

"How did it go?"

"It was okay. He wanted to know all about my life and how my job was going. We had a good chat. He asked for my new address as he wanted to write to me. I gave him mum's as well. I know how much she missed him."

"So did you not want to find him after all this kicked off?"

Amy closed her eyes, shaking her head. "When we were chatting, he seemed almost normal, except… I knew he wasn't. I could see it in his eyes. His words were thoughtful and caring, but there was no emotion there. Almost like he was reading from a script—one he had rehearsed meticulously. I knew it wasn't him anymore. When I walked out of there, I decided I'd never go back. Even now. I'm… scared, I guess."

Ben squeezed her hand. "Scared of what?"

"Scared of finding him dead. But also scared of finding out he's still alive."

"Do you think he'd try to harm you?"

"I don't know. I don't know what he's capable of anymore."

"Well, either way, you're safe with me. I won't let him harm you."

Amy offered him a smile. While she was grateful for his reassurance, she knew it wasn't enough. If her brother *was* alive, it would take more than Ben to stop him.

Five minutes later, she noted the familiarity of the vast countryside and its limited landmarks. Her grandparents' house gradually appeared as the sloping road levelled out. Everything looked exactly the same as when they had fled. The supplies that had been spewed over the ground from the upturned Transit van still remained, as did the HGV, which had smashed into the side of the house. Amy felt a beacon of hope light up inside. If they were lucky, the contents of the HGV had remained untouched.

They turned onto the long track leading up to the house, which was littered with crushed corpses. It was then they noticed there was no other lorry present. Frank's LGV had disappeared.

"They survived?" she gasped, looking around for signs of the abandoned vehicle.

"Must have," Ben replied. He slowed as they approached the carpet of bodies, dodging some, but driving over others. "I just hope they haven't been back for the food."

The thought had crossed Amy's mind as soon as she realised the LGV had made it out. Whilst Frank and his misfits had escaped, it didn't mean they were still alive. Over a week had passed—more than enough time for them to have met a grisly end.

She felt her stomach twist as Glen's corpse came into view.

"I still don't know how he got infected," she said, noticing Ben's gaze running over their former companion, too.

"Me neither, but I'm guessing he turned just before he crashed into the house. I doubt those things can drive."

They pulled up alongside the lorry and stepped outside, each grabbing a handgun. The air was hotter than ever, tinged with the stench of decay. Amy tried not to look at Glen's corpse as she followed Ben to the rear of the truck. The doors were closed: clearly a good sign.

"Are you ready?" Ben lifted his gun into view, positioning himself next to the heavy door. He grabbed the handle, waiting for Amy's response.

"Ready."

She aimed into the back of the lorry as Ben swung the door wide. There was nobody inside, but there were huge trolleys laden with food, water, and supplies.

"Oh, thank god," she sighed, lowering the handgun. She pulled the other door wide as Ben stepped back to appraise their haul.

"Holy shit. This is enough to keep us going for months."

"I know, but how the hell do we get it back?"

Ben walked a few paces to the side, inspecting the damage at the front of the lorry. "Well, I doubt we'll be able to drive it. We're going to have to get another truck and transfer it over."

"Do you think we'd be able to salvage that?" She pointed to the upturned Transit van. The windscreen had cracked from the HGV's impact, but apart from that, it didn't look too damaged. If they could get it upright, Amy had a good feeling it would be driveable. Before Ben could respond, a rumbling engine caught their attention.

A police SUV trundled up the road towards the cottage.

"Get the rifles, quick," Ben snapped. They ran back to their car, grabbing the weapons from inside as the vehicle rolled to a stop at the edge of the clearing. Amy crouched beside Ben, using their car as cover. She peered over the top as both driver and passenger doors of the police car swung open.

"Hello there!"

A man dressed in black tactical clothing called out to them. He wore a Kevlar vest and helmet, equipped with various items, and held a hefty rifle. His female partner was smaller. She didn't wear a helmet, but wore a similar vest and combat trousers, both of which appeared too big for her. She flicked her curly blonde hair out of her face as she looked through the sight of a submachine gun, pointing in their direction.

"Put your guns down, or we'll open fire," Ben ordered.

"Whoa, whoa, let's not get hostile. We mean you no harm. We only want to talk," the man called back.

"Put your guns down and then we'll talk."

Amy listened to the pregnant pause that followed, before the man finally spoke.

"You need to put yourself in my shoes, mate. How do I know you won't open fire on us?"

"You'll just have to risk it, or leave."

"Okay, as a gesture of trust, I'll put my gun down. But my wife is going to keep hers. Is that okay?"

"And you want *us* to trust your wife won't shoot us, is that it?"

The man chuckled. "Look, mate. If I wanted to kill you, you'd be dead already. I'm a sniper, and I had you in my sights from the moment you arrived."

Amy glanced at Ben, who gritted his teeth. "Can we trust him?" she whispered.

Ben said nothing.

The man called out again, "My wife is carrying an MP5. She could puncture that car like paper if she wanted to. Come on, we're on the same side here."

"Cover me," Amy said. "If they start shooting, make sure you fire back."

Before Ben could protest, she stood up, looking between the pair. The man had been honest when he said he'd put his weapon down, much to Amy's relief. His wife, however, still held a submachine gun, which she fixed on Amy.

The man smiled. "Thank you. We genuinely aren't here to fight."

"Then what are you here for?"

The man's smile faltered and he glanced at his wife, looking for an answer. Ben rose from his position, aiming his rifle at the policeman.

"She asked you a question," Ben said.

The man's wife gasped and pointed the machine gun at Ben, her hands trembling.

"It's okay, Donna," the policeman said, raising a hand toward her. "Put it down. They won't harm us."

Donna seemed unconvinced. She glanced at her husband before finally lowering the weapon.

The policeman turned back. "There, see. We aren't here to cause trouble. Please, put it down."

Ben lowered the rifle, but kept it in his hand as he strode around the car. "What do you want?"

"Help. Company. Survival. What about you?"

"We only want to get our supplies and get out of here."

The man looked past them at the HGV embedded in the remains of the house. "That's one hell of a parking job," he chuckled. "Is this your house?"

"No," Amy replied. "It belongs to my grandparents."

The man beamed. "Is that so? Well, I hope they weren't inside when that lorry crashed through their living room."

"No, they were dead before."

His smile dropped. "I'm sorry to hear that."

Amy studied him, unsure whether he was being sincere, or just saying the right things.

"I'm Kev, by the way," he continued. "This is my wife, Donna."

"I'm Amy, and this is Ben."

"Amy." The man's smile returned. "It's great to meet you."

"Likewise. I think. So, are you actually a police officer?"

"I am—well, I was, at least. Twelve years in the job, and four as an AFO."

"What's an AFO?"

"Authorised Firearms Officer. It's why I carry a big gun." He motioned to the sniper rifle at his feet.

Ben stopped beside Amy.

"So why did you come here?" he asked.

"We were passing and saw the lorry had smashed into the house. Things like that don't just randomly happen. We thought somebody might need help."

"That's nice of you, but you're a little late; it happened last week."

"Really?"

"Yeah, we just came back to get more supplies."

"So, you have a safe house, then?" the man asked, a look of hope appearing through the gap in his helmet. Amy looked uncertainly at Ben. While the couple seemed nice, and possibly trustworthy, she was unsure if she wanted to reveal their secret hideaway. Judging by the look on Ben's face, he was toying with the same dilemma.

"I don't mean to pry," the man went on, clearly able to read their expressions. "It's just that my wife and I have been on the road since all this happened. We haven't found anywhere safe yet. There are zombies everywhere, which is why we came out here. If you'd consider letting us stay with you, we'd be more than happy to pull our weight. Donna's a terrific cook, aren't you, love?"

Donna nodded enthusiastically. "Please, we're tired of running. We just want to be safe."

"And you know what they say, safety in numbers and all that," Kev added.

Amy glanced at Ben, who sighed heavily. "Do you mind if we discuss it in private?"

"Oh please," Kev said, "be our guest." He stooped down and collected his rifle before returning to the police cruiser.

"What do you think?" Ben asked, his voice low, his posture stooped.

"I don't know. They seem nice. And he's right; if they wanted to kill us, they could have."

Ben glanced over at the couple.

"It might be good to have someone with that level of training on our side, too," Amy added.

"Yeah, but I don't think she's trained. It looks like he's looted the armoury and given her some body armour and a gun."

"Maybe. But I think we could make it work."

"Is there room at the cottage?"

"Well, it's got three bedrooms. I'd say so."

"We took the floorboards out of the third bedroom, remember?"

Amy faltered. Her initial thought was to suggest he move into her bedroom and offer the couple the other room, but how would that look to Ben? They had shared a bedroom on the first night when he had kicked Glen out, but he had spent the entire time perched up against the door. Besides, they were closer now. What if he misinterpreted? *Would it be misinterpretation, though?*

"I suppose they'd be able to manage," he said, after a moment of deliberation. Amy nodded, her heart sinking slightly as she looked back at the pair.

"Are we good?" Kev called. He had taken off his helmet and placed it on the roof of the cruiser. His bald head gleamed in the sunlight, a stark contrast to the dark bushy beard that Amy surmised was compensating for the lack of follicles atop his smooth dome.

"Yeah, we're good," she told him. "If you help us unload this lorry and bring some of the food, you can follow us to the house."

"Oh, thank you." Kev and Donna embraced, the relief on their faces clear as day.

The heart-warming scene made Amy smile, almost forgetting her insecurities. She had a feeling they had made the right decision. The policeman's training would no doubt prove useful, even if she hadn't witnessed his firing ability. But, as the sound of another engine approached, she had a feeling they'd be needing it sooner than expected.

10

Frank groaned when he felt Lisa's warmth fade from his side. He shielded his eyes, taking in every inch of her flawless body.

"Time to go." She gave him a nudge and walked away from the lounger they had been lying on.

Frank groaned again, and sat up. Lisa walked over to her clothes, which were still piled in a heap near the showers. Only moments before, they were both curled up beneath a blanket of sunlight. It felt good—perfect, even: a brief reprieve from the horrors of the outside world. Now, it all came racing back as he watched her hop into her trousers crusted in mud, blood, and gore.

"And there I was thinking you wanted another go," Frank said. He didn't need to raise his voice; the vast, echoic nature of the spa carried the sound just fine as he walked towards his own discarded clothes.

"All in good time," Lisa replied. "We need food, otherwise we won't have any energy left."

"Oh, that'd be a big problem."

"Wouldn't it just," she laughed as Frank leaned in for a kiss. "Now come on, get your clothes on. We need to find this farmhouse again."

Frank hurriedly dressed, his attempts at getting clean nothing but a distant memory as he pulled the dirty clothes back on. He grabbed his rifle and followed Lisa out into the main reception area.

"Shall we go out the front?" he asked.

"No, let's stick to the window. We need to find a way of securing this place going forward as well."

"You don't like the fragile glass?"

"I mean, aside from potential zombie voyeurs watching us fuck, there's always a chance they *could* smash their way in."

"With 'could' being the operative word?"

"The sarcastic word," Lisa corrected. They made their way back to the first floor, retracing their steps to the window Frank had gained entry through.

"Okay, say goodbye to paradise for a few hours."

He helped Lisa out onto the LGV and slid down to the ground. The area was just as isolated as when they'd arrived, with only the new position of the sun offering any significant difference to their surroundings.

Before long, they were back on the road, their Shangri-La haven fading in the distance.

"So, do you remember where this place was?" Frank asked after a while.

"Not really. My sense of direction is rubbish. It has to be south, though. We travelled north to the army base, remember?"

"True. Let's keep an eye out for road signs, it might give us an idea where we are."

"It'd be nice if we had a map."

"Or satnav."

Lisa cast him an amused look. "Won't be using satnav anymore. We gotta go old-school from now on."

"Just how I like it," Frank retorted.

He turned onto another road. This one looked a lot more maintained, giving the impression it had been a regularly-used route prior to the apocalypse. Before long, Frank's instinct proved correct when a road sign offered them direction.

"Aha, we're on the right track," he announced. "Bealsdon is a few miles away. That's where we went to get all the supplies. Do you remember?"

"How could I forget?" Lisa said. "Might be best to find a way around. We were lucky to make it out of there last time."

"Yeah. Besides, I know where I am now. It'll probably be quicker to skip the town altogether and stick to the back roads."

"Safer, too."

Frank veered away from the sign pointing towards the town and took the narrow road leading through dense woodland. The blazing sun quickly vanished, replaced by a canopy of leaves and branches. The air felt cooler, prompting Frank to lean closer to the open window.

"That's better," he sighed. A single bead of sweat trickled down his forehead. He caught it on the bridge of his nose, sending a searing pain through his face.

"Sorry about your nose," Lisa said.

"It's okay. I've broken it more times than I care to remember."

"Yeah, looks like it, too."

He shot Lisa an acid glare.

"It's fine," she laughed. "It makes you look rugged, and *manly*."

She gave his thigh a squeeze and looked out to the woods. A damp, musty smell had developed in the air. The LGV batted aside low-hanging branches as it rumbled deeper through the woodland.

"So, what's the plan?" Frank asked. "Fill up with food and head back to the hotel?"

"No, we're going to have to go to the army base first."

"Why? We don't owe Gus and Zielinski anything."

"Not for them. All our weapons and ammo are there. We can't defend the hotel with a few rifle rounds and handgun magazines."

"If we go back, they'll want our food."

"Then we can make a trade. Or if they turn nasty, we can kill them and run."

"Ruthless," Frank sneered.

"Business is business," she shrugged. "Besides, it'll be good to see what supplies they've found. We could take some and use them to secure our place."

"Well, I'll leave that to the master thief. I'll distract them. You take the goods."

"No distractions needed," she grinned. "I'm a professional."

"Yeah, right."

The woodland came to an end, and they were back in the familiar landscape of the moors. In the distance, Frank spotted a lone farmhouse.

"Is that it?" he asked, pointing to the derelict building.

"I don't know. It looks pretty smashed up, but I don't think that's the same one."

"No?"

"No. Ronald's house had a roof, for one." She pointed out the exposed beams that looked warped and weather-beaten. The house had clearly been derelict for some time.

"Damn, I thought we were in luck."

"Just keep going. It's bound to be around here somewhere."

Doubt started to form in the pit of Frank's stomach, but after another five minutes, his uncertainty quickly resolved.

"There it is," he announced, recognising the balcony that overlooked the lush green fields. He saw the HGV still entrenched in the foundations of the house, along with the upturned Transit van Lisa had driven. Then he saw a familiar red sports car parked alongside.

"No way, look who it is."

"Shit. They're still alive?"

"And stealing our food. Fuck."

Frank pushed the LGV hard and turned onto the trail leading up to the farmhouse. They drove down the uneven track, rolling to a halt behind a police cruiser.

"Uh oh. The fuzz are here." Lisa checked the magazine in her handgun while Frank grabbed his shotgun. He leapt out just as a quartet of familiar and unfamiliar faces turned to greet him. Amy and her security guard boyfriend were recognisable, despite the latter looking like an old lumberjack in his new clothes. But the other two, he hadn't seen before. He eyed their matching outfits in wonder, trying not to imagine how sweaty they must be beneath them. Of the two, the man looked to be the policeman.

"Officer, I want to report a crime," Frank announced as he approached. He stopped when the man pointed his rifle at him. "Okay, *two* crimes."

He heard Lisa take up position with the rifle beside him, prompting the cop's female counterpart to brandish her own weapon.

"Christ, talk about handbags at dawn," said Frank.

"Who are you?" the cop snapped.

"Frank?" Amy stepped into view, her eyes darting between him and Lisa.

"Hey, if it isn't the nurse. And is that Rambo I see hiding back there?" Frank cast a cheeky smile at the security guard as he strode forward.

"You're still alive, then?" said Ben.

"For now." Frank looked back at the police officer holding the rifle. "Who's the muscle?"

"Do you know this guy?" the cop said, glaring at Frank.

"Yeah," Amy said. "Don't worry, we've met him before."

The cop nodded, but kept his weapon trained.

"As I was saying, officer…" Frank stepped forward. He could feel the defiance blazing in his eyes. "…I want to report a crime. But would you mind taking that gun out of my face?"

"No. This is for the safety of me and my companions."

Frank scrunched up his face. "Hmm, but you're not really safe, are you? You pull the trigger and that fine piece of arse over there will blow your head off."

He flicked his head in Lisa's direction, waiting for the policeman's gaze to follow, but it remained fixed on him.

"Yeah? And my wife will fill her full of holes."

"Who? Her?" Frank laughed, pointing to the blonde woman holding the submachine gun. "She's no fighter. Look at her, she can't even hold the gun still."

Frank longed for the cop to turn, to distract him long enough to disarm him, but it was no use. The man maintained his focus, his unwavering stare locked, his rifle rigid, his finger poised over the trigger.

"Okay, enough," Amy snapped, stepping closer to the pair. "Stop with the dick-slinging contest. Put the guns down, all of you."

"My gun isn't pointing at anyone," Frank said, stepping closer so his face was right in front of the cop's rifle. "So why don't you put *your* dick down, cuntstable?"

The man deliberated for a few seconds before conceding. He took a step back, his rifle held to his side.

"Now, as I was saying," Frank continued, "I'd like to report a crime. You see, it looks to me like you four are about to steal food which doesn't belong to you."

"What?" Amy snapped. "What are you talking about?"

Frank pointed to the HGV. "Half of that food is ours, and we've come to collect."

"*We* got that food. Not you."

"As I told you back then, there is no 'we.' There never was. *We* were a collective group. Now, since most of that group are dead, *we*, the surviving members, can split the food equally."

"Most of your group are dead?" Amy asked.

Frank shrugged. "Some are dead, others are MIA, presumed dead. Either way, we want our food."

He made to step forward, but Ben blocked his path.

"You're not getting anything."

"Ah, Rambo. How's that luck of yours holding out? Have you managed to give her one yet?"

Ben clenched his fists, his lips forming a thin line.

"Must be hard with old bacon bap here cock-blocking you. I feel for you. I really do. Especially after I did you a favour and dispatched young Demolition Man over there."

Frank looked at Glen's decomposing corpse. The bullet hole in his forehead had dried up, leaving a dark ring, clearly apparent in the middle of the pale white flesh.

"Ben, just let them have it," Amy sighed.

"What?"

"We can't carry it all. And one of their group did help us get it, even if she's not here anymore."

"We won't take much," Lisa offered, walking over to Frank. "There's literally only two of us now. I'm sure we could share it all equally."

"Is that what you want?" The cop turned to Amy, who nodded curtly. "And you?" Ben's gritted teeth and seething eyes said everything his silence did not.

"Then I'm sorry, but you're not having it."

He made to raise his rifle, but stopped as Ben stepped forward.

"Wait. It's fine. They can have some."

"Great." Frank clapped his hands together. "Come on, Lise, let's pull the van up."

"Manners," Lisa pressed, nodding towards the others. "They were here first. Let them fill up their cars and we'll get what's left after they've gone."

Frank groaned, taking a step back towards their LGV. "Fine. When did you become Miss Moral?"

"Fair is fair, my dear."

They stood and watched the quartet pack the sports car with as many boxes as it could hold. Once full, they turned their attention to the police cruiser.

"So where are you guys hiding out?" Frank asked.

"We've got a house somewhere," Amy replied.

"A big house?"

"Big enough."

"Secure?"

"For now. What about you?"

"We're at that old army base up north," said Lisa.

Amy stopped loading the car. "How did you get in there?"

"Frank knows the guys hiding out there. They let us stay."

"Really?"

"Yeah. Honestly, if you ever need somewhere to go, you'll always be welcome while we're there."

"Is that so?" Ben folded his arms.

"Yeah. We need to bury this animosity between us. We're all trying to survive, right?"

"Right." Amy smiled and nudged Ben, encouraging him to return the sentiment.

"Yeah—well. We're happy to let the past go and start anew."

Frank nodded slowly. "Agreed," he managed after a prolonged silence. He waited for Amy and Ben to walk back to the HGV for more supplies.

"What was that?"

"What?" Lisa said. "I just got us some allies. We need all the help we can get. I don't want to be worried about zombies *and* them."

"But you know fine well they're not going to be welcome at the base."

"I said while *we're* there. They don't know we aren't intending on staying."

Frank looked up as the policeman approached the SUV carrying boxes.

"I appreciate you letting us load up first," he said to Lisa. "That was a kind gesture, and I'm sorry for my aggression earlier."

"Don't sweat it." Lisa waved away his apology. "Water under the bridge."

They watched him prop the box on top of the others in the police cruiser. Then, carefully, he lowered the boot and turned back to Ben and Amy.

"That's about as much as we can carry," Amy said. "The rest is yours."

Frank climbed back into their lorry, with Lisa in tow. The rumbling engine drowned out the conversation between the quartet beside the police cruiser. He manoeuvred around the open space, before slowly backing up so the rear was almost flush with the trailer.

He jumped down as the other vehicles departed, the sports car leading, the SUV following. The policeman extended a hand in farewell as they trundled down the long trail.

"I've heard of pigs in blankets, but pigs in Battenburg is a new one on me," Frank grumbled, nodding towards the blue-and-yellow chequered pattern on the side of the police cruiser.

Lisa chuckled as she jumped into the back of the HGV.

"Hey, they've left us loads," she called, her voice amplified within the trailer.

"Yeah, not through choice, though." Frank looked in after her, surprised to see all the food stored in wheeled metal cages. It would be fairly easy to move it from one lorry to another.

"Wait here," he said. "I'll reverse up and close the gap, then you can push them over."

"Oh, so I'm stuck in the back left to do all the work? Charming."

"You're already in there."

Frank returned to the cab and reversed until the lorry met resistance. A dull thud shook his seat, telling him the two trailers were flush. He shut off the engine and looked out over the fields, watching the other two vehicles continue down the road until they disappeared from view.

Their hideout had to be somewhere nearby. And how the hell did they get lumbered with a cop and his wife? Perhaps they were hiding out in a police station. Or they'd found the couple's house and convinced them to let them stay. Whatever the scenario, he was sure it would be nowhere near as perfect as their idyllic hotel, their Eden.

A metallic clatter came from the trailer as the first cage trundled over. Frank guessed it came as a result of the height difference between the two vehicles. The cages would have to drop as Lisa rolled them into the back of their trailer. He heard her curse as a second clatter resounded.

"Are you okay back there?"

"Never better." Her indignant grumble became muffled, and was then lost completely as a third clatter shook the lorry.

Frank felt his heart sink when he heard a distant rumble. Across the moors, a herd of horses galloped across the next field towards them.

"Oh, shit."

Frank tried to identify an injury amongst the herd: a sign of infection, a hint of blood, but there were none. Yet, the horses still bounded toward him. He propped the shotgun against his shoulder, aiming out of the window—

The horses arced away from the lorry, galloping straight past as they made it into the next field. *They're not infected.* A mixture of awe and hope surfaced, replacing the grip of terror. The horses may as well have been unicorns. He had never anticipated he'd ever see a living animal again, let alone an entire herd of them. If they could survive in such dire circumstances, surely that put him and Lisa in good stead, too?

He retraced their route through the field until his roaming gaze found what they were fleeing from.

"Lise, we need to move!" He banged on the metal behind him, his eyes fixed on the horde of undead sprinting across the field. History was repeating itself. He sat in the same vehicle as before, with the same trepidation assaulting his heart, watching the same number of undead bearing down on him. Only this time, it was horses that had led them to the farmhouse, not an undead hippy.

"Lisa!"

He knew he had to move. If he didn't build up enough speed, the dead would swarm them, and the outcome could be a hell of a lot different than last time.

"Two more cages," she called.

"There's no time. Hold on to something!"

He set the lorry in gear and moved away from the farmhouse. This time around, they were facing the right direction, and picked up speed on the dirt track. The roaring undead had barely cleared the field, and were unable to reach them as they trundled on down the path.

He watched them in the side mirrors, enjoying the indignant chorus and the valiant attempts of some that pursued them. But others were more interested in the house. More still were interested in the HGV. A number of the corpses sprinted over to the trailer which lay beyond the scope of his mirrors.

His heart raced when a sudden notion stuck him. Lisa *did* get out. *Didn't she?*

11

Amy climbed out of the car, moving the boxes from her lap to the passenger seat. She reached inside and grabbed her rifle as the police SUV pulled into the drive. It rumbled over the loose gravel, slowing to a stop beside them.

Kev whistled as he got out, admiring the secluded cottage.

"Wow, nice place. How did you find it?"

"It took a while," Ben said from behind a stack of boxes.

"Here, let me help you with that." Kev dashed forward and lifted some of the boxes away.

They marched over to the house, where Amy held the door open for them. Donna was the last to cross the threshold.

"Shall we unpack while the boys bring the food in?" she suggested.

"Erm, do you not think we should all help bring the food in first?" Amy replied. "We need to limit the time we're outside. There could be zombies nearby."

"Ah, it's fine," Kev said, placing the boxes on the kitchen table. "Me and Ben can handle it, can't we, mate?"

Ben shrugged. "Yeah, can do."

Amy watched them leave. She and Ben had always worked as a team. It didn't feel right to put them at risk. And for what?

"Actually, I'm going to give them a hand," she told Donna. "The sooner we get everything in, the sooner we'll be safe."

She walked back out to the car.

"Is everything okay?" Kev asked. He carried a stack of boxes from the back seat, his eyes barely visible over the top.

"Yeah, I just think we should all chip in," Amy said. "It'll be quicker."

"Oh, okay. Well, there's a couple of boxes left in there." He trudged back to the house, easing through the doorway and out of sight.

"What's wrong?" Ben asked, appearing from the other side of the car. "You look ready to punch him."

"I don't conform to macho bullshit," she sneered. "The women stay in the kitchen while the men do the heavy lifting? Not a chance. At the expense of safety, no less."

Ben laughed as he heaved the food containers from the car.

"I'm perfectly capable of carrying a few boxes," she added.

"Oh, sorry, I didn't mean any offence." Kev appeared in the doorway, relinquished of his cargo. "I just didn't want to give you any hassle."

"I get that," Amy replied. "But it'll be quicker if we all chipped in."

"Of course. Me and Donna are probably just old-fashioned." Kev chuckled as he led the way over to the SUV. He pulled open the boot, catching a box that clattered out. "Oops. I guess I'm not very good at stacking."

"Good reflexes, though."

Amy took the box from him and waited for him to pass her another.

"Donna's emptying the boxes," Kev said. "I hope you don't think less of her, her back has been playing up these past few days."

"Oh, not at all. It's nice to have someone who knows what they're doing in the kitchen. I can't wait to try this terrific cooking you speak of."

"Oy!" Ben called as he left the house, feigning insult.

"Sorry, Ben. But you *did* manage to burn pasta yesterday."

"Burn?" Kev said. "You can cook here?"

"Yeah, it's got an external fuel tank round the back," said Amy. "Houses this isolated aren't connected to the main gas lines."

Kev's face lit up. "Wow, it's been days since we've had any hot food. Donna will be thrilled."

They spent another five minutes unloading the rest of the boxes. Once finished, they congregated inside. Amy locked the front door while Ben dragged the heavy chest of drawers against it.

"This place is perfect," Kev said, taking in their surroundings. "What happened to the owners?"

"We don't know. There was nobody here when we arrived." Amy took the seat opposite Kev.

"Really? How did you get in?"

"The door was open. Country folk don't usually lock their doors. I know my grandparents didn't." Amy scolded herself for bringing up the memory, which would no doubt prompt further digging from Kev.

Sure enough, almost on cue: "What happened to them? If you don't mind me asking."

"They were already dead when we arrived. Frank and Lisa, who you met earlier, were hiding out there with a group of people."

"*They* didn't kill them, did they?"

Amy shook her head. "No, they said my grandpa killed himself after they got there, and my grandma was already dead."

"Do you believe them?"

"They seemed genuine."

"For criminals," Ben added.

"Criminals?" Concern shrouded Kev's face.

"Yeah, Frank's a murderer, and I think I heard them mention Lisa being a thief."

Donna gasped. "Really?"

"Sound like model citizens," Kev scoffed. "No wonder you parted ways. Do you have any other family apart from your grandparents?"

Amy sighed, longing for the conversation to take a different turn. "Yeah, my mum. She... she didn't make it."

She glanced at Ben. He rested his elbow on the table, his head in his palm, averting his eyes. She could tell he was blaming himself. She reached across and squeezed his thigh reassuringly. He blinked away his reverie and smiled.

"I'm sorry to hear that." Kev's voice became solemn. "Anybody else? No brothers or sisters?"

This time, it was Ben's turn to offer reassurance. He squeezed Amy's hand gently as she took a deep breath.

Damn, he asks a lot of questions.

"Yeah, I had a brother, but I'd rather not talk about that. What about you?" she added hurriedly. "No family? No kids or anything?"

She regretted the words as soon as they had left her lips. The couple tensed up, as though she had leaned across the table and slapped them both. An awkward silence formed as they battled with a sea of emotion. Eventually, Kev cleared his throat.

"We—uh. We have a son. He's… somewhere else."

Amy's stomach dropped, overwhelmed with guilt as she watched the pair fight back tears. Kev put his arm around his wife, who looked close to breaking down.

"I'm *so* sorry," Amy said, tears forming in her eyes. She longed for a distraction. Something big enough to take them away from the situation. A zombie attack. An explosion. A nuclear bomb. Anything. But nothing came. Eventually, it was Ben who became her saviour.

"Why don't we show you to your room?" he offered. "There's a bit of an issue with the flooring, which I'm sure you'll be able to guess from looking at the windows."

He motioned towards the boards concealing the light from outside. It earned a snort from Kev and a nod from Donna as they both rose to their feet.

Amy mouthed *thank you* as Ben led them out of the room. He smiled back, leaving her sitting at the table alone. She listened to their dull footsteps ascend the stairs to the landing. Something Ben said earned a guffaw from Kev. There were a few more words exchanged before there were footsteps on the stairs again.

"Kev's going to readjust some floorboards to make a walkway and then they'll be down," Ben said.

"I feel terrible," Amy replied. "Note to self: don't mention their dead child."

"Ah, you couldn't have known. Don't beat yourself up."

"I know, but still. It must be awful."

"Yeah." He took a seat opposite her and scanned the countless boxes around the room. "I think we've done alright. Even with two extra people, this food should last for months."

"Hopefully, if we're able to plant more fruit and veg, we should be able to stay here in the long run, too."

"Y'know, there's that huge garden centre in Doxley. I bet we'd be able to find every fruit and veg plant going."

"Doxley?"

"Yeah, we could head there in a bit and see what we can find. I'll have to get my farmer's hat on."

"You're already wearing the clothes," Amy teased. "Oh, where are the new clothes we got?" she asked, suddenly aware she had not seen the bag since they got back.

"I put them in your room."

Amy jumped to her feet, desperate to get out of her tainted clothes and into something clean. "Be back in a minute."

She jogged up the stairs two-at-a-time. The bag of clothes was beside her bed—the messy, unkempt bed that in her previous life she wouldn't have been able to leave without remedying. It was bizarre how much somebody could change in such a short space of time.

Amy closed the door and quickly undressed. She still felt unclean—as though a thin layer of dirt covered her from head to foot—but as she tried on her new clothes, she instantly felt better. She thought back to the last time she had washed. It was two days earlier, under the trickling water pressure of the shower. Whilst it had taken an age, she had made sure to scrub every inch of dirt from her body.

Amy looked in the mirror, satisfied that the dark leggings and t-shirt fit. She readjusted her hair, untying it before slinging it back into a high ponytail. Content with her appearance, she left her bedroom and stood on the landing.

A quiet sobbing sound came from the third bedroom. It was Donna. Amy felt her stomach tighten with guilt. The door was ajar, offering a limited glimpse beyond. She could see the woman perched on the edge of the bed. Kev held her in an embrace, rubbing the back of her neck. His mouth was moving, probably offering soothing words, but she couldn't hear.

She moved forward slightly, but the old house offered her voyeurism no quarter. The floorboard creaked beneath her feet and she flinched. Kev pulled open the door.

"Oh, Amy." He smiled at her, but she could see moisture in his eyes.

"I'm sorry, I wasn't—I came up to get changed."

"I bet it's good to have clean clothes again."

He stepped closer, closing the door behind him.

"How is she?" Amy whispered.

"Oh, she'll be alright. We're just—I mean—I think she's struggling to come to terms with things."

Amy nodded, looking past him at the closed door. "I can't imagine how she's feeling. If there's anything we can do to help, just say the word."

"Thank you. I appreciate that. But you're helping far more than you realise."

"Really?"

"Of course. You've opened up your home to us. In a manner of speaking," he added with a laugh, looking around at the dated décor. "I can't tell you how grateful we are. We actually get to sleep in a *real* bed tonight."

"Well, if there's anything else you need, don't hesitate to ask."

"Thank you. I wouldn't mind a quick drink if there's one going? I'm sure I saw a bottle of whisky down there."

"Sure, c'mon."

Amy led the way downstairs, to the kitchen.

"Wow," Ben gasped, rising from his seat. "You look… great."

Amy smiled, tucking a loose strand of hair behind her ear. "Erm, thanks!"

"Doesn't she just," agreed Kev, stepping into the kitchen behind her. "You're a lucky man, Ben. I wish I scrubbed up that well."

Ben made to respond, but fumbled his words as Kev retrieved a bottle of whisky from one of the boxes.

"You don't mind if I pour myself one, do you?"

"No, go ahead," Ben replied, finally finding his tongue.

"Great, where are the glasses? I haven't done orientation yet."

"Your guess is as good as ours." Amy took a seat at the table while Kev searched through the different cupboards until he found one laden with glasses and mugs.

"Aha." He took out a glass and turned to the others. "Are you all having one?"

"No, I don't think it's appropriate," said Ben. He glanced at the boarded windows, almost expecting a sudden assault from outside.

"Not appropriate? You aren't expecting this place to come under siege, are you?"

"No. I just want my wits about me. Plus, we're heading back out soon."

"That's fair. I'll only have one to take the edge off. Donna will be down soon. She's looking forward to making us a warm meal. She's one hell of a chef as well."

Kev sat at the table, readjusting his body armour, which settled beneath his chin.

"You must be boiling in that," Amy said. "Are you sure *you're* not expecting us to come under siege?"

Kev chuckled. "Old habits. This thing is a pain to get in and out of. Once I take it off, it's off for the night."

"I see."

"You're right, though. It's mafting under here. I wouldn't stand too close if I were you."

The trio sniggered as Donna walked into the room, her eyes puffy and swollen.

"Here she is," Kev beamed. "How are you feeling, love?"

"Hungry." She offered a weak smile. "How about I make us some food?"

"Would you like a hand?" Amy asked.

"Oh, no. You've done more than enough for us already. It's the least I can do."

Donna pottered about the kitchen, gathering ingredients and utensils. When she realised the gas stove was still working, she gasped in amazement.

"External gas supply," Amy said. "Speaking of which, we should keep an eye out for gas canisters or even a tanker. We don't know how much fuel we have left."

"I tell you what," Kev said, leaning forward. "There are *loads* of gas tankers down at the industrial estate about twenty miles from here. We should go there."

"Really?"

"Oh yeah," Donna added. "I think that's a great idea. We should get it while we can."

"There's no rush." Ben took a sip of bottled water. "The dead don't seem interested in fuel."

"No. But the living certainly are."

"You think there are more survivors?" said Amy.

"I know there are. We've seen them, haven't we, Donna. And some aren't very nice."

Donna nodded. "Some are worse than the zombies."

"I didn't realise," Amy said. While she had considered there were probably other survivors out there, she hadn't imagined they might be hostile. Yet, her initial distrust of Kev and Donna proved that wasn't entirely true, either.

"Well, we're also planning on going to Doxley," said Ben. "There's that big garden warehouse. We figured we'd start growing our own food. The supplies aren't going to last forever."

Kev nodded. "Makes sense. Proactive approach. I like it."

"We could also see what else we can get while we're there. Depending how bad the town is, we might be able to get more supplies."

"Yeah, just be mindful of the time. We don't want to be out past sunset. It's hard enough to keep an eye on those bastards during the day."

"True. Well, maybe you two can go to the industrial estate and we'll head to Doxley?" Ben offered. "Saves doing two trips."

Kev and Donna exchanged a wary glance. "To be honest, it's probably best if we stick together," Kev replied. "We don't know what's out there, and I know four guns are better than two if anything goes wrong."

"Okay." Ben looked at Amy, who nodded in response. "That sounds good. We'll all head to Doxley after we've eaten, and then down to the industrial estate after."

"Then once we get those seeds planted, we can play farmers. See if we can find a bran' noo comboyne 'arvester." Kev adopted a thick Somerset accent, causing laughter from the other three.

Amy's body ached. She assumed it was from the bumps and falls from earlier that day, but it didn't dampen her spirit. She was happy—a welcome alternative to the doom and gloom she had become accustomed to.

The next hour passed quickly. They ate, talked, drank, and laughed. Kev and Donna made exceptional company, and as time went on, Amy's unease started to fade. She even allowed herself to experience a degree of normality. There was no apocalypse, just two couples enjoying a meal and a drink. Or at least one couple and a relationship she was still uncertain about.

She cast a glance at Ben beside her and saw genuine happiness on his face. It was good to see him so content, and she knew this was partly down to Kev and Donna's arrival. The burdens of life in a post-apocalyptic world seemed to lift when shared with others.

"Right then, shall we make tracks?" Ben suggested, getting to his feet.

"Yep, you two lead the way. We'll follow." Kev downed the contents of his glass and got to his feet.

"Hang on—I'll check the coast is clear," said Amy, jogging upstairs.

From her bedroom window, she looked out at the dirt track below.

"We're good," she shouted, picking up a box of bullets as she turned to leave, realising again that she had nowhere to put them. The leggings she had picked up had been a comfort choice over practicality. She went back downstairs and handed the box to Ben.

"Still no pockets?"

"Nope."

He had already moved the chest of drawers aside, and pulled the door open, bringing with it the searing heat from the sun. The quartet stepped outside, all shielding their eyes as they walked towards their vehicle.

"Thank god for air con, right?" said Kev, getting into the SUV.

"Right," Amy muttered, looking back at their sports car with distaste. The billowing heat escaped from the car, and once again, she begrudgingly sat inside.

"We need a new motor," Ben said, clearly sharing Amy's aversion. "It's too bloody hot without air con."

"Let's add it to the shopping list."

They reversed out of the driveway and back onto the country lane. After waiting for Kev and Donna to get behind them, they drove on. Amy held an open palm out of the window, manipulating the warm air between her fingers. She had never been to Doxley, but if Ben's words were anything to go by, it sounded like a large town.

I hope there isn't anybody there, she thought. Zombies were one thing, but after their conversation earlier, she found she was developing a newfound apprehension of survivors. Donna's words still sounded in her mind. *Some are worse than zombies.* Whilst she knew there were always exceptions, she prayed the town was deserted, and that it was only the dead they would have to contend with.

12

How long have we been in this fucking box?
An hour? Maybe more?
It's too hot. We're going to end up dying in here.
We're not gonna do shit. Gus Razor is not gonna die in a fucking paddy wagon.
No. Not until we've killed that fucker who put us in here.
And the rest...
And the rest.

Gus listened to the men outside the van laughing and joking. Every now and again, they would climb into the back, filling the other cells with plundered goods from the neighbouring buildings. Zielinski had fallen silent, no doubt sick of the abuse he received every time he voiced his disdain.

How many are out there?
Five. Too many to take in one go.
Bullshit.

We need to be smart. We pick them off one by one.

You do smart. I do mad. Let's see who spills the most blood.

I'm in control. Not you.

For now...

***

Frank pulled up outside the army base, surprised to see that Gus and Zielinski had not returned.

"Maybe they're dead?" Lisa suggested, reading the look on Frank's face.

"Ha. We're not that lucky."

He spotted Lisa massaging her shoulder, flexing her arm back and forth.

"Still hurts?"

"What do you think?" she chided. "You try having a cage full of boxes roll into you over and over again."

"I said I was sorry." Frank raised his hands in defence. "We had to get out of there."

"You didn't have to drive like a madman for a mile and a half, though."

"Some of them followed us."

Lisa rolled her eyes and turned her attention back to the army base. "Maybe they've parked round the side?"

"Maybe." Frank shut off the engine and jumped down. There were no new tyre marks in the gravel, and no noise coming from the base as he approached the large double-doors. They opened easily, with no barricading oil drums preventing his entry.

"They're not here."

"Shit. Maybe they *are* dead. What should we do?"

"We get our guns and leave."

"But we still need to find supplies to barricade the hotel. It won't be safe to stay there until we do."

"Okay," Frank sighed, "but I don't really want to stay here, either. What if they come back? We'll have to split the food. If we get the guns and run, we won't have that issue."

They ascended the stairwell side-by-side, their boots echoing off the high walls.

"We can't stay there in its current state," Lisa said. "There's too much glass. If the zombies even suspect we're inside, they could smash through, and then what? Barricade ourselves in one of the rooms while they roam the corridors?"

"There weren't any zombies there, though."

"Yeah, at the time. What's to say they aren't swarming around there now? They've already started roaming further afield. It's only a matter of time before they reach the hotel."

"Okay, well, we need to decide what to do."

"We could get the guns and go back to the hotel to unload?" said Lisa.

Frank glanced at his watch. "No. I think we should drive into town. If Gus and Zielinski *are* dead, they might have got the truck filled before they croaked. One of us could drive it back."

"But what if whatever killed them is still there?"

"Then we dish out a bit of revenge on their behalf," Frank sneered.

"If we go into town, it won't give us much time to secure the place."

"True. But we need supplies. Let's just see how we get on. If need be, we'll come back here for the night, especially if Gus and Zielinski aren't coming back."

They made it to their designated lookout point on the top floor. Frank stooped down and retrieved the two assault rifles perched next to the window.

"You get the ammo, I'll go and—"

"We've got company."

Frank groaned and headed to the window. He knew the pair being dead was too much to hope for. He looked outside, expecting to see the pickup truck trundling down the path. But he saw nothing.

"Where?"

Then he spotted them. Two women walking up the path towards the building. Their cautious approach told him they weren't zombies. There was a timidity in the way they walked, almost apprehensive.

"Survivors?" he gasped.

"Looks like it."

"What the hell are they doing here?"

"Surviving."

Lisa turned to the stairs, and Frank begrudgingly followed. If the women were expecting the army, they were going to be in for an unpleasant surprise.

"Let's chase them off and leave."

"We can't do that," said Lisa.

They reached the front entrance and threw the doors wide once more.

"Why not?"

"Because they might prove useful."

"How?"

The two women froze when they spotted Frank and Lisa.

"It's alright. We're not gonna harm you," Lisa called. "Frank! Put the guns away."

"Fuck that," he replied, eyeing the two women uncertainly. "They might have weapons. They might be infected."

"*Or* they might be reluctant to approach the big rugged bloke carrying a pair of assault rifles."

"Big and rugged, eh?" He nudged her playfully.

"I'll call you worse than that if you don't put the bloody guns away."

Frank sighed and propped the rifles beside the door. "How are these two going to prove useful?"

"I don't know yet."

The women approached cautiously, their eyes skimming over the huge building.

"Hi," Lisa beamed.

"You're not the army," said the dark-haired woman.

"Yeah, not through lack of trying." Lisa motioned towards the two rifles beside the door. "You're the first survivors we've seen for a while."

"Really?"

"Yeah. Why, have you seen others?"

"Unfortunately." The two women exchanged a glance, which Frank recognised only too well.

"I'm guessing you ran into Gus and Zielinski."

The women looked at him blankly.

"Two dickheads driving a pickup truck?"

"Oh yeah," the light-haired woman said. "They tried to proposition me."

"Sounds about right."

"I'm sorry," Lisa added. "They're arseholes."

"Oh, that's nothing compared to the others."

"Others?"

"Yeah. We were part of a group hiding in a house. Then these guys smashed their way in. They... killed our friend."

"Shit," Lisa gasped. "What were they doing? Looking for supplies?"

"No. They were looking for *people.*"

Frank scowled. *Looking for people?* The notion barely had time to register before another crossed his mind: *We're not on a scouting mission.* The woman they had killed in the shootout had uttered those exact words. She had also said, "He'll kill you." Whoever *he* was must be sending out groups to gather survivors. But why?

"How many were there?" Frank said, louder than intended, which caused the two women to step back.

"I don't know. Three, maybe four?" The dark-haired woman turned to her companion, who nodded in agreement. "They killed one of their own while we were there. He got infected, so they shot him."

"*Shot* him? They had guns?"

Whoever these people were, they clearly had access to enough firepower to arm their group. Frank thought back to the weapons they had recovered from the couple—both handguns. They wouldn't have been easy to come by.

"How did you escape?" Lisa asked.

"We hid in a cupboard. Once they started firing, they quickly left. We were lucky to get out before the zombies came."

"So why here?"

"It's the only other place we could think of that would be safe. We kind of hoped the army might be here."

Frank snorted. "Sorry to disappoint, but the last soldier died over a week ago." He thought back to the dead man still leaning against the vending machine. Why Gus had kept the corpse there was beyond him.

"How long ago did you see Gus and Zielinski?" he asked.

"An hour or two?" The dark-haired woman shrugged. "We walked from Doxley."

"So, they made it that far, then." Frank turned to Lisa. She seemed lost in thought.

"What are your names?" she asked.

The women appeared hesitant. They exchanged a brief glance before the light-haired woman spoke. "I'm Kara, this is Abigail."

"Nice to meet you. I'm Lisa, this is Frank. And you'll be pleased to know we aren't in the business of kidnapping people."

Her attempt at humour didn't seem to register.

"Can you shoot?"

"No. We've never even held a gun before," Kara said.

"Can you drive?"

The two women shook their heads.

"We're not completely useless," Kara urged. "In our group, we'd all take turns going on supply runs. We'd also clean, maintain the house, keep watch. We played an important part."

"I'm not suggesting you didn't," Lisa countered. "I'm just trying to find out what you can bring to the table."

"What do you mean?"

Lisa glanced at Frank before answering. "I'm gonna be honest. We're not hanging around here. We've found somewhere better."

Frank sighed, running a hand over his hair, turning away from the group.

"Somewhere that has the potential to keep us going for the long run," Lisa continued. "But ideally, we need some help."

"Where is it?" Abigail asked.

"It's not far. But it needs barricading. We've got food. We've got water. We just need more hands to secure the place quickly."

"And what if those other guys find us?"

"Then we kill them," Frank said, picking up both rifles and handing one to Lisa. "We're heading into town now. But if you want to come with us, you'll have to pull your weight. Understand?"

"Can we discuss it first?"

"You have as long as it takes for me to start that lorry and drive away."

Frank strode past them towards the LGV.

"If you're coming, you need to jump in the back."

He climbed into the driver's seat, and sat alone for a couple of seconds until Lisa jumped in beside him.

"What are you thinking?" he snapped once she closed the door.

"We need to be realistic. We can't defend that place ourselves. If there *are* crazy bastards abducting people, they're going to be more of a threat than mindless zombies. We need to start thinking tactically."

"And *those two* are tactical?"

"They can help us secure it, and with time, they can help us defend it."

"I don't trust them."

"Of course you don't. You've spent too much time in prison surrounded by criminals. Not everyone is out to get you, Frank."

The sound of rolling shutters came from the back. With a sigh, Frank started the engine and made off down the path.

"I hope this isn't gonna bite us on the arse," he grumbled, turning onto the narrow lane and picking up speed towards town.

"It won't. They want to survive, like us. They're going to be useful, trust me."

"Fine, but at this rate, we're gonna be running an actual hotel."

They drove in silence for the entire journey. Once Doxley came into view, they passed the man and woman they had killed earlier, prompting Lisa to voice her concerns.

"Who do you think this guy is? The one those two were talking about."

"I don't know. But it sounds like he has a lot of people working for him, and packing a decent bit of firepower."

"But why abduct survivors?"

Frank shrugged. "Maybe he's being a good Samaritan?"

"What kind of good Samaritan forcefully takes people away?"

"Don't ask me. I'm just a primitive criminal. I don't understand how the outside world works."

Lisa scoffed at his pettiness. "Are you going to be in a mood the entire journey?"

"What entire journey? We're here now."

He motioned around the desolate streets as they entered Doxley. The only sound emanated from their engine as they drove down the road, but an enigmatic roar soon followed. A bloodied teenager sprinted toward them, running diagonally across the road and into their path. Frank maintained their momentum, colliding with the zombie, sending him crashing into a parked car. A collective shriek followed, as more of the undead appeared.

"Quite the welcome party," Frank said.

Lisa worked on ensuring her rifle was loaded. Another loud bang came as a second zombie fell victim to the racing lorry, this time being crushed beneath the wheels. The lorry rocked as it mangled the corpse into the road.

"Well, there goes the stealth option," Frank said. They passed the remaining undead, who emitted a chorus of angry roars and disgruntled wails. "The entire town can hear us approaching."

He looked in his side mirrors, relieved to see their pursuers fading into the distance.

"Where do you think we should start? Where would they have gone?"

"Knowing those two, they probably bickered the entire time until they came across something that looked like a DIY shop."

They turned a corner, where Frank slammed on the brakes. The lorry screeched to a halt behind a familiar-looking pickup truck.

"Or they might've stopped randomly in the road," Lisa said.

"No. It wasn't random."

Frank climbed out of the lorry, shotgun in hand, watching the prison van further down the road.

"Oh, wow. Do you think it's Tina?" Lisa joined him at the front of the LGV, as the sound of rolling shutters came behind them.

"I hope not. We've already picked up enough stragglers." Frank motioned back towards the sound of the new recruits exiting the lorry.

"Where are we?" Kara asked, stepping up behind them.

"Doxley."

"What?" She turned to Abigail, a look of fear in her eyes.

"We're getting supplies."

Frank slowly approached the pickup truck, dismayed to find its trailer empty. *Well, they didn't manage to get anything.* Lisa walked beside him, rifle raised. When they reached the truck's passenger door, Frank stretched up and swung it wide. Nobody there.

"Where are they?" Lisa whispered.

Movement further down the road caught Frank's attention. He wasn't certain, but he could have sworn he'd seen a figure slip through the doorway of a terraced house. He motioned for them to proceed, scanning the area. He kept glancing back at the doorway, hoping to catch more movement, but it didn't come.

"Let's split," he whispered. "You take the prison van. I'm checking over there."

"What?"

"I thought I saw somebody."

"But—"

He held up a hand to silence Lisa, his eyes still fixed on the doorway. The silent street amplified their footsteps, causing his heart to hammer harder as he approached the house. He was sure he had seen somebody. It wasn't a zombie; zombies didn't hide. This was somebody alive, and potentially an even greater threat. He tried to steady his nerves as he drew close to the open door.

"Frank."

He felt a pang of irritation as Lisa spoke behind him. Any remnant of stealth left after the screeching zombies was now gone. But when he looked back, the irritation instantly turned to shock when he saw her being held with a gun to her head.

"Lisa!"

He raised his shotgun, but her assailant positioned himself behind her. The side door of the prison van stood open—his hiding place, where he had been waiting in ambush.

Frank snapped his aim to the right as Kara and Abigail cried out. A pair of men rushed them, one armed with a shotgun, the other with cable ties.

"Quiet, ladies!" one of the men sneered. "You'll wake the dead."

Before Frank could process what he was seeing, he was given something else to add to the equation. Cold steel pressed into the back of his head. He could feel the distinct circular indentation of a handgun muzzle.

"Hands up, sweetheart," his gruff-voiced assailant demanded. Frank obeyed, raising both hands skyward, watching the events unfold. The man holding Lisa stepped into view, forcing her hands behind her back where he bound them with shackles. Frank had seen them in use before. They were the same type used to transport prisoners to and from court. He looked back at the prison van, and his stomach dropped.

"Well, what have we here?"

The man behind him prised the shotgun out of his hands.

"This is a nice boomstick."

His shotgun replaced the handgun muzzle. Ahead of him, Lisa's captor bundled her into the back of the van. The vehicle rocked as she was thrown into one of the cells.

"Get in there!"

After the sound of a slamming door, her captor emerged and went over to help restrain the other women.

"No! Get off her!"

Kara screamed after Abigail, when the man dragged her toward the van. She cried out, fighting to get back to Kara.

"Oh, Carver's gonna have some fun with you," the man said. "Hell, I think we all will."

The two men cackled as they dragged Abigail into the van. Her wailing became muffled before ceasing entirely when the cell door slammed shut. Kara's cries remained, echoing down the street from her position on the ground.

"What are you doing?" Frank growled, finally finding his voice.

The gunman shoved him forward. "You're going to jail, sweetheart. Come and tie this one, Gaz," he called to his companion.

Frank watched the man approach, noticing the grey tracksuit. He was a former prisoner. They *all* were. Frank didn't recognise them, but he knew there was only one place they could have come from.

"You're from Harrodale."

"Oh, we've got a detective," Gaz sneered, baring his few remaining teeth. "I can't wait to see what happens to *you*."

He stepped past him and yanked Frank's hands behind his back. He felt the shredding bind of cable ties around his wrist, causing him to hiss in pain.

"Oh, does that hurt? That's nothing compared to what's coming, lovely boy."

His captor stepped into view, placing the shotgun beneath his chin. Frank glared at him. He had the same prison-issue tracksuit and close-cropped hair as the others, but a diagonal scar and large mole beneath his left eye helped distinguish him.

"Go on, Gaz. Put him in the back."

Frank stumbled forward as the man yanked his upper arm, leading him to the back of the prison van. He tripped up the step, eyeing all the doors. All closed, except one. He didn't have time to ponder who the occupants were before he was shoved into the last cell. He struck the wall face-first with a grunt, slumping down as the door slammed shut behind him. The narrow confines made it impossible to turn into the seat, leaving him with no option but to remain half-kneeling, half-standing, wedged between the chair and the wall.

"We're out of space, Mo." The voice belonged to Gaz. "We can't fit her in. Shall we just kill one of the blokes and leave them here?"

One of the blokes? Who else is in here? He immediately remembered the pickup. *Gus and Zielinski. Shit.*

"Nah, I've got a better idea," said the guy with the mole. *Moley Mo, how fitting.* "You three wait here with her. We'll get these pricks back and all the shit we've filled the other cells with. Then send another van for you. That way, we'll get to finish emptying this street and Carver won't be pissed."

"You want us to stay here?" Gaz protested. "We're sitting ducks."

"It'll literally be half an hour. Here, you can have this shotgun, as well."

"Half an hour is more than enough time for us to be ripped apart."

"Fuck off, there's no zombies here."

160

"We literally just heard them before those pricks showed up."

"Okay, fine," Mo conceded. "Kill one of them, but you can explain to Carver why he only has five things to play with instead of six."

The pair fell silent, with only Kara's sobs splitting the silent atmosphere. Frank strained his ears, trying to hear the outcome.

"Half an hour?" Gaz finally said.

"If that. Wait here and we'll come straight back."

Footsteps sounded around the front of the van as some of the men climbed in. The engine roared, the cell vibrated, and within seconds, Frank slipped further into his claustrophobic stance as the van took off. He fought against the biting cable ties, trying to readjust himself, but it was no use. He gave up, resigned to his fate.

After escaping the prison the first time, he thought he would never see it again. Now, here he was, being transported back to where it all began. And as the van rumbled on, the same pessimistic thoughts that had plagued him throughout his last tenure resurfaced. This time, there was no getting out. He was going to die in the prison.

13

They rolled to a stop beside the corpse, waiting for the police cruiser to catch up.

"What do you think?" Amy asked, looking between Ben and the dead man beside their car.

"It looks like Frank and Lisa beat us to it."

"How do you know it's them?"

Ben leaned across her lap, pointing out the bullet hole in the man's face. "How many people are running around with guns?"

"We are. And so are they." Amy motioned to the car that pulled up alongside them. The driver's window lowered, revealing Kev and Donna.

"What's going on?" Kev called.

"This guy has been shot. Somebody's been through here."

The door to the police cruiser swung open. Kev stepped out, adjusting his bulky vest. He stooped down and examined the corpse, then the broken window of a bright-orange SUV.

"It looks like the shot came from the back of this car," he said, rising to his feet.

"How can you tell?"

"The shot was fired outward, see?" He pointed to the specks of glass covering the dead man. "Whoever shot him was hiding in the back, but—"

Kev fell silent, his hand running across the bodywork of the SUV.

"What is it?"

"There's bullet holes all along here." He turned, scanning the rest of the area. "This was a gunfight."

Amy glanced at Ben with wide eyes before they both stepped out of the car. They watched Kev as he slowly walked away, his head darting back and forth.

"You think they were shooting at each other?" Amy called after him.

"No. This guy died from a blitz attack. Somebody else was firing."

"So he wasn't a zombie, then?"

Kev didn't reply, his attention fixed on a motionless form in the field beyond. They followed him as he jogged over, removing his helmet once he reached the body. After examining the corpse, he shoved it onto its stomach.

"She was shot in the back," he said, once the others were within earshot. "Somebody murdered her."

Amy placed a hand to her mouth, Donna's words taunting her once more. *Some are worse than zombies.*

"I told you some survivors aren't very nice," Kev said, reading Amy's expression. "We need to proceed with caution. How about we lead the way, and you guys follow?"

"Do you know where we're heading?"

"Yeah, that huge garden centre is in the middle of town. It's right next to a supermarket, too. We can have a look in there while we're at it."

Kev and Donna turned away, returning to their vehicle. Before Ben could leave, Amy grabbed his arm.

"We might've made a mistake coming out here," she whispered.

"What?"

She motioned to the dead woman nearby. "These were survivors, like us. They were killed by the living, not the dead. What if it happens to us?"

Ben took both of her hands in his.

"I'm not going to let that happen. The people who killed them are probably long gone. We're going to get a few more things, and then we can spend the next few weeks hiding out at the cottage."

"But it's not only zombies we're facing. What if other survivors find us?"

"Then they'll come up against that big beast." He nodded towards Kev. "We'll be fine."

Amy took a deep breath. She allowed herself to be steered back to the car, desperately trying to relinquish the pessimistic scenarios. She climbed into the passenger seat, her hand instinctively closing around the rifle propped in the footwell.

I should've taken this when we got out the car, she cursed. They waited for Kev to drive ahead before following at a leisurely distance.

Doxley was like every other town they had encountered so far: empty and ruined, a wasteland of suffering and destruction. They passed shattered windows, burnt-out cars, debris-strewn pavements with blood tainting almost every surface to differing degrees. The sights no longer affected her. They were the new normality. What bothered her was the prospect of having to be alert to a new type of enemy— one who was clever and tactical. One who was armed, with the ability to carry out long-distance attacks as opposed to the close-range attacks they had become accustomed to.

She watched the police cruiser meander around several abandoned cars before turning a corner, momentarily out of sight, before Ben followed. They drove past a familiar-looking LGV, then a large pickup truck.

Then the firing started.

Amy looked on in horror as the police SUV raced ahead under a hail of gunfire. Ben slammed on the brakes, both watching as a gunman ran out into the street. He had his back to them, firing after Kev and Donna. The SUV performed a handbrake turn, swerving behind a parked van. The man stopped to reload, his head snapping up and down, looking between his handgun and the space he had last seen the SUV.

Then he turned.

Amy gasped as the gunman locked eyes on their car.

"Shit." Ben shoved the car into reverse. A range of movement happened all at once. They lurched back. The man raised his gun. And Kev's SUV came into view down the street. Ben swerved the car behind the pickup truck as gunfire resounded once more. Amy flinched, but in her fleeting glimpse of the street, before the pickup obstructed them, she saw the gunman pitch forward, a cloud of red mist at his back.

Squealing rubber replaced the spray of automatic fire, and Amy could only surmise that Kev was coming back to help them. She leapt from the car, rushing round to Ben as the police cruiser screeched into view. Another handbrake turn spun the car around before Kev and Donna leapt out, rushing over to join them.

"Are you okay?" Donna gasped, grabbing Amy and looking her over.

"We're fine," she replied. "What the fuck's going on?"

"We've got a hostage situation." Kev leaned back against the trailer, sniper rifle in hand.

"What?"

"Two more left, and they've got a young lass tied up. Looks like one has a shotgun." He turned to Ben. "You with me?"

Ben nodded, swapping places with Donna.

"Okay, let's move."

Before Amy could protest, the pair disappeared around the side of the van. She made to follow, but Donna's grasp on her arm prevented her.

"What are you doing?" she hissed.

"This isn't time for chivalry," Amy spat, yanking her arm free. "We work as a team!"

Not waiting for a response, she broke cover, rifle poised. She saw Ben on one side of the street, and Kev on the other, both crouched behind splayed, abandoned vehicles. She hunkered behind the car nearest to her when she saw one man shuffle into view. He held a shotgun, his gaze fixed on the car Ben was hiding behind.

She wanted to warn him, but knew she would alert the gunman to her presence if she did. Instead, she aimed her rifle, looking down the scope, lining up the crosshairs with his torso. The biggest target.

Bang.

The shot thundered down the street, instantly flooring the man, and causing Ben to flinch. He looked around the car and then back at Amy. She didn't acknowledge him, her attention caught by more movement further down the street. The last gunman appeared, dragging a young woman by her hair, a handgun pressed to her temple. Seeing Amy, he crouched behind his hostage.

"Put your gun down or this cunt's dead," he spat.

Amy froze. If she ducked out of sight, he might shoot the woman. If she lowered her gun, he might shoot *her*. She glanced back at Ben. He was scrambling back, clearly unable to get a clear shot.

"I'm gonna count to three!" the man snapped. "One."

She looked to other side of the road for Kev, but he was no longer there.

"Two!"

"Okay!" she called. "I'm putting it down."

She lowered herself to a crouch.

Still no sign of Kev.

When she placed the rifle on the ground, she looked back at the gunman.

"Now, come here."

She didn't have to deliberate this time. No sooner had the words left his lips than his head exploded in a cloud of blood, brain, and skull fragments. The thunderous boom of Kev's sniper rifle reverberated down the street, causing Amy's ears to ring. He appeared out of his vantage point between the cars, rushing to the aid of the blood-spattered hostage.

"Are you okay?" Ben asked, finally reaching Amy.

"Yeah, you?"

"Yeah. Thanks, you saved my life."

"Think nothing of it," she said. "We're a *team,* remember?" She turned back to Donna, who timidly approached, looking at the floor.

"I'm sorry," she murmured.

"Don't be," Amy replied. "Just change your mindset. We're all equals on this team. We look out for each other."

Donna nodded, still avoiding eye contact. Amy turned back to Ben, who examined the dead man's shotgun.

"What's up?"

"This gun," he said. "It's the same one Frank took from the shop we raided."

"Could it just be the same type?"

Ben shook his head. "No. I remember Frank seemed pretty excited about it. He said it was a dodgy import."

Before Amy could contemplate the gun's owner, Kev led the sobbing woman over to them.

"Please, you have to help me," she cried. "They took her."

"Who?" Kev asked.

"My partner, they took her."

"Who took her?"

The woman shook her head, flicking away clumps of brain matter from her hair. "I don't know. There were about five or six of them. They all had guns. They took her from me."

"Where did they take her?" Amy pressed.

"The prison."

"The prison?" Amy said. "Are you sure?"

The woman nodded, wiping her nose in the crook of her elbow. "Please, you have to help me get her back. She's all I have."

"How long ago did they take her?" Kev asked.

"About ten minutes." She wiped the tears from her face, fixing the group with a steadfast determination. "They're in a prison van. If we hurry, we can catch them. Please, I'm begging you. Help me get her back."

"Of course." Amy rubbed her arm. "Is that okay with you, Kev? Donna?" The couple exchanged an uncertain look.

"Yeah, okay. Let's see if we can catch up with them. If they're actually *inside* the prison, we might have problems."

Ben nodded. "We don't know how many there are. We might be outnumbered."

"Okay, let's just go," Amy urged. "We'll meet you at the prison."

She ushered the young woman over to their car while Kev and Donna ran to the SUV.

"What's your name?" She swung open the passenger door, allowing the woman entry.

"Kara."

"Hi, Kara, I'm Amy. Can you tell us what happened?"

Ben spun the car around and raced back the way they had come.

"We—we were originally part of a group hiding in a house a few streets from here. Then some guys smashed their way in and took Leanne and Sam."

"Took them?"

Kara nodded promptly, as if she had already had to relay her story multiple times. "They take people. I don't know why. Me and Abigail escaped. We made it to the army base, where we found some more people."

Frank and Lisa.

"They told us they had found somewhere better and were getting supplies."

"Better than the army base?"

Kara nodded. "So we went with them. Then we got ambushed by loads of blokes with guns. They tied us up and put them all in the back of the prison van. They said there wasn't enough room for me, so they told those three to wait and they would send a van back in about half an hour to pick us up."

"And that was ten minutes ago?" Ben asked, looking in the rear-view mirror at the woman. She nodded again, running fingers through her hair, picking out skull fragments. Beyond her, Amy could see Kev and Donna bringing up the rear.

She turned back in her seat and reloaded her rifle, glancing at the speedometer. They were travelling at over a hundred miles an hour. Yet, with a head-start of over ten minutes, Amy knew it was unlikely they would catch the van before it reached the prison. Their only hope was that the prison was empty, and that the kidnappers would take their time, unaware they were being pursued.

14

The engine cut off. The floor stopped rumbling, and Frank could hear raised voices outside.

"Jimmy, go and get Carver. We've got a little surprise for him."

The van rocked as the men climbed in the back, where one of the cell doors swung open. He expected to hear somebody being dragged outside, but all he heard was the clink of bottles and the rustle of bags.

"Did you get much?" came a voice.

"Oh, more than you realise," Mo replied.

The unloading lasted a couple of minutes. After clearing the first cell, they moved onto the next. Frank tried to ascertain the number of people based on the various footsteps, but it was impossible. Aside from identifying three distinct voices, he was none the wiser. He heard another cell open, this time accompanied by a frantic voice.

"Get off me!" Abigail shrieked. The van rocked harder as they dragged her out.

Footsteps again. Then his door swung open. He twisted, locking stares with Mo, who grinned at him.

"Your turn, princess."

He grabbed Frank's forearm and yanked him out of the cell. Frank tried to gain his footing, but he was pulled too fast. Before he knew what was happening, he was being thrown out of the van. With his hands tied, he could not cushion his impact, and his face smacked against the asphalt, forcing the air from his chest. He wheezed, trying to fill his lungs with oxygen.

"Get your fucking hands off me!" Lisa raged from the van. Frank heard a scuffle before she hit the ground beside him. He twisted his head, relieved to see she had fallen on her side. She looked back at him, steely determination in her eyes.

"Keep your guns on this next one," Mo called from the van. "He isn't tied."

"Let him out, let's have some fun," ordered a new voice. Frank tried to look up from his prone position, but all he could see were two sets of boots as they stopped in front of him.

More noise came from the van as another cell door opened. Its occupant was quiet as he stepped outside. *That has to be Zielinski. Razor would be shouting to the rooftops by now.* Then the man spoke, confirming Frank's theory.

"You've gotta be shitting me," Zielinski said.

"Well, well, Polak, you've come back." This second voice sent ice coursing through Frank's body.

He tried to look up.

It can't be.

173

He tried to turn.

We left him to die.

"So this must be…" Frank felt a boot against his shoulder. It shoved him onto his back, the glaring sun blinding him. He longed to cover his eyes, but his bindings prevented it. Then the face he had despised for so long loomed over him, offering him shade.

"Hello, Lee."

Frank snarled. "Henderson!"

"The very same. You look like you've seen a ghost."

"You know these pricks?" the other man asked.

"Oh, you bet I do. Get them all up."

He stepped away from Frank as rough hands dragged him to his feet. He looked around, taking in the sights he had vowed never to see again. They were outside the main prison, within its chain-link perimeter. Henderson grinned at him, exposing dark yellow teeth beneath his thick moustache.

"We got one more," Mo announced. His footsteps sounded within the van as Henderson's partner stepped forward.

"So, Henderson, care to share who these lovely people are?"

"Well, Carver, I only know two of them. We've got Frank Lee, a former inmate who was doing life at Her Majesty's pleasure for murdering his wife."

Carver feigned a shudder. "Scary."

"And Zielinski over here has been in and out all his life. He was in the middle of a sentence for manslaughter. Bumped off an old biddy."

Carver held a hand to his mouth. "Jesus, we've got some hard nuts here."

A commotion from the van caught their attention. Frank turned to see Mo leaping from the van with Gus Razor in tow.

"Come here, you little fucker!" Gus spat. He chased him towards the others, where he stopped in his tracks, his eyes locked on the two men before them. "Henderson?"

"And this is Gus Razor," the guard beamed. "He was never supposed to see the light of day again. Lucky bastard."

"Really?" Carver muttered. "Why do they call you Gus *Razor?*"

"Give me a blade and I'll show you."

"Ooh," Carver cackled, taking a step forward. "You've got balls, I'll give you that. I'll look out for them when you're being ripped to pieces."

Gus sneered, but Carver took no notice, instead turning to the women.

"My, my, what a tasty morsel you are." Carver ran his fingers over Abigail's face. She recoiled under his touch, taking a step back until he grabbed her arm.

"Easy, darling." He pulled her closer to him. "Look around you. You're in a prison yard, surrounded by men with guns. You're not going anywhere." He turned to one of the men. "Jimmy, hold her for me. We'll be bringing her in."

Jimmy stepped forward, grabbing Abigail's arm. She fought in his grasp as he pulled her closer to the building.

Carver turned his attention to Lisa.

"Oh, and what have we got for dessert?"

Now it was Frank's turn to react. He lunged forward, stopping only when Henderson pushed a shotgun beneath his chin.

"Now, now, Lee. I've shot you with this before. Don't make me do it again."

"It fires rubber bullets, Henderson," Frank growled. "Be my guest."

"At this range, it'll still kill you. But if you don't like that, how about this?" He retracted the shotgun and pulled out a handgun, aiming that at him instead.

"Oh, so exciting," Carver whispered, watching the exchange.

"Where did you get that?" Frank snarled.

"This?" Henderson raised the gun, admiring it in the sunlight. "This is my little toy. It's amazing what you can get when you're surrounded by criminals."

Carver pulled Lisa close. "Look at you. Curves in *all* the right places." He ran his hands over her body. "Cracking set of tits, too." He cupped her breasts, prompting her to swing a headbutt at him. Carver sidestepped, dodging her attack by inches. In response, he kicked the back of her legs. Her knees gave way and she hit the ground.

"You fucker," Frank snarled through gritted teeth.

"Oh, is this your bird?" Carver sneered, dragging Lisa back to her feet. "She's feisty, isn't she? I don't blame you, though. She's got a peachy arse on her, too." His roaming hands ran between her legs. "I'll be having her as well," he announced, pushing her towards Abigail.

"Like hell you will." Frank lunged forward, only to be struck across the head by the handgun. He staggered and fell, the asphalt grazing his face once again.

"Last chance, Lee," Henderson growled. "Next time I put a bullet in your skull."

Frank staggered to his feet, noticing Carver now stood beside the former guard.

"Tell me, Henderson," Carver said, "are any of these cunts worth keeping alive?"

The guard looked between them all. "Frank Lee is scum. Zielinski is a waste of space. And Gus Razor…" he shot a calculated look at Gus "…has been unusually quiet so far. What's up, Gus? Cat got your tongue?"

"Just thinking."

"Thinking? That's a first for you. And what, pray tell, are you thinking about?"

"How did you survive?"

A grin spread over Henderson's face. "You mean after you left me to die? Well, thankfully, not everyone in this shithole was a heartless prick. You remember McAllister?"

Frank thought back to the kind-hearted guard who had released them. The same one they had beaten up and escaped from. At the mention of the guard's name, Carver walked away, an evil sneer on his face.

"McAllister let you out?" asked Gus.

"He did indeed. He released Carver and a bunch of the others, then came back and found me. Fortunately, he killed those fuckers you left trying to have a pop at me. He even earned a little nibble off one of them, bless his heart."

Frank's stomach lurched.

"Died soon after, of course. But when he came back as one of those things… well, we couldn't bear to kill him again." Henderson chortled, looking between the horrified faces. "So, we kept him as a pet."

Frank's eyes widened in horror. Carver returned, leading a bound, hooded figure before him. An angry growl emanated from the hood as the man started thrashing against his confines.

"You sick bastard!" Frank snapped.

"Nothing from you, Razor?" said Henderson.

"We all gotta die sometime, right?"

"We do indeed. Some sooner than others."

"So, let's get started." Gus held his arms out, looking expectantly from face to face.

Carver motioned for one of his men to take control of the zombie and walked toward him once more. "You ready to die, old man?"

"As ready as I'll ever be."

"Wow, you have changed, haven't you?" Henderson praised. "Tell me, Gus, what do you hold dear now that money doesn't exist?"

"That still awaits to be seen."

Henderson sneered. "I tell you what…" He offered out his handgun.

"What the fuck are you doing?" Carver gasped, producing his own gun. "He'll kill you!"

"No, he won't," Henderson replied calmly. "He knows if he kills me, he'll be blown to Timbuktu. It's time to show allegiance, Gus. You've always been a smart man. I'm guessing Frank's *debt* means fuck all now. So shoot him. Let's prove where your loyalty lies."

Frank's heart thudded against his ribs.

"Loyalty?" Gus sneered. "You know me better than that, Henderson; I'm loyal to nobody."

With that, he grabbed the gun and fired.

The loud blast accompanied a searing pain through Frank's body. He recoiled, partially in pain, partially from the bullet's impact.

He hit the floor, his ears ringing.

His body screaming.

His vision blurred.

He thought he heard Lisa scream, but it came from afar, as though his mind had already vacated his body.

He looked through a blurred lens, watching, almost in slow motion, as Lisa and Abigail were dragged towards the building. He saw Henderson clap Gus on the back, steering him towards the prison, with Carver in tow.

"Shit!"

Zielinski's voice resonated through his head. He felt the man's hand on his shoulder, shaking him alert. Frank blinked, trying to clear his mind, trying to focus on what was around him.

It worked.

His vision gained clarity, along with his hearing. But so did the pain.

The searing fire in his side where the bullet had struck scorched through his nerves. He fought for breath, taking huge gulps as Zielinski helped him into a sitting position.

Zielinski was saying something, but Frank couldn't hear—his attention fixed on the prisoner holding McAllister.

The man cut the bindings on the zombie's hands and removed the hood from his head. With wide, bloodshot eyes, McAllister scanned his surroundings until he was shoved forward. He whirled around, but his assailant was already sprinting back to the prison. Despite this, McAllister pursued, roaring in anger as the man made it inside, the doors slamming closed behind him.

Frank tried to shuffle back, but it was no use. The pain was too intense. The three men standing on the rooftop hollered and joked as the show unfolded. After a few agitated slams against the barricaded door, McAllister turned his attention on the two men stuck inside the fenced compound with him.

"Oh shit," Zielinski whimpered. He backed away, leaving Frank alone on the ground.

The zombie's eyes grew wide, his mouth salivating, his grin spreading as he raced forward.

***

Kill them! Kill them all!
Not yet.
Gus looked around the familiar sights as he stepped inside the prison. He could still hear Frank's cries of pain behind him, but it soon ceased when the door swung closed.

"Welcome home, Gus," Henderson said, motioning for him to step forward.

I want blood.

And you'll get it.

Now!

He felt the grip of the handgun and the worrying dissolution of his resolve.

"Here, you can have this back."

Henderson blinked, a look of wonder adorning his face as he took the weapon.

"You're full of surprises, Gus."

"Really? Last time I checked, they call me Gus *Razor*. Not Gus *Shooter*."

"And I can see why," Carver sneered. "You're a shit shot. You barely got him."

Gus glanced at the man with disinterest. "I didn't need to learn how to shoot. My lads did all the dirty work."

Let's kill him. He's nobody. Henderson's running the show.

We don't know that for sure.

Kill him and find out. Let's see his blood.

Not yet.

Now!

"Give me a blade," Gus snapped, his attention back to Henderson.

"We'll get you one."

"Now."

It took a moment, but Henderson's characteristic grin appeared once more. He reached into his back pocket, producing a cut-throat razor. Gus reached to grab it, but he pulled it back.

"Be careful with this. It's my only one."

You won't want it after I've finished with it.

Gus took it and opened the blade, admiring the razor-sharp finish. His gaze flitted to Carver's neck, pinpointing his jugular.

Slit it. Slice it!

Before Gus could act, a thunderous clap sounded outside the walls.

"What the fuck was that?" Carver snapped—

The sound came again, accompanied by distant, panicked cries. As it sounded for the third time, they identified the source: gunshots.

15

"What do you see?" Amy asked, craning her neck, trying to see more of the distant prison. A large chain-link fence ran around the perimeter, topped with barbed wire. An enormous wall within the fenced area encased the prison. A change in the structure at the front led her to believe they were looking at the entrance, but from where they stood, it was impossible to be certain. She looked down at Kev, who monitored the scene through the scope of his rifle.

"Kev."

"There's quite a few," he said. "All armed. They've got hostages."

"How many?"

"I don't know. They're bringing them out of the van."

"Abigail," Kara cried. She scrambled closer to Kev. "Is Abigail there? Long black hair, about five-foot-six?"

"Yeah, she's there."

Kara sobbed, running fingers through her hair. "Well c'mon, let's go rescue them."

"It's not that simple," Kev replied, still monitoring the scene. "They outnumber us. They've got guys on the roof and the ground. If they see us getting close, they'll open fire."

"Can't you pick them off from here?" Ben suggested.

Kev shook his head. "The minute I start shooting, they'll retreat inside. They could take the hostages with them, or kill them. Either way, not a desirable outcome."

"So, what are we going to do?" Kara whimpered.

"We need to attack from two angles. I can't get a clear shot from here. I need higher ground." He turned away from the scope and scanned the field behind them. "There."

He pointed to what seemed to be the shell of an old factory. Most of it lay in ruin, aside from a two-storey metal fire escape still intact next to a flimsy-looking wall. The prison and the structure seemed so far apart, but Kev had to know what he was doing.

"I'll take up position back there. Donna, you be the driver. I want the rest of you to stick to the treeline and get as close as you can." He pointed to the woodland running off to the side of the prison. "The minute you hear my first shot, I want you to attack. I'll take out as many as I can, but it's down to you to get the hostages out."

"And how do we do that?" Amy asked.

"Stay low and get across to the gate. It looks like the only way through the fence. I'll take out the ones on the roof. You aim through the fence. Hopefully, with all the confusion, we'll get to the hostages before they get them inside, but if there are more gunmen in there, we'll have to work fast. Donna, the minute you hear my shot, you drive down to help them. Get in, extract them, and get out."

"How are we all going to escape in the car?" Amy asked.

Kev looked through the rifle sight again, counting under his breath. "I see five hostages now. Just put the back seats down and pile in. Cling to the roof rack if you have to. Once the confusion has cleared, they might launch a counter-attack. I don't want to hang around long enough for that to happen. In. Rescue. Out. Are we all clear?"

The group nodded.

"Good, Donna, drive me to that factory. You three head for the treeline. Remember, wait for my first shot."

Amy turned and ran with Ben and Kara towards the woodland. They heard a screech of tyres behind them as the SUV raced away. Her heartbeat trebled as the realisation of their task started to sink in. Just over a week ago, she was a nurse working her first shift at the local hospital. Now, she was an armed apocalypse survivor on a rescue mission, about to storm a prison. She felt sick, her body trembling as they fought through the dense foliage. She followed Ben's path, trying to tread in his footsteps as they continued on.

After a couple of minutes, she heard a faint muttering.

"Please be okay, please be okay." Kara's whispers followed her like an audible shadow.

"We're nearly there," Amy said, trying to reassure her. Through the gaps in the trees, the prison seemed a lot closer now, and she could make out a gathering through the chain-link fence. They were all outside the main entrance. The figures were still indiscernible, but she felt reassured they were all alive.

"There's so many," she said. "Which ones do we fire at first?"

"The ones pointing their weapons at you."

She could hear the smile in Ben's voice. Despite not knowing how he could remain calm in such a tense situation, she felt reassured. It was a fleeting emotion, one displaced by shock as a gunshot resounded.

It wasn't Kev. The sound had come from the prison.

Kara whimpered, obviously drawing the same conclusion.

"Hurry!" Ben hissed. They pushed on through the overgrowth, batting aside shrubs and low-hanging branches. The crack of the gun still resonated in Amy's head. A pang of fear struck home when she considered they might have been discovered. She looked back at the prison, conscious they were at the edge of the treeline. Yet, no further shots came. If they had been discovered, they would have been dodging bullets by now.

So, who did they shoot?

They were almost at the prison, less than a hundred metres from the gate, when the next shot thundered. This time, it *was* Kev. The distinct difference in volume and ensuing resonance told her that much.

"Let's go!" Ben's words were barely audible as another shot came. The trio leapt out of the woodland and onto the open field, sprinting as fast as they could toward the prison. Amy looked to the roof, in time to see a third shot dispatch one of the gunmen.

One more remained.

She toyed with the idea of stopping to take a shot of her own, but Kev's stark warning overrode this thought. *In. Rescue. Out.* She raced on, scanning the rest of the building for signs of movement. She looked back up at the gunman on the roof, her stomach lurching when she saw him aiming at them. She stopped in her tracks, fumbling with her rifle before another shot thundered. The gunman disappeared from view—another victim of their police marksman.

"Amy, move!" Ben shouted over his shoulder.

She sprinted to catch up to them as they neared the chain-link fence. Through the gap, she could see Frank lying on the ground, clutching his side. Another man stood nearby, agitatedly darting back and forth. She looked back as a roaring engine quickly grew louder behind them. Donna raced into view, speeding past them and smashing through the chain-link gate onto the open part of the compound.

"Get in!" Donna shouted. The frantic man obeyed, rushing over to the SUV as Ben and Kara reached the entrance.

"Abigail?" Kara cried.

Amy rounded the open gates and rushed past her. Abigail wasn't there, that much was clear. But the others in the forecourt could still be helped. Frank writhed in agony, pushing Ben away as he went to kneel beside him. Another body lay nearby, clad in full body armour. His head had been obliterated, showering the asphalt in claret.

"They've shot him," Ben said.

"How bad?" Amy wheezed. She crouched down and pried Frank's hand away from his side. A huge red disc had formed through his shirt, with blood pooling beneath him. "Okay, help me get him in the car."

Ben draped Frank's arm around his neck, and together they hoisted him to his feet. He cried out in pain, trying to shrug Amy away as she pressed a hand to his side.

"Keep the pressure on or you'll die!" she snapped. Donna had lowered the back seats of the SUV, allowing them all to scramble in. Amy crouched beside Frank, holding his side.

"Kara, get in!" Ben yelled.

"Where's Abigail?"

"We have to go, now!"

She shrieked when Ben grabbed her around the waist. He dragged her into the car just as the prison doors flew open.

"Drive!"

The tyres squealed and the SUV shot forward, through the chain-link gate and back onto the road. Gunshots sounded from the prison entrance, occasionally interrupted by the boom of a countering sniper rifle. Amy flinched when a bullet ricocheted off the roof. She struggled to remain upright as Donna weaved back and forth across the road.

"We need to go back," Kara cried. "They still have Abigail."

"And Lisa," groaned Frank. He tried to sit up, but hissed in pain, falling back in a slump.

"We will. We'll get them back." Amy looked up at Ben and saw he shared her concern. *But how?*

"Is everyone okay?" Donna called over her shoulder.

"Yeah. Just make sure you get us back in one piece."

Donna slowed to a halt beside the red sports car. "Okay, let's split up," she urged.

"I'll stay here with Frank," Amy said. "Ben, you take Kara and, what's your name?" She turned to the man in the passenger seat.

"Zielinski."

"Right, you go with Ben and Kara in that car."

"Where shall we meet you?" Ben asked.

Amy racked her brain. "Frank. Do you have any supplies at the army base? First-aid kit? Anything?"

"Yeah. Just patch me up and get me back to the prison."

"We'll meet you at the army base," Amy said. Ben nodded in response and leapt out of the SUV, with Kara and Zielinski in tow. Once clear, Donna raced toward the distant, derelict factory. Kev had already descended the stairs and stood waiting for them.

"Is everyone alright?" he asked, jumping into the passenger seat. He looked over his shoulder as they drove away once again.

"Yeah, but Frank got shot," Amy said.

"I know." He looked down at Frank. "Who were those lads? Friends of yours?"

"How many *friends* do you know shoot each other?" he snapped.

"None. But then again, I'm not a criminal. What happened back there?"

Frank shuffled against the side of the SUV, wincing in pain as he tried to sit further up. "They ambushed us in

Doxley. Took us back to the prison. Looks like it's run by some guy called Carver and that stupid prick Henderson."

"I take it you know him?"

"We have history. He was a guard at Harrodale. Tormented me for years. We left him for dead, but he survived."

"Is that why he shot you?"

"*He* didn't. Gus Razor did."

"Who?"

"One of our group. He's joined them now. We need to get back there so I can kill him. And rescue Lisa."

"Where is she?"

"They took her and that other lass inside. We need to go back."

"You're in no state to return yet," Amy chided. "I need to check this wound and get it cleaned."

"We're getting more guns and going back."

"If your wound gets infected, you'll probably die."

"I'll be fine."

"Yeah. Sure. What do I know, right?"

"How many of them are there?" Kev asked.

"I don't know." Frank slid back down, his eyes closed. "How many did you kill?"

"Four or five, if you include that zombie they set on you. You're welcome, by the way."

Frank remained silent.

"What's the plan now, Amy?" asked Kev.

"We need to head to the army base. Once I've dressed Frank's wound, we can decide what we're going to do next."

"The only plan is to return to the prison," Frank countered. "If you aren't game, I'll go on my own."

"Then it'll be a waste of time patching you up. If you go back there alone, you're as good as dead."

"So, help me."

"We're not gonna leave them behind," Amy sighed, massaging the bridge of her nose. "I just don't know how we're going to do it yet."

"Well, you need to think of something quick. The only people in that prison are sex offenders and murderers. We don't have long."

***

Lisa struggled in the grasp of her captor. The cable ties bit into her skin as she twisted and turned, flexing her fists.

"Quit it."

She strained her neck to get a better look at Jimmy. He was tall and lean, with solid muscle stretching his tight-fitting shirt. He glowered at her, shoving her forward. Unable to stop herself, Lisa hit the ground hard, pitching from her knees onto her stomach.

"Leave her alone," Abigail whimpered. Lisa struggled back to her feet as footfalls approached.

"Well?" Jimmy asked.

"They got away." Carver stopped in front of Lisa. "Who else do you have with you?"

"Nobody."

He seized a handful of her hair and yanked her closer until they were almost nose-to-nose.

"Tell me."

Lisa smiled, offering nothing but a gobbet of spit in his face. Carver recoiled, wiping his eye. Then he retaliated with a knee to her stomach. Lisa doubled over, gasping to refill the air blasted from her body.

"You won't get anything out of her, kid," said Gus Razor. "She's as stubborn as an ox."

"Is she really?" Carver gripped her chin, forcing her to stand upright again. "I'm going to have fun breaking you." He then turned his attention to Abigail. "And you."

"That one's not worth your time," said Gus. "She isn't even part of their group."

Carver ran fingers through Abigail's long dark hair, sliding it beneath his nose. "Is that so? Or are you trying to protect her?"

Gus snorted, but the humour didn't reach his eyes.

A look of delight spread across Carver's face. "Jimmy, take them both to the doctor's office. I'll be along later. And remember, you lay a finger on them and you're dead. I get first dip."

With that, Jimmy shoved the pair forward, down a sterile white corridor and into a vast open area. The stench of death and decay became overwhelming, matched by the spatter on the walls and the floor. The macabre graffiti consisted of brain matter, old brown blood, and fresh red splats. Whoops and hollers accompanied them from the metal walkway above.

"Fresh meat!"

"We gonna get some pussy tonight."

"Jimmy, where are you taking that gash? Bring them up here!"

The crude outbursts and obscenities continued long after they left the hall, echoing through the corridor. Finally, they stopped outside a medical room, indicated by a green cross and a wall-mounted defibrillator.

"Get in."

Jimmy shoved them into the room, one at a time, before following them inside. The office was of a conventional nature. A pine desk topped with a computer and keyboard occupied one side of the room, with an examination bed against another. Aside from a filing cabinet next to the door—in front of which Jimmy stood—there was nothing else of note, and certainly nothing they could use to free themselves.

Lisa motioned to the bed on the other side of the room. Jimmy stood with his arms crossed, watching the pair as they leaned against it.

"We're going to be fine," she whispered, her back to the sentinel at the door, who stood watching, smirking.

"Fine? They're going to rape us."

"I'm going to get us out of here before that happens."

A light of hope illuminated Abigail's tear-stained eyes. "How?"

"I don't know yet," she admitted.

16

He's got her. He's got Miranda.

She's going to be fine.

He's going to hurt her.

Not while he's with us.

Gus glanced around the familiar corridor of HMP Harrodale. Flanked by Henderson and Carver, it was almost reminiscent of his time as a prisoner.

We are a prisoner.

Maybe for now. In time, we'll be running this place again.

We need to kill Carver before he hurts Miranda.

I told you, it's not Miranda!

Gus side-eyed the man to his left, enraged by the smug look on his face as he glanced around the prison.

"You seem to know this place well."

Carver turned to him. "A king needs to know every inch of his kingdom, wouldn't you agree?"

"How long have you been here?"

"Carver got transferred right before all this shit started," said Henderson.

"Explains why you don't know me."

"Should I?" Carver sneered.

"I'd say so. This used to be *my* prison. *I* ran this place."

"How things have changed." Carver smirked. "Now let's make one thing clear: *I'm* the host. And you? You're a guest in my court."

He swept his arm out, showcasing the long rec room. An enormous pile of bodies now stood where the ping-pong and pool tables used to be. Gus recognised one or two faces of prisoner and guard alike atop the macabre hill.

"I love what you've done with the place."

"Yeah, me too. It's artistic, right?" Carver strode forward, arms outstretched. "It's like a monument to the dead—A memory of times past."

"Or a pile of corpses."

Carver turned back. "You're just another uncultured cretin. Unable to appreciate true art when it's right in front of you."

"Yup. That's me."

Henderson stepped forward, obviously playing mediator. "Let's show him the other changes."

"Wait 'til you see what else I've done." Carver motioned for the pair to follow him as he strode through another door.

Our prison. Our kingdom. It's time to dethrone him.

Gus clamped his fingers around the blade in his pocket. He walked alongside Henderson, stopping as two prisoners dragged a third through the doorway in front of them. They each grabbed a leg and an arm, hoisting the man off the ground and swinging him onto the pile of corpses.

"What happened to him?" Henderson asked.

"Fell into a shiv," one man replied.

"Six or seven times," the other added.

The two men cackled as they walked away, dusting off their hands.

"I don't recognise them, either," Gus said.

"Of course you don't. You never mixed with the sex offenders."

"They're nonces?" Razor spat.

"Some of them, others are just rapists."

"And what's Carver?"

Henderson sneered. "He's a bit of everything."

He's a waste of space. Let's kill him.

Not yet. We kill him now, we're dead. He'll have all the rapists and nonces on his side.

"What are you waiting for?" Carver called down the corridor. "Fucking hurry up."

Henderson quickened his pace, with Gus strolling after him.

"Hungry, Gus?" Carver smirked.

"Not particularly."

"That's a shame. Wait 'til you see what we've got in the kitchen."

He needs to die. His blood needs to paint these walls.

And it will.

Now.

Not yet.

Kill him now, or I will.

Not yet.
Now!
"No!"

"What's the matter with you?" Henderson asked.

"I—uh, I left the iron on."

"You're a strange man, Gus Razor." Carver motioned for them to walk ahead, his suspicious gaze still fixed on Gus.

They entered the canteen, where a small group was gathered around the tables. The din of indignant chatter was periodically interrupted by a loud burp, or tobacco-induced cough. The men slurped the same lumpy gruel, all wearing the same look of disgust. Some of the murmurings trailed off as the trio approached.

"I see some things haven't changed," Gus said, following Carver past the disgruntled prisoners and into the kitchen.

"Maybe, but the recipe certainly has," Carver sneered, a delighted look on his face. "We have a gourmet chef now. He's—"

"Chomping Charlie!" Gus beamed, arms outstretched as if greeting a long-lost son. The chef looked up, wiping his hands on his bloody apron. He offered a toothy grin as Gus approached. "How are you doing, my son?"

"G-g-g-good, G-Gus," he stammered.

"Bloody hell, you still got that stutter? I thought you would've calmed down with all your fellow cannibals running around now."

The man chuckled, holding a bloody hand to his mouth.

"What's cooking? Or is that a daft question?"

The man laughed harder, leaning against the counter to support his trembling frame.

"You two know each other?" Carver asked, unable to mask the disappointment in his voice.

"Yeah, Chomping Charlie has been here longer than me. So, you're feeding these boys human flesh then?"

"No, not yet," Henderson said. "But we're considering it. Supplies are running out, and we've got a lot of mouths to feed."

"Is that why you've been abducting survivors?"

"Abducting survivors?" said Carver. "We haven't abducted anyone. Except you." His confused expression turned to one of delight. "Although, now you mention it, it *is* a good idea. We could use them for meat. We could even start with you." He looked past Gus towards the chef. "What do you say, Charlie? Shall we put Gus in one of your stews?"

Henderson stepped in. "Boys, boys. Stop with all this shit. We need to stick together. There's an army of zombies out there; we need to unite." He turned to Carver. "I kept Gus alive so he can help us run this place. He's not going to take over, but he *does* know some of the lads giving us grief. If anybody can get them on side, Gus Razor can."

Carver considered this for a moment. He fixed his eyes on Gus. "So why *do* they call you Razor?"

"Bring me the lads you're having trouble with, and I'll show you."

Carver smirked. "Okay, maybe we *can* find a use for him."

"Yeah, he definitely has his uses," Henderson said.

Gunshots sounded outside, prompting a hefty sigh from Carver. "If those bastards are back, I'm going to put their heads on pikes." He turned to Gus. "You're on our side? You're going to help us get this place in order, right?"

Gus nodded.

"Good. Then come with me. Let's see if any more of your friends are attempting a rescue mission."

"I don't have friends," Gus countered, following Carver out of the canteen and onto a long corridor. He couldn't see Henderson, but he could hear him at his heel.

"Why does that not surprise me?" Carver laughed.

They strode through a barred gateway onto another corridor. It was then Gus realised all the gates were open. "Do you not think this place is a bit insecure now?"

"How do you mean?" Henderson called from the rear.

"All the gates are open. What if the zombies get in?"

"Do you think these boys would want to stay if everywhere was still locked up?" Carver shouted, not looking back as they rounded a corner and ascended a stairwell. "They get free rein in this prison. That's part of the deal. In return, they maintain, supply, and defend it."

"Sounds like you're too soft on them."

Carver stopped and whirled to face Gus.

"You think you can do better?"

"I *know* I can. Don't worry, son, with me at your side, I'll have them eating out of the palm of your hand.

Carver studied him, as if he was trying to find a visual flaw in his statement. When none was forthcoming, he turned and continued up the stairs. Despite the stairwell looking vaguely familiar, Gus struggled to place where they were heading. It was only once they emerged onto the roof that the memory hit.

He had been up there once before, having incited a riot a few years back. After being told the prison was no longer stocking Yorkshire Tea, Gus provoked a series of mass violence towards the guards, which culminated in the prisoners taking an entire wing. The two-day siege ended when the army arrived, but by that point, Gus had already returned to his cell. The guards had met his demands after the first few hours, and, with no further cause to protest, he had left the prisoners to it.

Now, they were on the roof again, but in completely different circumstances. He followed Carver to the edge, where a pair of prisoners fired at a group of zombies below. What was left of those previously manning the roof lay scattered around. A dead body at his feet only had the lower part of its skull remaining.

Sniper fire. Where the fuck did they get a sniper from?

The huddle of zombies stood at the metal fence, yanking at the mesh, each being dropped one after the other by the riflemen.

"Any sign of those bastards that attacked?" Carver asked.

"Nah, just this lot. The noise must have attracted them," one of the men replied. "We haven't seen any sign of the cars."

You won't see anything if they've got a sniper, Gus mused. Shielding his eyes from the sun, he looked out at the endless fields, fixing on the solitary speck in the distance.

"What's up?" Henderson asked.

"That building over there. What is it?"

"Just old factory ruins. Why?"

"Because they've got a sniper."

"A *sniper*?" Carver spat.

Gus nodded. "And the only vantage point I can see for miles around is that factory over there. That must have been where he was."

"They did drive over that way," one rifleman offered.

"That must be it. I'd advise you get some of your men to tear it down before they come back."

Carver glowered at the distant factory. "How do you know it's a sniper?"

Gus kicked the corpse at his feet. "Had to have been a high calibre to take most of his head off like that. And from his position, he could only have been taken out by somebody from a similar vantage point."

"You know your guns, then?"

"Of course I do."

"Yet you barely hit your buddy earlier."

"Like I told you before, I don't need to shoot. Why learn to bark when you've got a pack of dogs?"

Carver sneered and looked back down at the corpse. "Yeah. Well, that's some good work, Gus."

"I'm not just a pretty face."

"Clearly. Henderson, take some lads over there and tear that piece of shit down."

"Me?"

"Yeah. You know what they're like—barely a brain cell between them. They might end up rebuilding the fucker if they're not supervised."

"How do you propose we tear it down?"

"Well I'm guessing *you* have more than one brain cell. Figure it out. Just make sure they can't use it again."

"Maybe Gus should—"

"No," Carver interrupted. "I wanna chat to Gus. Go on, hurry up before more zombies come."

Henderson seemed ready to protest, but thought better of it. He strode past them, back inside the building, leaving Gus, Carver, and the remaining gunmen on the roof.

Now's our chance. We've got him alone.

Are you forgetting about those lads with the rifles?

No. We can kill them, too.

Not without a good chance of being shot.

"You're a peculiar man, Gus Razor." Carver stared out at the vast countryside, his hands clasped behind his back.

"Took you a while to work that out."

"It's taking me longer to work out if I can trust you or not."

Gus tightened his grip on the blade in his pocket.

"What about Henderson? Can I trust him?"

"I think you know the answer to that," Gus sneered.

"Yeah, once a screw, always a screw, right?"

"Exactly."

"So why did he keep *you* alive?"

Gus studied Carver's deadpan face. "You know why. You need me to convince some lads to join you."

"I *heard* what he said, but that's not the same thing. What does Henderson have to gain by keeping you alive?"

"Apart from the reason he gave? Fucked if I know."

"Hmm."

They fell silent, watching the desolate fields for any sign of movement. The unrelenting sun prompted every pore in Gus's body to expel sweat. He wiped away a film across his brow, plucking his shirt from his back. Carver appeared oblivious to the heat, lost in a world of thought. Before long, they heard a commotion at the front of the prison.

"Sterling, you can come as well," Henderson called. "Hurry up, let's get this done. A trio of doors slammed shut in conjunction with a rumbling engine. The prison van trundled into view as it left the yard and set off towards the derelict factory.

"What would you say if I told you Henderson's days are numbered?" Carver asked.

"I'd say I'm surprised he lasted *this* long."

A grin creased Carver's face. "He was useful in the beginning—helped me secure this place, and get people onside. But now, he's made the mistake of bringing you in. If you can get the remaining lads to step in line, he'll no longer be useful."

"Which lads?"

"Just some wannabe gangsters and smackheads, really. But they're showing reluctance to follow me. Henderson has tried different ways of convincing them, but it hasn't worked."

"Why don't you just kill them?"

"Oh, I'd love to. But it's not that simple. Y'see, they're well-liked in here. If I kill them, I risk an uprising. All my hard work would be for nothing."

"So that's where I come in?"

"Possibly. You convince them to join me, then we'll get rid of Henderson and you can be my second-in-command."

"And you expect *me* to just fall in line?" Gus snorted.

Carver turned to him. "I don't have any qualms about killing *you*. If you don't want to help, let me know."

"What's in it for me?"

"Aside from continuing to draw breath, not a great deal."

Gus sneered, looking back out at the prison van in the distance.

Make him promise not to hurt Miranda.

She's not *Miranda.*

Do it!

"Okay, I'll help you. But I want something in return."

"Which is?"

"The woman."

Carver grinned, his eyes lighting up once more. "I knew it. What is she, your bit on the side?"

"Not quite."

Carver sucked air through his teeth. "But to ask me to give away such a delicious morsel...I was looking forward to ploughing her."

"There's always the blonde one, and the other one still waiting to be picked up."

Carver frowned. "What other one?"

"Didn't you notice only half your boys came back? They're waiting for the van to pick them up. They've got another lass with them."

"What? Why am I only hearing about this now?"

Gus puffed out his chest. "We'll have to get these boys in line, won't we?"

Carver gave him a calculated look. "Okay, Gus Razor. You have my word. You can have the tart, providing you help me get this place in order. Put it there."

They shook hands. "Deal."

"Good. I'm going to find that prick, Mo. You enjoy the view a little while, and make sure Henderson does his job. With any luck, he'll die out there and save us the hassle."

Once Carver had left, Gus looked back out at the distant ruins, contemplating his options. Which would he benefit from more? Partnering with Carver, or Henderson? Both came with various risks and rewards. And while it was a troubling decision to make, it would only be a temporary measure, anyway. By the end of the day, both would be dead and *he'd* be the one running the prison.

17

"This place was empty when you got here?" Amy asked, taking in the vast structure as they approached the army base.

"No," said Frank. "There was a soldier hiding out when Gus and Zielinski turned up. They had him restrained by the time me and Lisa arrived."

"So where is he now?"

"Dead."

Amy tore her gaze away from the building to look at Frank. "Did you kill him?"

"No. He shot himself after becoming infected."

The SUV lurched to a stop outside the double-doors. The others had already arrived and were standing beside their car.

"Okay, let's get you inside."

Amy offered a hand to assist, but Frank ignored it, instead shuffling to the edge of the door and gingerly easing himself outside. He hissed in agony when he rose to his feet, increasing the pressure on his side.

Zielinski entered first, closely followed by the others.

"This place is huge," Kev said, looking around the great hall. "How did you keep it secure?"

"With these," Zielinski answered. He stood beside the front doors, manoeuvring one of the heavy metal barrels. "Give me a hand, will you?"

"That won't be necessary," Frank said, hobbling to one of the side rooms. "Once I'm patched up, we're heading straight out."

"Don't you think we should come up with a plan first?" Amy asked. She followed him into the room, where an overpowering smell of decay greeted her. The stench of rotten flesh had endlessly assaulted her senses over the past week. Yet, it was something she felt she'd never get accustomed to. The thick, cloying acid hit the back of her throat every time, prompting her to cover her mouth. The boarded windows offered minimal light, but coupled with the glowing swathes coming through the front doors, she could make out most of the room's contents. A number of chairs lay haphazardly around the floor, with a powerless vending machine in the corner. When she saw the mutilated body resting against it, she realised the source of the foul smell. Frank strode past, seemingly unperturbed by the grisly corpse.

"I'm guessing this is your dead soldier?"

Frank said nothing, retrieving a first-aid kit from the table and shuffling back towards her.

"What's going on?" Kara stepped into the room, pinching her nose to ward off the rotten stench.

"We're going to get Frank patched up and then work out how we're going to get Lisa and Abigail back."

"I told you, we don't have time for that," Frank said. "We need to get back there *now*."

"And do what? Go rushing in there, guns blazing?"

"They're going to be killed."

"And so will we if we run in there. We need a plan." She walked back into the hallway, where Ben and Donna stood waiting. "Where's Kev?"

"He's gone upstairs to check what's here."

"Tell him to keep his hands off the guns and ammo," Frank snarled, hobbling after Amy.

"Relax," she chided. "Take a seat."

She righted an upturned chair in the middle of the hall and took the first-aid box from Frank. The contents were sparse, with only a couple of rolled bandages, gauze, surgical tape, and a bottle of saline solution. She eased his shirt up, assessing the injury.

"It's just a flesh wound," she said. "The bullet has gone straight through."

Frank scoffed. "Terrific."

"You should count yourself lucky."

"*Lucky*?"

"If the bullet had struck any of your organs, you'd probably be dead. If the blood loss didn't kill you, shock or infection certainly would. So yeah, you're lucky."

She ripped open the gauze and pressed it against the wound.

"Hold this for me."

She ripped some strips of surgical tape free and secured the gauze in place.

"There. That should keep for now."

"Thanks," Frank muttered. He rose to his feet, leaning to his left so as not to stretch his side. "Now let's head back."

"I agree," Kara added. "Please, we can't wait any longer."

"Guys, we need to think of a way in," Amy sighed. "Frank, you know that place better than anyone. It's a *maximum-security* prison. It's designed to keep people in and would-be rescuers out."

Frank crossed his arms.

"Kara, I'm sorry," Amy said. "I know you want to rescue Abigail. We all do. But we need to be strategic here. How are we going to do it?"

Kara nodded, tears falling from her closed eyes. After a few moments of silence, Frank turned his back on them and shuffled down the hall.

"Where are you going?" asked Amy.

"I need a drink."

She exchanged a glance with the rest of the group. "C'mon, let's go after him. We need to think of something. Let's put our heads together and work out how we're going to do this."

"I'll go and find Kev," Donna offered, and went for the stairs.

Kara morosely walked towards the room Frank had entered, her jerking shoulders betraying the sobs she tried to conceal. Amy replaced the contents of the first-aid kit, listening as Ben stepped closer.

Jerking

"Are you sure about this?" he whispered. "You wanna go back there?"

"We can't leave them, Ben. It's a prison filled with sex offenders and murderers. They won't stand a chance."

"Nor will we if we try to attack that place. You saw how many there were, and that was just on the outside. They're armed, too."

"So are we."

"You want us to risk our lives trying to save two people we don't even know?"

"I'm a nurse, Ben. My job—No. My *calling*—is to save people I don't know."

"And my job was to keep people safe. If we attack that place, it won't end well."

Amy fell silent, staring into the deep green pools of his eyes, desperately trying to find an ounce of compassion.

"What if it was Fran?" she asked. "What if it was me?"

There it was. The compassion became clear when his brows slackened and his eyes widened. The realisation hit home.

"I—uh." He considered his words before emitting a long sigh of acceptance. "I'd do whatever I could to save you."

Amy felt her heart swell. She placed a hand on his arm, still staring into his eyes.

"So, are we gonna do this, then?" Kev called from the top of the stairs. Amy quickly took a step away from Ben, who offered a kind, reassuring smile. Kev and Donna made their way down towards them.

"Yeah. Frank and Kara are in there. Let's go and work out how to do this."

She led the group over to the side room Frank and Kara had entered. Despite the gloom, she could make out a bar area. A pool table stood in the middle of the room, with a number of bar stools positioned around it. Frank sat behind the bar, cradling a large bottle that seemed to be some sort of spirit. Kara sat opposite him, holding another bottle. They both looked up as Amy approached.

"So, how are we going to save them?" she asked, placing the first-aid kit on the pool table.

"I don't know." Frank looked back at his bottle. "You said yourself there's no way in."

"They'll have the entrance secured," Kev said. "I couldn't see much, but they've boarded the glass doors. It also took them a while to come back out, which suggests they might have had to remove barricades blocking the door."

"Is there no other way in?"

"I doubt it," said Kev, hoisting his large frame onto the pool table. "We could get through the metal fence easy enough, but that wall runs around the perimeter of the prison."

"How did you escape, Frank?" Amy asked.

He took a long swig from his bottle before answering. "We stole a prison van and went through the garage."

"Could we get in that way?"

"I doubt it. Henderson has been a guard there for years. He would've made sure it was secure."

"So, we can't fight our way in?"

Frank shook his head, the liquid sloshing as he drank.

"The prison van!" Kara gasped, jumping from her stool.

"What?"

"They were supposed to send another van out to collect me, remember? Along with those guys you killed."

"Yeah. That's an idea," Kev said. "We can pick them off, steal the van, and head back to the prison."

"Okay, but how does that help us?" Ben asked.

"They'll open the doors if they think we're one of their own. Almost like a Trojan horse."

"Okay, so they'll open the front door. The minute they see it's us, they'll run back in, or blow us to pieces."

"Which is why we kill them as soon as they open the door."

"Then what?" Frank asked, no longer interested in his bottle. "What do we do when we're inside?"

"That's when we draw on your expertise," Amy said. "You know that place better than any of us."

"I don't know where they'll be holding them. It's a *prison*. There are hundreds of cells in there. They could be using any of them."

"Then we work our way through until we find them."

"You think seven of us are going to stand a chance getting in and out?"

"*Six*," came a voice.

The group turned to look at Zielinski in the corner of the room.

"What?"

"You've got six people. I'm not going back there."

Frank tightened his grip on the bottle, causing the liquid inside to tremor. "You're not going to help?"

"Why would I? You think I'm going to risk my life for a pair of tarts who're probably already dead?"

That's enough! No longer content with venting his anger on the neck of the bottle, Frank hurled it at Zielinski. He ducked out of range as it smashed into the wall, showering the room with shards of glass.

"You pathetic little cunt!" Frank spat, making his way around the bar. Ben and Kev intervened, each grabbing a shoulder and wrapping an arm across his torso before he could reach Zielinski.

"You need to save your strength," Kev warned.

"He's not worth it," Ben added.

Frank stepped back reluctantly, his glare fixed on the Polish man. "Get the fuck out of here, you piece of shit!"

Zielinski slunk silently out of the room, avoiding all eye contact.

"That leaves us with six," Frank snarled. "It's going to be even harder now."

"I'm trained in tactical infiltration," Kev countered. "As long as you all follow my lead, we should be fine. I'll need you up front with me to navigate. Ben and Amy can bring up the rear, with Donna and Kara in the middle."

"I've never fired a gun before," Kara said.

"It's okay. I'll give you an overview on the way. Now, how long did they say they'd be?"

"Half an hour."

"That doesn't give us much time. Let's hope the chaos we caused has delayed them. If we miss the pickup, we're screwed."

"Then let's go." Frank pushed away from the bar and made for the hall. He stopped in the doorway when Ben came to meet him.

"You might want this back." Ben offered Frank the recovered shotgun. "Take better care of it next time."

Frank sneered and snatched it from his grasp. "Thanks."

"You've got quite the armoury here," Kev called after him as he went into the hall. "We'll need that if we're going to save them."

"Whatever it takes."

"Well, that machine gun can come for a start. Then there's the shotgun, and—"

"Grab whatever you need," Frank said. "Let's just get on the road and get this done."

"Donna, get some bandages," Kev said. "Just in case. I'll go and get the stuff upstairs."

Frank sighed in exasperation as they dashed in different directions. He knew they were running out of time. He could feel it.

***

"What are you staring at?"

After enduring Lisa's studious gaze for a couple of minutes, Jimmy had finally had enough.

"You," Lisa said. "I'm trying to work you out. But I gotta admit, I'm struggling."

"Yeah. You will."

"You've got that mysterious bad-boy vibe going on. Hasn't he, Abigail?"

Abigail nodded sheepishly.

"Is that right?" he sneered.

"Definitely. That shaved head, tribal tattoos over those *bulging* biceps. I wouldn't want to mess with you."

"Then don't."

"See, that's where I'm conflicted." Lisa pushed away from the wall and walked towards him. "Whilst you *do* seem like a tough guy, I'm pretty sure I could take you."

This earned a hearty laugh, to which Lisa responded with a sweet smile.

"I'm tougher than I look," she continued. "I've floored plenty of guys in the past who were the stereotypical tough guy."

"Appearances can be deceptive," Jimmy murmured, leaning in close to Lisa, who had stopped in front of him.

"Indeed. So how about a wager?"

"A wager?"

Lisa nodded. "You cut these cable ties off my wrist and we engage in a fair fight. If I win, you let us go."

Jimmy hissed through his teeth, portraying a look of turmoil, but his eyes gave him away. "That's an awfully risky wager."

Despite the condescension in his voice, Lisa persisted. "The greater the risk, the greater the reward."

"And what do I get if *I* win?"

Lisa looked back at Abigail, who regarded her with wide, horrified eyes. "You get us."

This time, Jimmy threw his head back, laughing harder than ever. He leaned against the wall for support, wiping a tear from his eye. His dramatic flair told Lisa everything she needed to know. She felt her stomach sink as it dawned on her.

"Of course, that would be worthless to you, wouldn't it?" she said. "On account of us both missing a cock."

"Bingo!" Jimmy chortled. He yanked her shoulder, spinning her to face Abigail, his bristled cheek brushing against hers. "Now," he whispered, "if your pitiful attempts at seduction are over, get back over there."

He shoved her forward, and, without being able to use her arms to steady herself, Lisa ploughed into Abigail. They fell to the ground, clattering against the metal bed frame.

"You couldn't tell he was gay?" Abigail whispered as they tried to get back to their feet.

"Obviously not. Could you?"

"I guessed, seeing as he hasn't raped us yet."

"True." Lisa steadied herself against the bed and struggled to her feet.

"So what now?"

"Now, we think of something else."

18

Gus strode through the familiar halls with a new sense of wonder. Whilst the prison still looked predominantly the same, the experience of roaming the corridors alone and unchallenged felt completely alien. He rounded the corner and saw the long metal walkway overlooking the hall below. It felt like a lifetime since he had run across it with the others to escape the prison.

He stepped onto the metal grating, walking across the bridge until he reached the centre. The hall below, previously riddled with corpses of prisoner and guard alike, was now clear. *They're probably all in that pile of dead bodies,* he mused.

He failed to see the logic of keeping the corpses inside. Not that it mattered. Once he was running the prison again, the 'monument to the dead' would be the first to go, with Carver's body added to it.

"There you are, Mo!" a voice echoed up from the hall. Gus leaned over the railing, watching as a prisoner strode across the room. He approached three men, one of whom looked familiar.

The one from Doxley.

"What is it?" Mo demanded.

"Carver's looking for you. He seems pissed."

"What have I done now?"

"I dunno, something about another lass needing to be picked up."

"Oh, fuck." Mo slapped a hand to his forehead. "I completely forgot. We left the other three lads with that tart." He turned to the others. "One of you needs to get out there now. If I tell him somebody's on the way to pick them up —"

"That won't work," the newcomer said.

"Why not?"

"Because he's stood out front with the vans."

"Vans? I thought Henderson took a few lads out in one?"

"Yeah, they've just got back."

"Shit," Mo hissed, sliding his hand down his face.

"It's alright," one of the men said. "I'll head out and pick them up. It'll be fine."

"That's not what worries me. I'm just wondering what those horny bastards will have done to her by now. I doubt Carver's gonna want sloppy seconds."

"If they're daft enough to have had her already, then Carver will deal with them."

Mo chewed his thumbnail, contemplating his options. "Well, let's not keep him waiting."

The trio quickly shuffled out of the hall, like troublesome schoolboys sent to the headteacher's office.

"Are you lost, sugarplum?"

Gus turned as somebody stepped onto the walkway, heading towards him. The man puffed his chest out, walking with a strut that reminded Gus of a peacock brandishing its feathers. His once-white string vest was now a faded grey, with yellow discs staining the armpits.

"Not lost," Gus replied, standing his ground. "I'm exactly where I want to be."

"Is that right?" The man didn't slow, and as he came within reach, he swung a fist towards Razor's face. Gus stepped back, leaning aside as another came his way straight after. The momentum of the punch sent the man into the side rail, allowing Gus to make his move. With all his strength, he shoved the man hard, causing him to roll over the top. His attacker yelped in alarm. He grabbed the ledge with one hand, his other dangling aimlessly.

"Help me," the man pleaded. "Don't let me fall, please."

Gus shook his head and retrieved the cut-throat razor from his pocket. He pulled the blade out of the handle and ran it across the railing. His attacker screamed as it sliced over his fingers—a noise which ended abruptly as he fell from the bridge and struck the ground with a sickening thud. Gus kept walking, not looking down, as he wiped the blade clean and placed it back into his pocket.

He reached the other side and followed the corridor around.

He won't make that mistake again.

It's strange. So many people here don't know who we are.

It's a prison full of nonces and rapists. Our people are gone.

Exactly, they don't know us.

They will.

Gus made it down a flight of stairs and through another corridor before he saw anybody else. Henderson rounded the corner, followed by a pair of greasy-looking prisoners.

"Ah, there you are," Henderson said, holding up a hand to halt his progress. He turned to the others. "Go and find Carver and tell him we pulled the factory stairway down. There's no way they can climb back up. I'll be in my office if he needs me."

With that, he motioned for Gus to follow him down a corridor and up another flight of stairs. The route looked vaguely familiar, and it was only once Henderson opened the door to an office, Gus realised where they were.

"Oh ho, you've set up in the Governor's quarters. Showing who's in charge, eh?"

Henderson closed the door behind him. "Sit down, Gus."

"We've played this charade before, Henderson. In this very room. You asked me to kill Frank back then. Do you remember?"

"Oh, I remember. I also recall your response."

"Yeah, well, I shot him today, didn't I? So now what do you want?"

Henderson motioned towards the seat opposite him as he sat down behind the desk. "I need help."

Gus stared, waiting for the punchline. In all the years he had known him, Henderson had been brash, abrasive, and full of confidence. Any time he needed something, he would offer a 'deal.' But not once had Gus ever heard him asking for help.

"You're serious?" He lowered himself into the chair, studying the embarrassment on Henderson's face.

"What I've told you already is true. McAllister released Carver and a few others before coming back for me. I got Carver onside and convinced him we needed to take the prison. McAllister wasn't onboard. So, we pushed him into a cage with the zombies and watched them eat him. Or at least *try* to eat him."

"I bet he put up a fight."

"And then some. Plus, that armour was tough to get through, but they managed to nick him and he inevitably turned. Anyway, after that, we released the rest."

"Sounds like you've got a nice little setup."

"It might look like I'm in control here, but I'm not. I'm a pawn. Carver runs everything. True, he gave me a reward for my loyalty…" Henderson's gaze drifted to the other closed door in the room. Gus suspected it led to a closet, given that the one they had entered through led onto the corridor. "…But I need to get rid of him before he gets rid of me."

"Why would he get rid of you?"

"Come on, Gus. Use your loaf. Carver doesn't need me anymore. The prison is his." Henderson traced his moustache with his thumb and forefinger, as if considering his words. "But I can't kill him. I don't have any support here; I've got nobody. If Carver's gone, somebody else will take his place, which won't bode well for me. It might surprise you to hear I'm not particularly well-liked."

Gus scoffed, shaking his head as Henderson continued.

"They're offering me *some* allegiance since I let them all out, but I can already see that's starting to wear thin."

"So, you need me to get them back onside?"

"There's a few who hate Carver. But he can't kill them, as they're heavily involved with some of the other lads. Killing them will cause an uprising, which he can't risk. We need them onside. We get them in our camp. The others will follow, leaving Carver vulnerable. That's how we take this place over."

"So, what do you want me to do?"

"Just be you. You ran this place for years! I need your help. Help me take over, and I guarantee no harm will come to you or that tart you seem to have a fondness for."

Gus felt his stomach lurch.

Agree. Miranda mustn't be harmed.

Carver already said he won't touch her.

I know, but he definitely *won't if he's dead.*

But side with Henderson?

For now. Eventually we'll slice that moustache clean off his face.

"Miran—I mean—Abigail needs to be kept safe at all costs."

"Of course, providing you keep your side of the bargain."

If we go with Carver, he'll want to rule this place. He's in a perceived position of power. He thinks he has leverage. We can easily manipulate Henderson; he's desperate.

Gus nodded. "Deal."

"Good. Now, tell me your secret. How did you run this place? I've tried your tactics and they haven't worked. I've tried fear. I've locked them up in solitary, beat them, starved them, even threatened them with a zombie: nothing."

"After doing all that, you still think I can persuade them?"

"Oh no, they're dead. They weren't the big players. Nobody even realised they're gone. Just some of the lesser shitbags. I did what you do, but I couldn't create that *fear*."

"That's your first mistake. I don't control people through fear alone. It's my unpredictability that does it. Psychological manipulation."

"What?"

"You step out of line, you die. Stay in line, you might still die, but you might also be rewarded."

"That's it?"

"Mostly."

"That doesn't make sense. Why wouldn't they just rebel?"

"They'd be stepping out of line, and they'd die."

Henderson twisted his face, clearly unimpressed with Razor's hypothesis.

"Trust me. That, coupled with some added muscle, and the trademark Gus Razor charisma, will always equal success."

"The Gus Razor charisma? So you're telling me it won't work if I do it?"

Gus sighed, leaning back in the chair, enjoying Henderson's uncertainty. "Let's be real. You know fine well everyone in here hates you. Most would rather die than have you running the helm. You need me to take this prison over."

"You?"

"Me. Under my rule, you'll be safe. You can sit in your little office, out of the way, and nobody would bother you."

Henderson shook his head. "I'm not relinquishing control."

"You already have, the minute you sided with Carver. If we're going to do this, we do it my way, or not at all."

Henderson scowled. "How do I know you'll keep your word?"

"You don't. That's the uncertainty that will keep you in line like the others."

"I'm not a fucking dog, Razor! You forget—*I'm* the one keeping you alive here. One word to Carver and you'll have a bullet in your head. Hell, I could do it now."

He produced a handgun, propping it on the desk.

"You won't kill me, Barry. You need me. And I'm sure you'd prefer a slight chance of survival under my reign, than a certain death under Carver's."

Henderson stared at the desk, deliberating his options.

"In fact, he's already told me he's going to kill you," Gus continued, unable to mask his delight. "He wants me to convince the lads giving him grief to join him. Once I've done that, he's going to have you bumped off."

A flash of alarm appeared in Henderson's eyes.

"Don't get me wrong, I'd much rather kill Carver. But if you're not going to conform to my methods, you really don't give me much of a choice."

Gus leaned back in his chair, studying the tormented look on Henderson's face.

"Okay," he conceded after a brief silence. "We do it your way."

"Good. Now, I have a few more stipulations. First, we get rid of the nonces. I'm not having any kiddie-fiddlers alive in this prison. Understand?"

Henderson's eyes grew wide. "That's most of the blokes down there. That'll only leave about twenty rapists."

"And?"

"We need numbers, Razor. You can't start taking the moral high ground. Who gives a shit, anyway? Some like them hairy, others like them smooth."

"We kill the nonces or we call it off."

Fire blazed in Henderson's eyes. He breathed heavily, leaning against the desk. "Fine," he snarled.

"Good. Second, I want that shooter."

"Why?"

"Crowd control. It's amazing how easy it is to get a person's attention when you're pointing a gun at their face."

Henderson nodded and shoved the gun across the desk.

"Good. Now, why don't you introduce me to the flock?"

They left the office, with the guard locking the door behind them, before leading the way down the corridor.

Ready for some blood?

Always.

19

Lisa glanced over at Abigail as a soft sob escaped her lips.

"Hey," she whispered. Unable to use her arms to comfort her, she resorted to rubbing her foot against her calf. "Are you okay?"

Abigail shook her head, nervously glancing at Jimmy to see if he was listening. Whilst he continued to stare at them, Lisa was sure he couldn't hear them talking under their breath, especially once she stood in front of Abigail, blocking his view of her mouth.

"He won't do anything. We're not his type, remember?"

"I'm not worried about us. Well, I am, but that's not what I'm upset about. It's—"

"Kara?" Lisa asked.

Abigail nodded, her head drooping as tears trickled down her cheeks.

"Tell me about her."

"What?"

"Talk to me. How long have you two been together?"

Abigail sniffed, rubbing her chin against her shoulder, catching the tear that had made it to the bottom of her face. "Just over five years. We met when we were nineteen."

"That's sweet. Was it love at first sight?"

"Not exactly," Abigail laughed. "She punched me in the face."

"What?"

"It wasn't on purpose. I was in a bar with some friends. It was on St. Patrick's Day, so it was packed. Some guy grabbed Kara's arse when she walked past, and she swung a punch at him."

"Sounds like my kinda girl," Lisa grinned.

"Yeah, well, she missed him and clocked me on the chin. Next thing I know, I'm lying on the floor with Kara crouched beside me. She asked to buy me a drink to say sorry. The rest is history. We've been inseparable ever since." Abigail's smile waned. "Until now, at least."

Lisa nodded, fighting back her own grief. All the time Abigail was talking, her mind had wandered to Frank. It dawned on her that despite only knowing each other for the better part of a week, the only time they had been apart was when they had split up for supplies. Even then, it had been an hour at most. Now she didn't even know if he was alive, or if she would be by the end of the day.

"I guess it's for the best," she said, realising Abigail was waiting for reassurance. "As long as she's not here, she'll be alright."

"That's the thing—I don't know if she *is* alright. She's tied up, at the mercy of those bastards. They could've done anything to her by now. Or zombies could've attacked."

227

"Or she could've got away," Lisa said. Her voice rose unintentionally, prompting her to look over her shoulder. Jimmy remained up against the door, his arms folded, his eyes unblinking.

"How could she have got away?"

"You said yourself, zombies could've attacked. In all the chaos, she could've slipped past them. There's a chance, quite a good one, in fact."

"How do you mean?"

"Well, someone started firing at the prison, right? Who was it? How did they know we were being held captive?"

Abigail shrugged.

"What if zombies *did* attack and Kara got away? Flagged the shooters down and told them what happened? She could be safe. Trust me, as long as she's out there, she's got a good chance. Or would you rather she was in here with us?"

Abigail shook her head, her puffy red eyes fixed on Lisa. "No. Whatever happens to us, Kara *has* to live. She can't come here."

"No news is good news. Just remember that."

Abigail smiled weakly. "I keep thinking about this morning. I got upset, and Kara was there to comfort me."

"Well, I know I'm not her, but I'm trying my best." Lisa nudged her playfully, trying to inject a bit of humour.

"No, it's what we said. I asked her to promise not to leave me. And promise not to die."

"And did she?"

Abigail nodded.

"And does she keep her promises?"

"Every time."

"Then you've got nothing to worry about."

"I'm worried that she thinks she's already broken that promise. The first one, at least. And I'm worried she's going to break the second by trying to right the first."

Lisa knew the chances of Kara being alive were slim, almost as slim as Frank's. She also knew that if either of them *were* alive, they'd be doing whatever they could to rescue them. Even if it meant dying in the process.

***

Frank sat in the SUV with his knees up to his chest. Opposite him, Kara sat in the same position, her head drooped, dazed eyes staring into space. They swayed as Kev sped over the uneven road, bouncing occasionally over potholes or debris. Each time, Frank hissed in pain, pressing down on the searing fire in his side.

"How is it?" Amy asked, beside him.

"About as painful as you'd expect."

"When we get to town, we can look for painkillers, there'll be a—"

"There's no time," Frank interrupted. He didn't know how long Lisa had been in the prison, or even if she was still alive. All he knew was the longer the wait, the more likely she would come to harm.

The trees outside flitted past as the SUV raced on. There were no other vehicles, aside from those abandoned every now and again. Every time a new one came into view, Frank felt his heart beat harder. But none of them were the prison van.

"We'll find them," Amy said, reading Frank's expression.

"What if they've already been and gone?"

"Then we'll find another way," Ben replied. "Don't give up hope."

"Hope?" Frank repeated. "They're locked in a prison with potentially hundreds of convicts. What hope do they have?"

Kara let out a sob. She wrapped her arms around her knees, her head still bowed.

"We'll find a way," Amy said. "They might have numbers, but we've got the superior firepower. Right, Kev?"

"That's right. I doubt there are many in there, but even if there are, I reckon only a handful will be armed."

"That doesn't help us get inside."

"There are other ways we could try." Kev watched Frank in the rear-view mirror. "If the prison van doesn't show up, we'll consider them."

Frank turned his attention back outside as the treeline ceased and vast fields began; it was a sign they were nearing Doxley.

"How many bullets have you got left?"

Frank turned and realised Ben was staring at him.

"Enough. How about you?"

Ben glanced at the rifle propped by his side. "Yeah, I should be alright. If I run out, I've always got a backup." He reached back and retrieved his handgun.

"You learn quick."

"Yeah right," Ben smirked. "Don't worry, I've got your back out there if you get into any trouble."

Frank laughed, which sent a shooting pain across his stomach. He winced as Kev shouted back to them.

"Okay, we're approaching the pickup location now. I'm going to park further down the road so we don't draw any suspicion. We'll have to walk the rest of the way."

The SUV slowed to a stop behind an abandoned bus. After a quick scan of their surroundings, the group got out, leaving the refuge of the cool ventilated air and stepping into a blazing hell.

Frank looked up and down the road. There was no sign of the prison van.

"Here, take this," Kev said, offering Kara a handgun. "This is the safety. If that's flicked on like this, you can't shoot. If you flick it down like this, then you can."

Kara nodded, studying the weapon as Kev highlighted its various parts.

"You hold it like this." He adopted a firing stance, feet apart, one hand clamped around the grip, the other providing a platform to rest atop of. "Keep your trigger finger resting on the side of the gun. It should only ever be over the trigger when you're ready to fire. Okay?"

"Okay."

"Now to reload, you need to…" Kev's instructions faded to nothing as movement down the road averted Frank's attention. It wasn't a prison van. It wasn't even a vehicle. It was a person. Based on his stature, Frank was sure it was a man. Then, when he turned into the road, revealing a crimson pulp of a torso, Frank realised he wasn't amongst the living.

"Get back," he hissed, interrupting Kev's demonstration to usher them against the wall. They stopped beside a storefront—one of the few with its windows intact.

"What is it?" Ben asked.

"Is it the van?" Kara pressed.

"Shh." He held a hand up to silence them, peering back into the street. The zombie meandered closer, now with an undead woman at its back.

"We've got company, and it's not the living kind."

Kev shrugged. "Okay, let's shoot them before the van turns up."

"If we shoot them, we'll draw attention to ourselves. The last thing we want is to use up all our bullets."

"So what do you suggest?"

Frank looked back down the road, scanning the surrounding buildings. Most housed broken windows with doors that stood ajar. Whilst there were only two zombies in view, there could be countless concealed all around them.

"We wait for them to get closer. They're not moving fast. If we're lucky, they might go another way. Or better yet, the van could show up and distract them."

"But if we're not lucky?" Ben asked.

Frank clapped him on the shoulder. "C'mon, Rambo. You know fine well you're our lucky charm."

The zombies had both stopped, and stood swaying in the middle of the road. Neither seemed in a hurry to move, unaware of their presence. Frank sighed and retreated to the pavement. Then another movement caught his eye. One beyond the group, inside the shop they'd gathered around. He tried to raise his shotgun, but it happened too fast. He saw the zombie sprinting out of the gloom towards the group and towards the window, where it hurled itself against the glass.

"Fuck." He staggered back onto the road as the zombie collided with Ben and Donna, amidst an explosion of glass shards. The others steered clear, but the confusion was clear on their faces. Kev was the first to react. With a bellowing cry, he lunged for the undead man, dragging him away from Donna.

Frank raised his shotgun, but shrieks came from further down the road. The other zombies sprinted towards him, their eager cries echoing around the street. He propped the shotgun against his shoulder, waiting for them to run closer.

A loud crack sent the first crashing to the ground. Frank lurched away from the rifle that appeared beside him. Amy held it aloft, firing at the second zombie.

"Shit," she hissed, the bullet sailing past the creature which had almost reached the abandoned bus. Frank aimed, and this time fired before her, causing the zombie to snap back, its legs swept high as it hit the ground.

A trio of rapid gunshots beside them ended Kev's scuffle. He clambered free and kissed his wife, who was training her machine gun on the corpse.

"Thanks, babe," he said. He followed the others into the road when a series of shrieks enveloped them. Some cries seemed muffled. Others distant. But all feral, eager, and hungry.

"Hope you packed enough ammo," Frank said. Kev didn't get a chance to answer as the first figure darted out of an alleyway in front of them. It managed a few feet before a series of bullets brought it down.

"We need to conserve ammo," Kev urged. "A tactical retreat may be in order."

"No!" Frank snapped. "If we leave now, we might miss the van."

Ben fired at another, emerging from the nearby alley. "If they keep coming, we'll be dead before the van gets here."

Another series of shots resounded through the street as more of the undead ventured out of the shadows. Whilst many of the bullets hit the zombies, the majority hammered into their surroundings.

"Preserve your ammo!" Kev snapped, his voice almost lost beneath an increasing roar. Frank spun around and found more of the undead racing toward them from the top of the street.

They were trapped.

"We need to move!"

"In here!" Amy shouted, motioning towards a nearby door which stood ajar. The group rushed inside, entering a dark, narrow corridor that offered a fleeting glimpse of a staircase at the far end. When Ben slammed the door, darkness consumed them.

"We need a light!" Frank snapped. He could hear a fumbling nearby, then a click as light burst out of Kev's flashlight. The white ray darted around the thin corridor, fixing on the staircase at the far end, then back to the door as a mass of bodies slammed against it.

"We need to move!" Ben urged. "The stairs. Move!"

Frank slipped past Amy, shotgun held high. If the dead were going to break in, he certainly wasn't going to be at the back of the group. He quickly ascended the stairs, watching the top, waiting for a zombie to lurch out at him. But none came.

As the group followed, the brilliant light of the torch revealed an empty landing, with adjacent doors further down the corridor. The shrieks of the undead diminished slightly as they strode further into the building, but didn't fade completely. Frank expected them to break through the door at any second, stumbling over each other, making for the stairs in a race to the top.

"Which door?" Amy wondered aloud.

"Try them both."

Frank walked towards the first one, shotgun pressed against his shoulder, aiming at the dark wooden panels. He motioned for Ben to try the handle, expecting a disparaging retort. Instead, he stepped forward and swung the door wide. Kev aimed the torch into the room, but found it was light enough.

A large window granted the sunlight entry, allowing it to illuminate various items of furniture in the room. It looked like a bedsit. A worn leather armchair—faded over time—stood in front of an old TV. A small kitchen area housed a breakfast bar, refrigerator, and integrated oven, while a double bed stood against the wall, with a prone figure lying beneath a tangle of sheets.

Frank snapped his aim at the motionless form, stepping aside to allow the others entry. They all gathered at the foot of the bed, all except Ben, who quietly closed the door. He reached across and placed a chair beneath the handle before joining the others.

Frank eyed the figure warily. He suspected it was a woman. Long golden tresses concealed her face, with a pale shoulder visible above the duvet. The bedside table comprised various medicine containers—all empty. Then Frank noticed the white vomit caked into the sheet beneath her face.

The woman was dead.

Frank leaned forward and prodded her with the barrel of the shotgun, finger poised over the trigger, just in case.

The woman remained still.

"Well, now what?" he asked, looking back at the group. Kev was no longer standing amongst them. Instead, he had taken up residency beside the window, watching the gathered horde below.

"Is there a way out?" Frank asked.

"Maybe. There's a ledge we could shuffle across. That'll take us over to the next building."

Frank looked out, feeling his stomach drop at the sheer number of zombies below them. There had to be at least two dozen, all trying to gain entry. He placed both palms against the windowsill, pressing his forehead against the warm glass. He could feel the adrenaline subside, reigniting the searing pain in his midriff.

"Or we could get into the loft," Ben suggested, motioning to the ceiling hatch.

"Yeah, that's a plan," said Kev. "We could break a hole through the roof and scramble across to the next building. Those dead pricks will be none the wiser."

"We don't have time," Frank said. He jabbed a finger into the windowpane, pointing to the prison van that trundled onto the street.

20

Gus followed Henderson back into the canteen. He quickly counted thirteen men. Fourteen including Chomping Charlie, who was still fervently chopping meat in the kitchen area.

Gus placed his hands behind his back, the razor blade in one, Henderson's gun in the other.

"Mo, have you seen Carver?" Henderson called.

"He's out front organising a pickup. We still need to collect that other tart from his group." He nodded toward Gus, who smiled in return.

"How are you fitting in, sweetheart?" Mo asked, taking a step forward.

"Oh, I'm having a blast."

"Really? That means you're not pulling your weight."

"Why would I need to do that?"

"This is *our* prison. You're here to serve *us*. And if you're not pulling your weight, you're not gonna be alive much longer!"

Gus snorted. The men behind Mo had started to take notice.

Good. An audience.

"Hmm, see, I've got a problem with that." Gus stepped forward, careful to keep both hands behind his back. "I don't take orders. Especially not from a child molesting cunt like you. Not in *my* prison."

"Your prison?"

"That's right. I'm back. And I'm here to stay. If you boys want to keep breathing, it's time to pledge allegiance."

Mo cast a bemused look at the other prisoners behind him. All shared the same astonishment. One of them stepped forward, standing in unity beside Mo, who chuckled under his breath.

"Oh, I knew you were crazy the moment I saw you," Mo sighed. "If you wanted to die, all you had to do was ask."

He brandished a knife and swung it towards Razor's face. Gus sidestepped, slicing the man's arm with the razor blade, before raising the gun and shooting Mo's companion. The bullet struck the centre of his forehead, immediately dropping the prisoner. With a single, fluid movement, Gus yanked Mo's jogging bottoms down, exposing his genitals amidst a bush of wiry hair jutting in front of two pasty white legs. He held the razor blade to his testicles, and, as Mo instinctively reached down to pull his trousers back up, shoved the handgun beneath his chin.

"Well, well," Gus shouted, ensuring everyone heard him. "We've got a situation here, haven't we?"

Mo whimpered, his trembling arms outstretched, looking down at Gus.

"It's about time we inject some order into this place," Gus bellowed, his voice bouncing off the walls. "We're going to start by incorporating some life lessons." He glanced up at Mo. "Do you want to lose your Jacobs?"

Mo shook his head, whimpering, as Razor pressed the blade harder against his testicles.

"Lesson number one! You need to learn to obey orders. If you want to keep these jewels, you better sing like a canary."

The trembling man looked down. "W—what?" he stammered.

"Whistle for your walnuts!" Gus bellowed. He slit the soft tissue, causing a trickle of blood to run down the blade. Mo cried out, spluttering and sobbing, desperately trying to whistle. But all he could muster was a raspberry, spraying spit across the room. Gus grinned and sliced the fleshy sack wide open.

The onlookers recoiled, clenching their legs together. Mo screeched, falling to his knees, his hands cupping his groin.

"If you don't follow the rules," Gus yelled over the screams, "you face the consequences!"

He reached down and yanked Mo's hands aside. Blood pooled onto the floor beneath him, spurting from the gaping wound where his testicles used to hang. He grabbed Mo's flaccid penis and, with a single swipe, sliced it clean off. The pitch of his victim's screams intensified. The gory spectacle caused one onlooker to vomit, adding to the smell of blood, piss, and despair.

"Here you go, Charlie," Gus called to the man in the kitchen. "Some sauságe for the menu."

He hurled the organ across the room, landing with a clatter amongst Charlie's pots and pans. He looked back down at Mo, satisfaction coursing through his body as he stooped beside the man's head.

"Looks like you've annoyed somebody before, *sweetheart*." He traced the thin scar down Mo's face with the blunt side of his blade. "This must be like opening old wounds."

"Please," Mo whimpered, but his plea turned into another scream as Gus turned the blade and ran it over the scar tissue.

"You're gonna keep us fed tonight, chump," Gus shouted. "And if you don't like sausage, you can have some guaca*mole*."

He sliced off the large mole beneath the man's eye and shoved it into his mouth. The scream cut off as Mo choked on the fleshy growth. Gus could hear more stunned murmurs from the gathered spectators. He looked up, eyeing each of the unfamiliar faces, until he stopped on one he recognised.

He's one of the pricks who ambushed us.

And he's laughing.

Gus brought the handgun up and effortlessly shot the sniggering man between the eyes. The gunshot echoed around the hall, silencing the crowd.

"Lesson number two: you should never laugh at another's misfortune."

Mo curled up into a foetal position, hands between his legs, his tortured sobs causing his body to hitch. Blood poured out of the gaping wounds in his face, covering most of his skin.

"Lesson number three." Gus crouched beside his victim's face. "*Never* cross Gus Razor."

With that, he ran the blade across Mo's throat, bringing with it a bloody torrent spurting through the thin slit. He stood up and regarded his congregation, feeling the warm spray of blood soaking his legs as Mo spasmed beside him.

"Now you know who I am, you have a choice. Join my band of Merry Men and live to see tomorrow. Or stay loyal to Carver and kiss today goodbye."

He looked from face to face, noticing defiance in some, but acceptance in others. Gradually, the men fell, each kneeling side by side, almost in a domino effect. He looked at those still standing, watching with joy as the blaze of defiance extinguished. The rest fell to their knees, leaving only two still deliberating.

With a sigh, he raised the gun and fired twice. "Took too long."

The pair fell, leaving Gus and Henderson the only two standing. He turned to the guard. "Well?"

"Well, what?"

"Choose, Henderson. Live or die."

Don't give him a choice. Slice him!

No. You've had your fun. Now I'm back in charge.

Not for long.

The guard snarled, baring his teeth, before sighing in resignation. He fell to his knees, his head bowed.

"Good. Now get up, all of you. We've got work to do."

***

An abrupt knock came from the door, prompting Lisa to sidle next to Abigail.

"Who is it?" Jimmy demanded.

"It's Jacko," a voice returned. "We caught another skirt from their group. Carver told me to bring her here."

"What?"

"He said to bring her here and keep her with the others."

Jimmy looked back at Lisa and Abigail, suspicion causing his brows to furrow.

"You have another lass in your group?"

"Kara," Abigail whimpered. She held a hand to her mouth, a fresh wave of tears escaping her eyes.

"Hurry up, Jim. You know what these fuckers are like. They'll have my hand off in a minute," the man called, hammering against the metal pane.

Jimmy sighed and unlocked the door. He swung it wide, revealing two grinning men. Lisa recognised them as those who had shouted obscenities earlier. Then she saw the blades.

"What the fuck are you doing, Jacko?" Jimmy took a step back as the men entered the room.

"We've come to have a pop at these two," Jacko replied, brandishing the shiv towards Lisa and Abigail. "It's been too long since I've had a bit of gash."

"Carver will kill you. He'll kill all of us." Jimmy held a hand up to stop their progress, but they paid him no heed.

"Fuck Carver, you can't keep a predator from his prey."

Jacko took another step closer until Jimmy shoved him away.

"I said get back!" he shouted. "I'm not getting killed because of you."

Jacko looked at his companion, who mimicked his sneer.

"Well, Jim, it looks like you're gonna die one way or another."

Lisa looked on in horror as the two men attacked. Jimmy caught the first shiv in both hands as it swung for his face. He kicked out at the second, wrestling with Jacko.

Lisa ushered Abigail into the corner as the violence drew closer. The blade skittered across the floor in their direction, then Jacko yelped in pain as Jimmy yanked his arm behind his back. He used the man as a human shield, fending off the other attacker who still held a shiv.

"Lisa," Abigail hissed, motioning to the blade nearby.

The fighting continued, with the trio moving around the room, Jimmy holding one man flush to his body, the other darting back and forth, looking for an angle of entry.

Lisa lowered herself to the ground and shuffled along the floor. The cable ties clasping her hands behind her back proved cumbersome, but she managed to reach the shiv without detection. Stretching out her foot, she dragged it beneath her. Her fingers groped the floor until finally resting on the handle.

A shriek of pain resounded around the room as Jimmy yanked his victim's arm higher. An audible snapping sound came, prompting Jacko to scream even louder. Unsettled by the cry, his companion lunged forward. Jimmy dodged to the side, shoving his human shield into the path of the blade. The knife plunged into Jacko's abdomen.

Jimmy allowed him to fall, then grabbed the second man's wrist and yanked it sideways. Another scream pierced the air. This one was short-lived. Jimmy wrestled the blade from his fingers and plunged it into the man's throat. The prisoner fell beside his counterpart, but Jimmy continued stabbing. The wet slaps continued long after the man had exhaled his last breath.

"Oh god," Abigail whimpered. Lisa stared, watching the bloodbath continue. Satisfied the man was dead, Jimmy got to his feet. He turned to face them, his upper half soaked in blood. He regarded them in silence, not even attempting to wipe himself clean. Then he turned and positioned his bulk in front of the door once again.

Lisa shuffled back to Abigail, her back to the wall, the shiv concealed in her palm. Then, with the slightest of movements, she began to cut.

21

"They're slowing down," Donna whispered.

"Of course they're slowing down," Frank retorted. "They're not going to drive into a crowd of zombies, are they?"

"What if they realise their friends are dead? What if they turn around and leave?"

The group watched the van roll to a stop halfway down the road. It was too far away to make out the faces of the occupants, but Frank could tell they were watching the horde, probably weighing up their options.

They're going to leave. Any second now, they're going to turn around and drive away.

No sooner had the thought crossed his mind than the van started to perform a U-turn.

"Shit. They're leaving!"

"Move out of the way," Kev ordered.

The group backed up as he produced his handgun and fired at the window. The glass exploded out, showering the horde below with glistening shards. The sound caused the zombies to roar louder, and the occupants of the van to stop. It was only momentary. As soon as they saw Kev position his sniper rifle on the window ledge, the prison van lurched round, completing its U-turn amidst a cloud of burning rubber and squealing tyres.

Kev fired, striking the side of the van as it raced down the street. The commotion attracted the horde below, and some of them broke away, sprinting after the fleeing vehicle.

Kev fired again; this time a further bang accompanied his thunderous shot as the front nearside tyre disintegrated. The van lurched violently to the left, and then the right, with the driver struggling to maintain control. But it was no use. The momentum caused the van to tip. Before their eyes, the vehicle flipped onto its side and screeched to a halt, colliding with an abandoned car.

"Nice shooting," Frank said, leaning against the wall to ease the pain in his side.

"I had to do something," Kev countered. "That was our only shot."

"Yeah, and you blew it."

"Maybe we can pull it upright," Donna suggested. "If we get it back up, we—"

"It won't drive," said Frank. "Your sharpshooting husband didn't just blow out the tyre, he disintegrated half the wheel."

"He's right," Kev sighed, running a hand over his smooth head. "We won't be able to get it back to the prison."

"So what do we do now?" Kara asked.

The group exchanged a glance, but nobody was forthcoming with a solution. They all looked to the window as a series of screams sounded above the undead chorus. Further down the road, the zombies had reached the van and were now devouring its occupants. They had intercepted a man trying to clamber up through the passenger door. He cried out when they dragged him to the ground, his screams fleeting, replaced by the ravenous moans of the undead.

"Why don't we wait until they've gone, then check out the van?" Ben suggested. "It might not be as bad as you think." He looked at Frank, who scoffed, shaking his head.

"The wheel's fucked. It's not just a case of changing a tyre. And disregarding that, how do you propose we pull it upright? Are you suddenly packing muscle under that old man's shirt?"

"Here we go again with the tough guy act. Yet you were screaming like a bitch when a bullet grazed your side."

Frank shoved himself from the wall and approached Ben. "How I about I shoot you in the side and we'll see who's a bitch then."

"Enough!" Amy snapped. "If you two keep arguing, you're going to bring the zombies back." She motioned outside, where the undead had gravitated toward the van, seemingly forgetting about the elusive meal in the bedsit above. "Let's take a step back. Relax. And wait it out."

"The longer we wait, the more likely they're going to come to harm."

"I know," Amy sighed. "Really, I do. But we don't have a choice. Even if you wanted to drive up there, guns blazing, there are too many zombies outside to make it to the car."

Frank closed his eyes. He knew she was right, but it didn't make the prospect easier to come to terms with. He sat down on the windowsill, his back pressed against the remaining pane of glass. Kev busied himself in the kitchen, searching through the cupboards.

"Aha," he said, holding up an orange packet. "Crackers. Let's get some sustenance while we can." He opened the wrapper and held it towards Donna.

"Shame we don't have any cheese," she mused, taking three crackers and passing the packet to Ben.

"There might be some in the fridge, but with no electricity for the past week, you'll probably have to shave it before you eat it."

Frank watched the crackers being passed from person to person until Amy presented them to him.

"I'm good," he said, waving them away.

"You need to eat. If you don't keep up your strength, you're not going to be any use to us when we hit the prison."

Frank sighed. He wanted to argue, but the pain in his side had coupled with a pang of hunger, intensifying it tenfold. He took the crackers and nodded. "Thanks."

They ate quietly, their crunching in unison with the undead outside who had slaughtered their living meal, and now feasted diligently. When he had finished, Frank rose from the windowsill and ventured over to the dead woman in the bed. His throat was dry, the wound more painful than ever. When he examined the bedside table, he knew he could kill two birds with one stone.

He picked up the blister packs of codeine. Despite the woman's suicide, she had only ingested half of them, as well as the contents of the medicine bottles, which now stood empty. He picked up the glass and swallowed the tablets, chased by the remnants of water as he downed the liquid in one gulp. He looked back at the rest of the group and saw Amy consoling Kara, who had her head in her hands.

"How are you holding up?"

"I'm not," Kara sniffed. "I keep thinking about Abigail. It's my fault she's there."

"It's not your fault. You had no idea those guys would ambush you."

"No, you don't understand. It was my idea to go there. Abi wanted to hide in another house, but I convinced her the army base was safer." Kara shuddered as she wiped tears from her face.

"We're going to rescue her. We just need a bit of time. But you need to remember, she's got Lisa in there with her. I've not known her long, but I know for a fact she's a badass. Right, Frank?"

She turned to Frank for support, but he was unsure if he could give it. His mind continued to torment him with the different sufferings Lisa could be enduring, each more harrowing than the last. But if there was one thing he was sure of, there was no breaking her. She definitely wouldn't go down without a fight.

"Yeah," he managed.

Amy turned her attention back to Kara. "We *will* get inside. And we *will* get her out of there. I promise."

Kara sniffed, wiping her nose with the back of her hand. "Promise? I promised Abigail I wouldn't leave her. Now she's alone because of me." She looked into Amy's eyes, fixing them with an unblinking stare. "Don't make promises you can't keep."

22

"How many blokes are actually left in here?" Gus asked Henderson, as they marched through the corridor.

"I dunno. About fifty?"

"*Fifty?*" Gus gasped, stopping to look at the guard. "How the hell did you hope to keep fifty people here?"

"We had a week's worth of food and drink when this shit happened." Henderson shrugged. "Even more for just fifty lads. But the food went quicker than expected. Those greedy bastards had it all. We've got enough water to tide us over, but the food is the problem."

"If you had killed them all, you wouldn't *have* a problem."

"Carver wanted them alive. He said we needed numbers."

"For what?"

Henderson shrugged again. "Security."

"Fuck me, Henderson, it's a *prison*. And in the middle of nowhere. You're hardly gonna have an undead army knocking at your door, are you?"

Henderson sighed, a flicker of annoyance creeping over his face.

"And even if they did," Gus continued, "you just need to stay quiet and pretend nobody's home. Fifty fucking people. No wonder you're low on food. I'm guessing that's why you're chopping folk up?"

Henderson glanced up and down the corridor, ensuring they were alone. "We're not eating people. It was a gimmick to make the lads go out and collect food for us."

"So you genuinely haven't been abducting people?"

"No. Why?"

"Nothing. Just something that Abigail lass said. Speaking of, where the hell is she?"

"I don't know. Carver didn't say where he was sending her."

He's lying. Let's kill him.

Killing him won't help us.

It'll help me. Kill him.

No.

Look what I did to Moley. I know you enjoyed that. Let's do it again.

Not yet.

Your resolve is weakening. I can feel it. If you don't do it. I will.

"Well, we need to find her. Either that or get to Carver first."

"I wouldn't advise it," Henderson said. "You've only convinced a handful of lads back there. Any of them could run to tell him what's happened. We need more support."

I'm going to slice that moustache right off his face. Cut it in two and stick the pieces over his eyebrows.

"What weapons do you have in here?" Gus asked, fighting to keep the voice at bay.

"We started out with the riot guns, and I stashed a Glock a few weeks back."

"Of course you did."

Henderson continued, ignoring the comment. "I used that for control at first, but after sending the lads out, they came back with a few firearms—rifles and a shotgun."

"Where did they get them from?"

"Fuck knows. You know how resourceful these lads are. Once Carver had those, I knew my time was short."

Guns are too impersonal. Let's slice them up.

A wall-mounted light flickered as they approached. Gus suspected it would fade to dark, but it returned to its full brightness.

"How are you keeping the power on?" he asked.

"Generators. For now. They'll be running on empty soon."

"Have you not had your boys out siphoning diesel?"

Henderson twisted his face. "That's a good idea, Gus. Shame you weren't here from the start."

"Yeah, tragic."

They entered the rec room, greeted by the growing pile of corpses.

"Your boys seem to be doing a good job of killing their own," Gus said, as they strode past the gruesome mound and entered another corridor.

"Food's short, tensions are high; you know how it is."

"I do. Which is why we need to act quickly to maintain order."

Oh, look what I've found.

Gus glanced down and realised he had retrieved the razor from his pocket. "Listen, we're going to split up," he said, shoving his hand behind his back.

"What?"

"Find Carver, tell him I need to speak to him and that I'll meet him in the interview room."

"Okay. What are *you* going to do?"

"I'm going to look for him as well. We can cover more ground if we split up. We need to make sure he doesn't know anything."

"Okay."

"And while you're at it, if you see any boys loyal to Carver, send as many of them out in the vans."

"What for?"

"Reduced numbers. The fewer people he has on his side, the better. Just send them down to Doxley and tell them to look for more food and supplies."

Henderson nodded in agreement.

"And if you see Miranda, keep her safe."

"Who?"

Gus squeezed his eyes shut, clasping a hand to his head.

Ha ha ha, I was only helping.

Back off. I'm *in control!*

If you say so.

"Uh—*Abigail.* Keep her safe."

Gus didn't wait for a response. He hurried to the end of the corridor and turned onto the wing leading to solitary confinement.

Slow down, Gustav. You'll give yourself a coronary.

You need to stop.

Stop what?

You know what. I'm *in control. Me!*

Doesn't look that way. You need to accept we're in this together. I'm you, and you are me. Together for eternity.

You're a poet now?

No. Just a philosopher. As well as a killer. A psychopath. A schizo. And whatever else those quacks called us.

Gus marched towards the first cell and peered through the viewing compartment. The room was dark, despite the radiant light in the corridor. He made for the next one.

You remember this cell? This is where Henderson put you.

Yeah, before you came back.

Just because you didn't hear me when you were on that medication doesn't mean I wasn't there. Watching. Waiting.

What I'd do for some Solenian now.

You won't get those shitty pills now. It's the end of the world. It's time you accepted me. I'm coming through loud and clear and I'm not going anywhere. Look what I can do.

Gus gasped when his right arm shot forward. He seized the tiny door to the viewing compartment and felt himself move closer. He looked on, unable to move as he dragged the viewing slide open. Wide bloodshot eyes greeted him. He leapt back as the zombie slammed against the door. The noise prompted a collaboration from the rest of the closed doors. All emitted a metallic clang as their occupants tried to break free of their confines.

Whoa, they've got zombie prisoners.

Henderson said he'd threatened the ones in solitary with a zombie.

He sure did. Looks like he went through with his threat.

Gus tried to turn away, but found his leg locked.

Ah, ah. What's the magic word?

"Just get the fuck out of my head!" Gus' voice bellowed down the corridor.

Easy, Gus. You're nothing without me.

"Shut up."

You need me.

"Need you? You're the reason I got banged up in the first place. You're reckless."

I get results.

"You're going to get us killed."

Me? What about the crazy bastards you're allying yourself with? They're keeping zombies in the seg—

Gus whirled around as footsteps approached from the end of the corridor.

"Who—Who are you talking to?" a young prisoner asked, glancing uncertainly at the cells. Gus recognised him as one of the men present in the canteen when he had butchered Mo—one of those who had pledged loyalty to him.

"Did I give you permission to speak?"

The prisoner scowled. "What?"

Gus brandished the handgun, holding it by his side. "Do you struggle with English, son? Or are you just thick? I said, 'Did I give you permission to speak?'"

The man's eyes widened. He slowly shook his head.

"Then you'd better come bearing good news, or these dogs in here will be in for a feast."

He booted the nearest metal door, the clamour prompting the zombies to roar louder as they continued slamming against the cells.

"You—you told us to tell you once we find Carver," the man stammered.

"And?"

"We found him."

Gus sighed. "I can surmise that much! *Where* is he?"

"He was heading to the hospital wing ten minutes ago."

"And you're only just telling me now?"

"I couldn't find you."

"Convenient." Gus stepped forward, raising the gun. "You wouldn't be looking out for Carver, would you?"

"No." The man trembled, both hands raised in front of his face.

"What's your name?"

"Matt."

"Matthew, this is your lucky day." Gus lowered the gun. "I'm going to give you a chance to prove your loyalty. I want you to wait here."

"W-wait?"

"Yes."

"For how long?"

"Until I tell you otherwise."

The man cast him a quizzical look. "Okay."

"If you do that, you can join my band of Merry Men. But if you don't…"

The man cowered as Gus raised the handgun once again. He clicked his tongue, moving his hand in a shooting motion, which caused Matt to flinch.

Satisfied his message had sunk in, Gus walked out of segregation and headed towards the hospital wing.

***

Lisa pushed her hands as far as the cable ties would allow. Her arms shook, yet she tried not to allow the exertion to show in her face. If Jimmy suspected she had the shiv before she managed to free herself, all hope would be lost.

The plastic cuffs shredded her skin, with no sign of them breaking. She readjusted her grip, feeling for the groove she had cut and then feeding the blade back into it. She froze when Jimmy scowled at her.

"Y'know, if the wind changes, your face will stay like that," she said.

He continued to scowl, his unblinking eyes fixed on hers. She felt a trace of unease form in her stomach. It was most probably down to his blood-soaked t-shirt and the pair of bodies at his feet. It certainly gave him a more foreboding appearance, yet she still tried to lighten the mood.

"C'mon, Jimmy. Crack a smile. I bet you've got a beautiful set of teeth under there."

The man grimaced, revealing a row of yellow incisors. Some were chipped, with one or two missing altogether.

"I guess not," she said. She broke eye contact as she dug the blade deeper into the plastic cuffs, hoping he would turn his attention on Abigail. But she could still feel his eyes burning into her.

"Why don't we play a game?" she suggested.

"A game?" Jimmy sneered, finally breaking his silence. "Let me guess. Hide and seek?"

"Well, that wouldn't be very fun, would it?" She glanced around the room to clarify her point. "How about charades?"

"Why not?" Jimmy grinned, raising his middle finger.

"That's just rude. Come on."

"You want a game? How about we see who can stay silent the longest?"

"Fine."

Lisa watched her captor, dismayed to see him staring right back at her. She tried to cut into the restraints again, but feared her movements would give her away.

"Oops. I guess I lost that one," she said, breaking the silence before it had a chance to settle. "What next?"

Jimmy growled in dismay. "We play again, and this time the loser gets a boot to the face."

"I admire your faith in my kicking abilities," Lisa said, "but if you think I can get my boot up that beanstalk you call a—"

"Enough!" Jimmy spat, taking a step forward. His outburst caused both women to flinch. Lisa felt Abigail shudder beside her. She sniffed quietly, her head bowed.

"Now you've upset her," Lisa scolded, staring at Jimmy defiantly. "Can you take my cuffs off so I can comfort her?"

"What do you think?"

"Please?"

"No." Jimmy stepped back over the corpses and returned to the door.

"Fine. Here, Abigail, get behind me. I can at least hold your hand." Lisa shuffled forward, keeping her bound hands out of sight. She waited for Abigail to move, but she clearly didn't understand Lisa's motive.

"C'mon," Lisa said, tapping her hand against the floor. "Don't let this prick upset you. Let's go back-to-back and I can hold your hand."

Jimmy sneered, watching as Abigail obliged and shuffled herself around to face away from Lisa. She scooted back until their hands were touching. It was then that Lisa handed over the shiv. She kept her eyes fixed on Jimmy's as she manoeuvred Abigail's fingers over the blunt end of the blade, positioning it against her restraints. She pushed her fingers down, signifying where to cut.

"You must think I'm stupid," Jimmy sneered. Abigail had interpreted the cue and started cutting. "Holding hands? That's the best you could think of?"

"What else could I have meant?" Lisa asked.

"You're wasting your time, girls. It doesn't matter how sharp your nails are, you won't be able to cut through those cuffs."

His grin gradually faded when he looked around the room, scanning the floor. Realisation contorted his face as he rushed forward.

"You sneaky little cunt."

Lisa slammed back against Abigail, hissing in pain as the shiv pierced her lower back. She brought her legs up as Jimmy neared and lunged with all her strength. Both boots connected with his groin, causing him to double over. In an instant, Lisa swung her boot up again, this time connecting beneath his chin. Jimmy staggered back, tripping over the outstretched legs of one of the corpses.

"Quick!"

Lisa prayed for him to lie still, for the kick to have been a knockout blow, but then she had never believed in God, nor genuinely expected her prayers to be answered. Sure enough, almost as soon as he landed, Jimmy climbed back to his feet with fire in his eyes.

Lisa prised her hands as far apart as they could go. A warm sensation coated her knuckles as they rubbed against her lower back—smearing the blood that trickled out of the knife wound.

"Hurry!"

Her hands shook. The plastic sliced into her wrists. She could feel Abigail rocking back and forth, feverishly slicing at the cuffs.

"Stupid bitch," Jimmy snapped.

Lisa made to reply, but she suddenly broke free. Both arms sprung out like a crucified messiah, just in time to embrace Jimmy as he forced her from the ground. She wrapped her arms around his neck, pulling his head tight to her body as he heaved her into the air. She lunged to the side—the momentum throwing them into the desk.

The computer monitor smashed to the floor, as both of them wrestled to gain the upper hand. She grabbed his throat, digging her fingers into his neck until he batted her arm aside. Then he reciprocated—clasping her throat with his right hand while swinging a punch with his left. The impact snapped Lisa's head sideways. She rolled off the desk onto the floor. The room spun, now a colourful exhibition of dancing lights.

A rough hand grabbed her hair and yanked her to her knees. Her arms instinctively came up to protect her face from an inevitable blow, but nothing happened. She blinked, trying to compose herself, trying to clear her vision, trying to focus on the other man who now stood in the doorway.

"What the fuck's going on in here?" Carver demanded, taking a step into the room. He slammed the door behind him, processing the scene.

"She got free," Jimmy wheezed.

"And what the fuck happened to these two?" Carver kicked a corpse at his feet.

"They tried to have a go before you."

"Cheeky fuckers." His eyes roamed over Lisa. "You've battered her a bit, haven't you? What did I tell you would happen if you laid a hand on them?"

"She came at me with a knife."

"Really? And where's this knife now?" Lisa felt the grip on her hair loosen. She looked around the room, trying to find the shiv. Then she saw Abigail, whose wide eyes betrayed its location.

"You!" snapped Carver.

Abigail cried out as he darted forward. He shoved her onto her stomach, exposing the partially severed cable ties and the shiv clasped between her fingers.

"Jimmy, tie the blonde up." He hurled plastic cuffs in the man's direction. "You've knocked all the fight out of her. She won't be any fun yet. But this one…"

Abigail cried out as Carver dragged her to her feet. He shoved her over to the side of the room, and bent her over the desk. Jimmy stepped in front of Lisa.

"Get up."

Not allowing her to stand of her own accord, Jimmy yanked her up and bound her hands behind her back. Lisa's vision began to clear—at a time when she didn't want to see what was happening. She squeezed her eyes shut, trying to control her breathing.

"Oh no, I want you to witness this!" Carver shouted. "Jimmy, force her eyes open. I want her to watch. I want her to see what's going to happen to her."

Coarse fingers forced her eyelids apart just as Abigail's scream pierced the room.

23

"How many are left?" asked Ben.

"A few," Frank said, turning away from the window. "Let's get down there and check that van."

"Still some lingering," said Kev, scanning the road. "I'm not convinced it's safe."

"I couldn't care less what you think. We've waited long enough. We need to move." Frank looked around the room for support, but met only uncertain faces.

"I agree," Kara stated. She took a step forward and stood beside Frank.

"If the crowd is still nearby, we won't be able to use the guns," Amy said.

"So we'll use the manual method." Frank flipped his shotgun and rapped the stock with his knuckles. "We've left them inside too long already. We need to get them out. Now."

"Okay." Ben nodded, taking a step forward. "We get to the van, we assess the damage, and then we retreat back here. Deal?"

"Deal."

Ben turned to Kev. "I'd feel a lot safer if you were covering us from here."

"Yeah, you and me both. If it goes tits-up, I'll start shooting. But the minute a gun is discharged, you need to get back here. We don't know how far they've gone."

Frank nodded, subconsciously patting the handgun in his holster for reassurance.

"I'll need someone to stay, ideally," Kev continued, "to keep an eye on the other end of the road. I won't be able to do both."

"I'll stay," Donna said. "If that's okay?"

"Sure." Amy slung her rifle over her shoulder and stood beside Kara. "Is the door clear?"

Kev glanced down at the street below. "Yeah, you're good."

"Okay, let's head out."

Frank led the way out into the gloomy hallway. He could make out the door opposite, but nothing beyond that. He was tempted to call back for Kev's torch, but strode on. The trio followed him as he stepped cautiously through the darkness, running his hand along the wall. Chipped paint broke away beneath his fingers until he finally reached the balustrade.

"Watch the stairs," he whispered, before descending towards the door. The others followed, their tentative steps scraping across the worn carpet until they found footing on the stairs.

Once he reached the bottom, Frank marched toward the door and swung it open. Brilliant light poured into the hallway, allowing the others to finish their descent with ease. The hot, clammy air wrapped his body as he stepped outside. He checked both ends of the street for any immediate threats as the rest of the group joined him.

"So far, so good," Ben said.

"Yeah, you just keep your finger off the trigger there, Rambo. If that van is salvageable, which I doubt, we won't be able to reach it if you're taking potshots."

"Less talk, more walk." Ben made for the other side of the street, but stopped when only Frank followed. He turned back to Amy. "What are you doing?"

"We'll stay on this side." Despite her voice barely surpassing a whisper, the silent street carried it across with ease. "If we all stay on the same side, we could get surprised by a zombie jumping out of an alley or something. This way, we'll have a better range of vision. We can watch each other's backs."

Ben glanced at Frank, his thoughts clear in the look of repugnance on his face.

"Suck it up, buttercup," Frank sneered. "You've got me for this little endeavour. Now let's move."

He led the way down the street, eyes darting left and right, shotgun held aloft, despite his previous warning to Ben. He imagined the zombies leaping out from any number of concealed spaces: the abandoned cars, the ruined shop-fronts, the narrow alleyways, even raining down from the rooftops. Glancing skyward, Frank felt satisfied the only thing above him were the punishing rays of the sun.

"Slow down," Ben hissed from behind him. Frank looked back and saw him motioning to Amy and Kara on the other side of the street. They were no longer parallel, with the two women opting for a more cautious pace.

"What are they doing?"

"Treading carefully."

"They need to hurry the fuck up." Frank looked back at Ben, just in time to see the rifle swinging toward his head. Frank ducked low, overwhelmed by an amalgamation of alarm, confusion, and rage. The swing would miss, and the momentum would carry Ben over the top of him. Then, Frank could smash his head in while he was on the ground.

Yet, Ben didn't miss. His rifle struck its target, and a yelp of rage followed as the undead corpse fell to the ground. Frank looked on, aghast, as Ben followed up his strike with a second, then a third. After the fourth, he replaced the rifle with his boot, stomping on the dead man's head.

Frank rose to his feet, scanning the street for more movement. It came in the form of Amy and Kara, but there were no further undead.

"Thanks," Frank said.

Ben wiped the rifle and the underside of his boot on the corpse's shirt. "No problem. I'm sure, despite all your talk, you'd do the same for me."

"Yeah." Frank looked back at the bedsit where they had left Kev and Donna. He could see the broken window and the motionless sniper beyond it. "Although, I'm not sure old sharpshooter has my back."

Ben followed his line of sight. "Must have been watching Amy and Kara."

"He needs to be watching *all* of us, not prioritising his favourites."

"He's a cop," Ben shrugged. "He's naturally going to favour two women over a criminal." He cuffed Frank on the shoulder as he stepped over the corpse at their feet.

Frank remained still, watching the man in the window. The sniper rifle had moved and was now fixed on him. "Yeah, funny, that."

He caught up to Ben, aware that they were now in sync with Kara and Amy on the opposite side of the road. He couldn't help but feel annoyed by his lack of awareness, especially when Lisa's survival rested on his shoulders. That's if she was still alive.

After passing shattered shop-fronts, a couple more abandoned cars, and a blood-spattered phone box, they finally reached the upturned prison van.

"Shit." Frank stooped beside the disintegrated wheel, which had ground into the floor.

"How bad is it?" Amy asked.

"The hub is warped. We can't replace the wheel."

"So, we can't get to the prison?"

"Not in this."

Kara let out an exasperated groan, which married with another sound. It was a grumbling engine, and it was getting closer. A Transit van turned the corner, stopping short when the driver spotted the quartet staring at him. He shut off the engine and jumped out, joined by a woman from the passenger side.

"They're armed," Frank snapped, noticing the machete at the broad man's side. He aimed his shotgun, detecting the others doing the same in his peripheral vision.

"Whoa," the man gasped, holding both hands aloft. "We come in peace."

"We mean no harm," the woman added. She, too, held both hands up, but held a crowbar in one, as opposed to her counterpart's machete.

"What do you want?" Frank asked. He kept his voice low, surprised that the zombies in the area had not encroached already. Between the Transit van and the man's outburst, he was sure they would've picked up on the sound by now.

"To help you."

"Help us? Help us do what?"

"Survive."

The group kept their weapons trained on the couple. "I think we're in the better position here," he said.

"For now. But where are you hiding? How much food and water do you have access to?"

"Enough."

The man shrugged. "For how long? Aren't you sick of living day-to-day? What if we told you that you won't have to anymore?"

"What do you mean?"

"We've got a community," the woman said. "There's just over seventy of us, with more survivors joining every day. We've got a ready supply of food, water, and electricity."

"Where?" Amy asked, lowering her weapon.

"Nearby. We can show you, if you like?"

"I think we'll pass," Frank said. "Unless you're hiding out at the prison?"

"The prison?"

Frank nodded.

"No." The woman shot a look at her counterpart, who shared her confusion.

"Why?" the man asked. "What's at the prison?"

Frank didn't know how to respond, but it didn't matter. No sooner had the question left the man's lips than a thunderous clap disintegrated them, as well as the rest of his head. His body crumpled, blood spurting from the stump on his neck.

The group remained rooted to the spot, all except the man's companion. With a shriek, she whirled around and ran for the Transit van. Another thunderous crack resounded down the street, and she slammed into the ground—a consequence of losing her left leg below the kneecap. She grunted, but a crescendo of shrieks drowned any further noise as the roars erupted all around them.

"Move!" Frank bellowed. He shoved Amy ahead of him and ran after her as movement seemed to come from every direction. Bodies spilled out of the alleyways as they sprinted down the middle of the road. The woman Kev had shot had now found her voice, and screamed in pain—a sound that quickly diminished as zombies engulfed her.

Beside him, Kara fired her handgun as she ran, the staccato cracks serving only to join the cumulating noise as her bullets missed their mark. Frank raised his shotgun and blasted a zombie that almost had her, smashing it into the ground.

"Keep going!" he snapped.

Ben caught up to Amy ahead of them, running alongside her as they neared the SUV and the refuge of the bedsit beyond. But as they approached, an undead woman darted out from behind the wreckage of a car, colliding with Ben, dragging him to the ground.

Frank stumbled, on course to trip over the grappling pair, until he lowered his body and slammed into the dead woman. They rolled across the street, settling with Frank atop the zombie, which screeched in his face, its snapping teeth desperate for flesh. He attempted to readjust his shotgun beneath its chin, but a gunshot snapped the undead woman's head aside, cutting short her aggressive protests.

Frank looked up at Kara, the handgun trembling in her hands.

"Thanks." He jumped to his feet and pulled her towards the door of the bedsit, closely followed by Ben and Amy.

The thunderous shots of Kev's sniper rifle continued, obliterating any zombies that stood in their way, and those pursuing them. But it wasn't enough. No sooner had they shoved open the door and made it into the hallway than the zombies spilled in after them.

"Keep going!" Ben yelled. He turned and fired at the closest zombie, causing the others to stumble in the narrow passageway.

"Ben!" Amy called from the top of the stairs, beckoning him to follow. As he ran up, the floored zombies reached out for him, while others stumbled over their companions.

He made it halfway before turning and shooting one of his pursuers. The zombie fell back down the stairs, taking with it all those standing behind.

Ben reached the top, where Frank and Amy waited. Frank looked past him at the mass of churning bodies regaining their feet. Their shambling frames blocked most of the light through the open door, casting the hallway into a gloom and rendering their escape impossible. They were trapped.

24

Lisa stared blankly, guided by Jimmy as he shoved her into an unfamiliar room. She knew tears were streaming down her face, but she couldn't feel them. She was numb—nothing but a shell, trapped in a memory she longed to forget. The scene replayed over and over, almost as a punishment for her failure.

I told her we'd be fine. That I'd get us out of here before anything bad happened.

Abigail's tortured screams rang through her mind, almost as a mocking response to her thoughts. Lisa lowered herself against the wall, only vaguely aware they were in a small padded room.

Probably where Carver is going to do the same thing to me.

Abigail's face appeared. And her eyes... those begging, pleading eyes.

Lisa sniffed hard, wincing as pain spread through her face—a pain that had saved her from the same fate as Abigail, if only temporarily.

She looked up at Jimmy—her captor and saviour. If he hadn't beaten her before Carver had arrived, she would probably be lying next to Abigail in the doctor's office, being preyed on by the beasts of Harrodale. The thought sent a shiver through her body.

No. That's not happening to me. I'm going to die fighting.

"What are you looking at?" Jimmy growled.

Lisa blinked, refocusing. "You."

"And that's causing you to shudder? I'm flattered."

"Don't be. Someone cringing at how grotesque you are isn't a form of flattery."

"I'll take it," Jimmy sneered.

"I bet you would. Is that why you're gay? Take whatever you're offered? Do you tell yourself you're gay to feel better? To make the man-love easier to accept?"

"Shut the fuck up."

"So that when you're getting passed around the showers, you can trick your mind into thinking you actually enjoy it?"

"I said shut up." Jimmy took a step forward, his fists clenched. "Or do you want me to beat the shit out of you again?"

"Try it, Jimmy. I doubt Carver will let you off a second time. Imagine what he'd do."

"Probably the same thing he did to your friend."

The verbal blow struck hard. The scene replayed and Lisa felt the tears form once again.

"Yeah," she replied, keeping the tremor from her voice. "So, it's probably best you be a good little boy and keep your hands to yourself. Plus, you don't want a woman to kick shit out of you again, right?"

Jimmy took another step forward.

"I knocked you on your arse with my hands tied behind my back," Lisa sneered, rising to her feet. "You're pathetic."

She waited for another punishing blow to the face, but, as the door behind Jimmy opened, she knew it was too late.

"Fuck," she whispered. But when she saw Gus Razor standing with his back to the door, she was just as confused as Jimmy.

"Afternoon," Gus beamed, looking around the room, both hands behind his back.

"What the fuck do you want?" Jimmy snarled.

"Carver, is he around?"

"What do you think?"

"I think he was seen around here and I want to talk to him," Gus continued. "Where is he?"

"Go and find him yourself."

Gus sighed and brought one arm from around his back. He held a razor, which glimmered under the harsh fluorescent lights. "Where is he?"

"Are you fucking kidding me?" Jimmy sneered. "Put that blade away before I stick it up your arse."

Gus sucked air through his teeth. "Oh, kinky. But I think I'll pass. Last chance, wanna tell me where he went?"

Jimmy marched forward, shoulders back, fists clenched.

Gus chuckled and brought his other hand into view—holding a gun, this time, now pointed at Jimmy's forehead. "How about now?"

Jimmy stopped in his tracks and instinctively raised his hands.

"He—he went to the canteen."

"Feeling a bit peckish, was he? Shame you couldn't have told me that from the beginning."

With that, Gus fired.

The sound faded into the padding of the cell as Jimmy's body crumpled to the floor.

"Blondie, you look like shit. What's behind your back there, you hiding something from me?"

"My hands are tied." Lisa turned to show the plastic cuffs binding her wrists.

"Oh, let me help you with that." Gus stepped smartly over the corpse toward her. With a flick of his blade, he cut her free.

"Thanks."

"All part of the service. Now I need to go and find Carver." He turned, but stopped in his tracks as if hit by a sudden recollection. "Oh, and the dark-haired lass. Where's she being kept?"

"She's dead." The words alone prompted the scene to replay in her mind.

Razor's smile vanished. "What?"

"She's dead. Carver raped and murdered her."

Gus changed. It was only subtle, but something about him faded. Whether it was a slight change in posture, a minor curl of his lip, or the light in his eyes extinguishing, Lisa couldn't tell. What she did know was that she no longer felt comfortable with the man in front of her.

"What happened?" Gus asked, his monotone voice almost alien.

"What?"

"Tell me what happened!" He punched the padded wall beside her face, his body looming over hers.

"He raped her!" Lisa shrieked. "He bent her over a desk and cut off her clothes. Then he raped her. Is that what you want to hear? Do you want to know what her screams sounded like? Do you want me to describe the pleading look in her eyes? They forced me to watch!" Lisa spat on Jimmy's corpse. "Then when she stopped crying so much, Carver started using his knife. The more she screamed, the more he'd get off. Is that good enough for you?"

Razor's eyes lowered. "How did she die?"

"He stabbed her in the side. Multiple times. Then he pulled her hair back, reached around, and slit her throat."

Gus closed his eyes, his breathing heavy. "Then what happened?"

Lisa studied him, unsure if she was witnessing genuine remorse or something else entirely. "He told that piece of shit to bring me here. Said he needed to refuel before he had his way with me. Then he shouted for all the other fuckers to have their turn with her while she was still warm."

Gus bowed his head.

"I'm going to kill him," Lisa snarled.

"You're not going to do shit. You're going to stay here and wait for all this to blow over." He offered her the handgun. "There's a few bullets left. Use them wisely. I'm going after Carver."

"Without a gun?"

"Oh, we aren't gonna need guns." He lifted the blade into view, an evil grin on his face as he made for the door.

***

Gus quickly pounded through the corridor, trying to work out which route Carver would have taken. His footsteps echoed through the vacant hallway, but he didn't process any sound. The white noise in his head was all he could hear. No more voices. No more instructions. No more threats of unification. They were one.

He reached the end of the corridor and stepped through an open gate that led back towards the rec room. He passed a couple of men, but none of them seemed familiar; neither did they seem interested in who he was or where he was going. That was until one man halted his progress with an outstretched arm as soon as he entered the rec room.

"You must be Gus Razor, the one who reckons he can—"

He didn't get to finish. No sooner had he started talking than Gus slashed the blade across his throat. Blood sprayed all around the room until the prisoner clasped both hands to his neck, falling to his knees. Gus grabbed the man's collar and dragged him over to the huge pile of bodies. The wet, guttural choking caught the attention of others in the room, but none attempted to intervene as Gus yanked his victim to the foot of the corpse mound, where he left him to see out his final seconds.

He walked away, down the corridor he had first walked with Henderson and Carver only a few hours earlier. He reached the canteen, which now stood empty. Even Mo's corpse had been removed, as well as his valiant ally, but the pools of blood remained. Gus stepped between them and made for the kitchen area, ensuring that Chomping Charlie had left. Sure enough, the kitchen was empty.

Gus turned to leave, when the rhythmic thud of boots met his ears. He stepped back into the canteen as Henderson entered.

"Ah, there you are." A sigh of relief, giving the words an airy quality. "I've got Carver. He's in the interview room like you asked."

"Good. Is the door locked?"

"No need." Henderson grinned. "I broke the handle off from the inside. He isn't going anywhere. I've also sent five of his close allies out in a van to pick up supplies. They're heading to Doxley as we speak."

"Good work, Henderson. You're starting to impress me."

"Yeah, be sure to remember that when Carver's gone."

"Oh, I will. But now I've got another job for you. Before they brought me here, I was in possession of a toolbox. I would really like it back."

"Where is it?"

"The best person to ask is now sitting in a dead heap." Gus motioned towards Mo's pool of blood. "Ironically missing his own tool." He chuckled.

"They unpacked the stuff they brought back in the loading bay," Henderson said. "I'll go and find it."

"Good. Bring it down to the interview room. I'm going to go and have a little chat with Carver."

The interview room was deep in the prison, but before he could confront Carver, Gus had another destination in mind. Leaving Henderson behind, he made his way back to the segregation cells.

25

"What the hell was that?" Frank demanded as he stormed into the bedsit. The door slammed behind him, before Ben and Amy heaved a chest of drawers in place. Once they had covered the doorway, Ben rushed to help Kara push the armchair up against it, further strengthening their barricade. Frank paid them no heed as he stormed towards Kev.

"What?" The man shrugged from his perch on the windowsill. A flurry of strikes against the door stole their attention. Ben pressed his body against the armchair, pushing it into the drawers as Amy and Kara shoved the refrigerator onto its side. Together, they lifted each end and staggered over to the door.

"Don't worry, you three," Amy snapped, "we've got it."

They heaved the fridge on top of the drawers and slid it over the doorframe, diminishing the roars and thuds coming from the other side. Frank turned back to Kev and Donna.

"Well?"

"Well, what?" Kev frowned. "They were armed. I waited for them to put their weapons down, but they didn't."

"They had a machete and a crowbar!" Frank snapped. "We were hardly in danger."

"You were standing in range of the machete, with your gun lowered. He could've hacked you before you knew what was happening. Then Amy walked closer, which meant two of you were within range."

"They weren't hostile."

"Oh yeah, they didn't look it either, brandishing weapons," Kev scoffed.

"They weren't," Amy said, stepping away from the barricade. "They were telling us about a community with over seventy people."

Kev frowned, glancing at Donna before responding.

"A community? Did they say where?"

"No, they said it's nearby and they'd show us."

"Sounds like a trick to me. You need to remember, civilisation has gone. There are no rules, no laws. It's survival of the fittest. Those two probably wanted your weapons."

"Well, I guess we'll never find out," Frank said. "You want to ease up on that trigger."

"It's not that bad when I'm saving your life, is it?"

"Just stop," Donna sighed, wrapping an arm around Kev.

"She's right," Amy said. "We need to decide what to do now."

"You mean sit around waiting to die isn't an option?" Frank sneered.

"I thought you wanted to save Lisa?"

"I do! But what hope do we have now? We're stuck in this shithole with zombies blocking the only way in or out."

"Ben said we could climb into the loft," Donna offered, glancing uncertainly at their makeshift blockade. The piled furniture shook with every strike, but not enough to topple.

"I don't care about escaping," Frank groaned, rubbing his eyes. "I care about how we're going to get in the prison now."

Nobody was forthcoming with any solutions.

"We're just going to have to take the place by force," he said.

Kev shook his head. "That's suicide."

"And what else do you suggest? It's your fault we're in this situation in the first place!"

"I know. And I'm sorry about that. But we can't go storming the place. It's a *prison*. We'd be dead before we got inside."

"Well, that's our only option."

"I can't agree to do that," Kev said. "I want to save them. Really, I do. But we're not dying in order to accomplish it. It's a fool's errand."

"He's right," Amy added. "We need to be realistic here. We're never going to get inside if we open fire on the place."

Frank growled in dismay, swinging a kick at the television, toppling it off the table with a loud clatter.

"We need to do *something*," Kara pleaded, glancing around the room. Kev sighed and leaned back on the windowsill, as the zombies in the hallway roared louder than ever.

"I don't suppose there was a tank at that army base?" Amy asked hopefully.

Frank shook his head. "We have fighter jets. If any of you fancy having a go at firing some missiles?" He looked around the room. "No?" He stared at Kev, who was looking through the sight of his sniper rifle out of the window. "What about you, big man? Know how to fly a plane?"

"No, he doesn't," Donna said.

"That's given me an idea, though," Ben said. "We could blow up the outer walls. Drive a car or a van filled with something explosive, right up to the side. Set fire to it, then *boom*."

"That could work," Kara gasped, her voice filled with hope.

"Yeah," Frank nodded. "We could have a look for some propane tanks. There must be a DIY shop or a caravan site or something near here, right?"

"Right."

"But which lucky sod is gonna drive it to the prison?"

Ben offered Frank a knowing look. "You're the one pushing for a solution. I've given you one."

"Oh, terrific, so I have to drive the bomb?"

Ben shrugged. "Why not?"

The group flinched as a gunshot thundered from the window. A roaring engine and the screech of rubber preceded an almighty crash outside.

"What the fuck was that?" Frank demanded, rushing over to Kev. He didn't get the chance to peer outside, as a series of gunshots shattered the windows. Kev lunged back, shoving Frank with him, as shotgun fire peppered the ceiling.

"It's a second chance," Kev beamed. "And I wasn't going to fuck up again."

Frank made to approach the window, but Kev stopped him.

"Not yet," he urged. "Just wait."

"For what?"

The gunshots sounded again, only this time they were aimed within the street. The yearning cries of the undead droned through the series of booms and cracks of shotguns and rifles. The thunderous assault on the door stopped, as the zombies in the corridor became preoccupied with the commotion outside.

"What's going on?" Ben asked, cautiously approaching the window.

"They've sent backup," Kev laughed. "And, more importantly, they're in another prison van."

The trio looked out at the carnage below. Frank immediately spotted the van, which had smashed into a parked car below them. A gaping hole in the windscreen revealed a blood-spattered driver's seat. The driver's remains were draped over the passenger side, where the door stood open. Zombies huddled around the side of the van, ripping organs and flesh from an unseen source at the centre.

Away from the van, three men retreated down the road, firing at the unwavering army that spilled out of the doorway after them.

"Shall we shoot them?" Ben was already unslinging his rifle.

"No." Kev placed a hand on the weapon. "Look."

The men continued their backtrack, unloading their guns on the roaring crowd. After a few seconds, one man hurled his empty rifle aside. He turned to flee, but ran straight into the path of his companion's shotgun. The blast almost severed him in half, and hurled his body into the path of the ravenous zombies.

"Shit!" the gunman bellowed. Some of the undead horde dived onto the grisly remains, while the others sprinted after the remaining two, who turned and ran down the middle of the road. Before long, they reached the end of the street and disappeared around a corner, with the majority of the undead close behind.

"Now's our chance," said Kev.

They quickly gathered around their barricade, listening for sounds in the hallway beyond.

"We can't be sure they're all gone," Ben whispered. He turned to Amy. "We'll move the stuff out of the way. You be ready to fire."

Amy pointed her rifle at the door as the others set about shoving the barricading furniture aside. Kara stood beside Frank, turning the handgun back and forth.

"What are you doing?" he asked.

"How do I see how many bullets are left?"

Frank took the gun and released the magazine. "You've got six shots," he said, sliding it back into place. "Make them count."

"Ready?" Ben asked. Frank rested the stock of the shotgun against his shoulder. He prepared for the worst, but when Ben swung the door open, all that greeted them was a gloomy hallway.

"Let's move."

Frank stepped through the doorway and into the darkness. The undead in the hall had all dispersed, allowing light to stream in from the open door below. Frank made his way down the stairs and outside.

The smashed prison van obscured one side of the road, but looking down the other, he could see there were no threats nearby. The rest of the group congregated behind him as he stepped past the van. Further down the road, the zombies continued to feast on the gunman, oblivious to the newcomers watching them.

"Let's get in the van and get out of here," Kev whispered, ushering them back into concealment behind the large vehicle. They gathered around the driver's door, which allowed a glimpse of the devastation within.

"Are you sure it can still drive?" Kara whispered.

"Only one way to find out." Kev eased open the door and reached for the ignition. The ravenous moans and the squishing, tearing flesh further down the road proved to be the perfect cover for the engine as it burst to life. Kev jumped into the driver's seat, disregarding the blood-soaked interior.

"Get in the back, quick."

The group edged to the front of the van, peering around the side, ensuring the road was still clear. The zombies continued their feast, unaware of the rumbling engine.

"Okay, get in," Frank ordered, opening the side door, allowing the others to jump in. He checked in the passenger side, greeted by the remains of the driver draped over the seat. Placing both hands on the man's shoulders, he yanked the corpse onto the street and took its place inside.

"You don't want to travel in the back?" Kev asked.

"I've spent enough time in a cell. Figured I'd ride up front."

"Suit yourself. Is that everyone in?"

Frank stuck his head out of the window, looking back as the side door slammed shut. The noise finally caught the attention of one of the feasting zombies. It looked up from the tangle of organs, its wide eyes regarding the prison van.

"Yep," Frank said, leaning back into the vehicle. "And the zombies have seen us, so let's move."

Kev pulled the van into reverse as an eager screech resounded behind them. He manoeuvred onto the road and floored the accelerator, racing to the end of the street where he took a sharp turn.

We're coming for you, Lisa. We're coming.

26

Gus approached the solid door that led into the interview room. It had been a while since he had last found himself in the small, contained room, but he could still remember the layout. After all, it wasn't hard: a table pressed up against a wall, with a chair either side of it, all secured to the floor to prevent any unruly prisoners using them to cause harm. But, as Gus stepped inside, he knew the harm that was about to be caused would surpass anything a table or chairs could create.

"Gus! Don't let the door close—no—no—" Carver dashed forward, but clasped his head in anguish as the door slammed shut. "You stupid prick!"

"What?" Gus asked, looking in surprise at the door.

"It's a trap! Henderson's locked us in here."

"Really?"

"Yeah, he must've found out we were going to kill him." Carver ran his fingers through his hair, his gaze directed at the ceiling. "Let me guess, he told you I wanted to have a chat?"

"No."

"Huh? How did he get you in here, then? He told me you wanted to speak to me."

"I do."

"And now we're locked in here. I knew that smarmy cunt was up to something."

"You can't trust anyone in here, can you?" Gus sneered, taking a seat.

"No. And right now, I don't trust *you*. Why aren't you more pissed off about being locked in here?"

Gus shrugged. "I came here to have a chat with you, and that's what I'm going to do. The fact we're stuck here is irrelevant."

"Irrelevant? You really are batshit crazy, aren't you?"

Gus shrugged. "Depends who you ask. My diagnosis seems to change with every person I kill."

"Oh, terrifying." Carver gave a mock shudder, an unrelenting smirk plastered across his face.

"I wasn't always this way. I had a wife."

"Really? And here's me thinking you were a poof."

"She was murdered," Gus continued, lost in a daze. "After that, everything changed."

"You became a lean, mean killing machine?"

"Precisely. I killed. I maimed. I inflicted as much pain as I could. It became an irresistible urge."

Carver slapped the table. "Yes! I knew we were cut from the same cloth. Pain's my kink, too. I get off on it. Hell, I can't get off *without* it."

"So I've heard."

Carver's smiled dropped. "Oh, you heard about your little tart, did you? Yeah, sorry about that. I know you wanted her to yourself, but I couldn't resist." He leaned back in his chair. "If it's any consolation, she was totally worth it. You've got a good eye."

Gus smirked, retrieving the blade from his pocket and holding it beneath the table.

"She had a cracking set of tits on her," Carver continued, "and the tightest pussy. Honestly, it was like a vice grip. Good set of pipes on her as well. You should've heard the screams. It's a shame you weren't there."

"Yeah," Gus nodded. "If only."

He brought the blade into view. A flicker of alarm flashed in Carver's eyes, rendering him silent. He watched Gus retrieve the box of matches from his pocket. He tipped them out onto the table, picked up the nearest one, and leaned back into his chair.

"Go on," Gus said. He turned the match around and began whittling the bottom into a point.

"What are you doing?"

"Just passing the time. So, you decided to kill her?"

"I would've kept her alive," Carver said, "but then she stopped screaming. I was ploughing away and all I got were moans. So I introduced a knife; that got her going again. Have you ever stabbed a bitch while you were fucking her?"

Gus shook his head. He placed the pointed match back on the table and retrieved another.

"Oh man, you're missing out. Every time I stabbed her, that pussy got even tighter! Then the grand finale came.

You need to try this, Gus. You pull their hair all the way back, then reach round and slit their throat while you're still inside. It's absolutely…." Carver closed his eyes, moaning in ecstasy, "…divine; the ultimate orgasm."

"Really?" Gus picked up another match.

"Yeah. She was flopping around like a fish out of water. I can't describe how good it feels. It's a shame it only happens once." He sneered, exposing dark, decaying teeth.

"I'll take your word for it."

"No, you don't have to. That blonde bitch is still up for grabs. You can have her if you like. My way of apologising for screwing your bird."

Gus lined up the pointed matches and picked up another. "That's very kind of you. But I think I'll pass. I don't get off on raping women."

"But you just said—"

"Killing. Pain. It's an irresistible urge—one I have to fulfil. But I don't get off on it. I'm nothing like you perverted fucks. I'm not a sexual predator. I don't cream my pants at the thought of rape. I don't kill for sexual gratification."

"Then what do you get out of it?"

"So much more." Gus grinned, placing another pointed matchstick on the table. He picked up the tenth when the door swung wide. Henderson strode into the room, carrying a toolbox and a shotgun.

"Henderson!" Carver spat. He jumped to his feet and made to rush the guard until the barrel of a shotgun stopped him in his stride.

"Easy, Carver," Henderson chided. "You don't want to be on the receiving end of one of these." He dropped the toolbox onto the table with a metallic clatter. "There you go, Gus."

"What's this?" Carver glared at the two. "Doing a bit of DIY? Or is something else afoot?"

"Oh, something is definitely afoot," Gus said, placing the tenth match back on the table. He aligned them neatly side-by-side and rose to his feet. In an instant, Carver slapped the shotgun aside and lunged for Henderson. His move caught the guard by surprise, but not Gus. As soon as Carver sprung forward, Gus grabbed the toolbox and smashed it over the back of his head.

Carver hit the ground with a thud, where he met Henderson's boot.

"Get him up," Gus snarled.

Henderson dragged him to his feet and hurled him into the chair. He tried to stand, but fell back when Henderson's fist connected with his jaw.

"Hold him," ordered Gus.

Henderson rounded the chair and held Carver in place as Gus retrieved a roll of duct tape from the toolbox. He yanked the tape, the shrill sound permeating the room as he wound it around Carver's torso. As if suddenly realising what was happening, Carver made another desperate attempt to jump up.

"Sit the fuck down!"

He jolted forward as Henderson's fist connected with the back of his head, but the duct tape kept him in place. A slurred noise escaped his lips, but he offered no further resistance as they secured him to the seat.

"There," Gus said triumphantly. "Now lean him forward. Place his hands on the table."

Henderson yanked Carver as far as his taped restraints would allow, gripping his wrists tightly, forcing his palms against the tabletop.

"Now, let's see what we have here." Gus busied himself emptying the contents of the toolbox. He retrieved a hammer and a handful of nails, before noticing a small box of fence staples.

"Aha." He picked up one of the curved nails, admiring its double-ended point. "These will do nicely. Henderson, spread his fingers."

Carver emitted a mumbled protest, trying to focus, but Henderson's unwavering grip kept his hand against the table.

Gus positioned a staple over Carver's finger, the metal points sitting on either side. "Hold still."

He hammered the nail into the table until it was flush with Carver's finger. Then he moved onto the next.

The first three went in without incident, but the fourth pinched his captive's skin. Carver hissed in pain as blood pooled around the injured finger.

"Gus…" Carver wheezed, finally finding his voice. "Please."

"Oh, don't start begging yet. Save that for later."

He moved onto the next hand where he hammered in the rest of the staples. Two caught Carver's skin, prompting further cries of pain. Henderson grinned, watching the show with a malicious stare. Once all the fingers were secure, Gus took a step back.

"Now then, how shall we secure your wrists?"

"Why not hammer a nail right through the middle?" Henderson suggested.

"You really are a sick bastard, aren't you?" said Gus. "I always knew you belonged in here with the rest of us."

"It's the least he deserves."

"Fuck you, Henderson!" Carver spat. "Gus, don't—"

"Relax," Gus scolded, picking up the duct tape. "I'm not risking you bleeding out. That'll spoil all the fun."

The harsh sound ripped through the room again as he wound duct tape over Carver's wrists, running long strips above and below, securing him to the table.

"There." Gus beamed, admiring his handiwork. "Now the real fun can start. Henderson, get out."

"What?"

"Out. Now."

Henderson looked crestfallen. He turned on his heel and marched to the doorway. "Do you want me to keep this door open?"

"No. Let's keep his screams in here, for now at least."

Gus waited for the door to close before turning back to Carver. Their eyes locked. The fear had faded from his gaze, replaced by a smug acceptance.

"Well, I've had a good innings," Carver sneered. "Go on, then, kill me and get it over with."

"Kill you?" Gus repeated. "I'm not going to kill you. I mean, you *might* die, but that's not my intention. It all depends on whether your body gives up."

Carver swallowed. "So, what are you going to do?"

"What I do best."

27

Kev peered through the scope of his rifle, sweeping it back and forth in the direction of the prison.

"There's nobody there."

Frank squinted at the distant building, but it was no use. They were parked so far away, the prison was a small speck, and any people in or around would be even smaller.

"Nobody on the roof, or just standing out of sight?"

Kev shook his head, adjusting his scope. "Nope. Nothing."

Frank scowled. What were they planning? Was it a trap? Had they found out they'd stolen the prison van? *No. How could they?* He thought back to the two men who had fled on foot. Even if they had survived, they would never have been able to get back to the prison before them. There had to be another explanation.

Frank jumped down from the van and walked around the side.

"Okay, we're here," he announced, stepping into the back, looking between all the cell doors which stood open.

The group sat in the individual chairs, all except Ben, who stood at the rear.

"But judging by the look on your face, it's not going to be as easy as we thought?" Ben readjusted his rifle, allowing him to lean against the back wall.

"No. Quite the opposite," Frank replied. "It looks *too* easy."

"What?"

"There aren't any lookouts. There's literally nobody outside at all."

"Well, that's good, right?" Kara said, from the cell closest to Frank. "Less chance of us being detected."

"I guess. It just seems… odd." Frank looked around at the uncertain faces peering back at him from each of the cells. "It's probably nothing to worry about."

"So we're going ahead as planned?"

"We go as planned. We'll drive up to the entrance. As soon as you hear the first shot fired, you all jump out and we storm that place. Agreed?"

The group nodded.

"Good. Let's do this."

***

"Miranda and I met in a cafe, of all places." Gus stared at Carver in the seat opposite him. He ran his fingers along the matchsticks as he spoke. "She was a waitress, a couple of years younger than me, and I was a young thug just starting to make my mark on the parish. I asked her out, she accepted. Six months later, we were married."

"Is this your idea of torture?" Carver said. "Listening to you ramble?"

"She hated the life I gave her: constantly worrying, always looking over her shoulder, afraid we wouldn't live to see tomorrow. I showered her with money, but she refused to give up waitressing." Gus grinned at the memory. "She was ballsy like that—always wanted to make her own way in life.

"Then, one day, a rival outfit found out about her: where we lived, where she worked—everything. And, to get at me, they locked her in the café and burned it to the ground."

"Tragic."

"Indeed." Gus leaned forward. "I found out who did it and ripped him to pieces with my bare hands. But it wasn't enough. Miranda was dead. Gone forever. Or so I thought... Today, I saw her again. The same dark hair, the same eyes. She was alive."

Carver's sneer faded. "Wait, you think that dark-haired tart was your wife?"

"I had the chance to make it up to her, to right all my wrongs, but you took that from me."

"Hold on!" Carver snapped. He tried to sit back, but the tape and nails kept his hands pinned to the table. "When did this happen? Your bird would be as old as you now. That slag I killed was early twenties, at most. It *couldn't* have been her."

"My only two pleasures in life were Miranda and torture. You've enjoyed one of them. Now, you can enjoy the other."

Gus rose from his seat, scooping up the pointed matches, and strolled around to the other side of the table.

"No, wait."

Ignoring the plea, Gus positioned the matchstick underneath the nail bed of Carver's index finger. He began to push.

"No!"

Carver's plea became a shriek of pain as the match slid beneath his nail. Gus smiled and picked up the hammer.

"Please!"

A swift strike forced the wood further into his finger, forming a rectangular mound beneath the flesh. Gus struck again until only the head of the match protruded beneath his nail.

"There!" Gus shouted over Carver's cries. "Only nine more to go!"

He repeated the procedure meticulously until all of Carver's fingers sported red matchheads at their tip. Some blended perfectly with the blood that trickled out of his nail beds. That was until Gus started to light them.

Carver's shrieks escalated in pitch as the flames scorched his fingertips, hungrily devouring the wood beneath his nails. He rocked in his seat, desperately trying to prise his hands free, but the crushing fence staples kept him pinned.

"You won't be going anywhere with those little digits stuck in there," Gus laughed. He reached inside the toolbox and retrieved a set of pliers. "Here, let me help you out."

Before Carver could protest, Gus pinched a finger in the pliers' crushing grip, and snapped it skyward. More wails of pain followed as he worked his way along, breaking each finger backwards at the point of the fence staple.

Carver breathed frantically, his eyes squeezed tight, spittle drooling from his mouth.

"I don't know what it is," Gus said, eyeing the ceiling in a moment of reflection. "But the sound of a tortured scream. It's... something else. You see, I'm an artist. A composer. You're my instrument. And together... Oh, the music we'll make."

Carver's eyes snapped open as distant gunshots sounded.

"Don't worry about that," Gus said, perching on the end of the table. "I arranged a little surprise for the boys. I found the zombies you were keeping in the seg, you little scamp." Gus wiggled one of Carver's broken fingers, prompting him to cry out.

"I know how it feels to be locked in those cells."

"You... let them out?" Carver gasped through gritted teeth.

"Not me. I had one of the youngsters do it. Gave him strict instructions to wait ten minutes and then release the hounds. I guess it's been ten minutes." Gus looked down at his watch. "Doesn't time fly when you're having fun?"

"You stupid bastard. You've killed us all."

Gus sneered, brandishing the blade once again. "Don't get your hopes up. *You're* not dying any time soon."

He grinned as the distant roars and cries of pain drew closer.

***

Frank scanned the prison rooftop as they raced on. It was still empty. No prisoners. No riflemen. Nobody.

"Something's not right," he said, his grip tightening on the shotgun.

Kev nodded, but remained silent as he pulled up in front of the entrance. He swerved the van around so the side door was facing the prison, then beeped the horn.

Frank took a deep breath, trying to steady his nerves. He knew a group of armed prisoners were probably going to come out, most likely removing the barricade from the door while they sat and waited. Yet, as seconds passed, a flicker of dread began to burn.

Something's wrong. They should be out by now.

Different scenarios formulated in his mind, everything from a zombie invasion to mutiny and mass suicide. Yet none of them proved beneficial to the prisoners within. Then his mind drifted to Lisa. None of them would benefit her, either.

"We need to move," Frank urged. He jumped out of the van and opened the side door. "Everyone out, now."

"What's happening?" Amy asked as she stepped out of the cell.

"Something's wrong. I don't know what it is, but I can feel it."

"Where's Kev?" Donna gasped, following Amy out.

"Don't worry, I'm here." Kev stepped into view beside Frank, his rifle cradled in both hands. "I think he's right. Something's off."

They stepped back to allow the others to exit.

"We need to stay on our toes," Kev continued. "Same plan as before. We go in, keeping the formation as discussed, and see what we're dealing with."

The group nodded, some checking their weapons, others staring with a steadfast determination.

"On me. Let's move!"

***

"Do you like nursery rhymes?" Gus asked, taking a cigarette out of his pocket and clasping it between his lips. He struck one of the remaining matches, sucking the hot smoke into his lungs before blowing it in Carver's face. "I asked you a question. If it wasn't obvious already, you disrespect me, you're going to be punished."

"No. I don't," Carver growled.

"Really? I do. I think they teach kids a valuable lesson from an early age. If only my dear mother had sung to me instead of beating me, I might've turned out better." Gus hoisted himself onto the table.

"Ring a Ring o'Roses taught them about the Great Plague. Mary, Mary, Quite Contrary, tells them about that psycho bitch Bloody Mary. Know any others?"

Carver ignored the query, distracting himself with the ceiling tiles. Gus took another drag of his cigarette. He waited, counting to three in his head, before pushing the burning end into Carver's hand.

"Fuck!" Carver tried to pull away, but it was no use.

"I've got one for you." Gus said. He retrieved a large pair of wire cutters and positioned them at the bottom of Carver's index finger.

"No, please!"

"This little piggy went to market!" Gus forced the handles together, creating a satisfying crunch that prompted Carver to scream louder than ever. His finger broke away, but remained in place beneath the staple as Gus made for the next one.

"This little piggy stayed home!"

He sliced the next finger off.

"This little piggy had roast beef!"

He severed the third finger, but it remained intact. He eased off the handles and snapped them together. This time the finger broke cleanly.

"This little piggy had—"

Gus stopped when he saw Carver had squeezed his eyes shut, tears streaming down his face.

"Oh no. No. No. No." He put the wire cutters down and retrieved the razor. "I'm not letting you miss out on the visual. That's part of the experience."

He stood behind Carver, running a hand through his hair. With his other, he dragged the smooth side of the blade over his face.

"For an artist to make music, he needs to make sure he tunes his instrument."

With that, he seized Carver's head, pinning it against his chest, the razor blade lingering over his left eye.

He began to cut.

Carver screamed as Gus sliced into his eyelid. The thin strand of flesh dangled down until he reached the end, at which point it fell into his lap.

"Now for the bottom lid."

Carver cried out again when the razor ran across the bottom of his eye. He jerked his head as the blade neared the bridge of his nose.

"Steady on!" Gus snapped, peeling the rest of the lid off his face. "I could've had your eye out there! Now, only two more lids to go."

He started to slice again, only this time, he dragged the blade through his cornea.

"Oops!" Gus sneered over Carver's squeals. "I'm such a butterfingers."

A translucent goo ran from the socket, merging with the blood running down his face.

"I think we'll forget about that one. At least you can still see out of the other." He returned to his perch on the table and picked up the wire cutters once more. "Now where were we? Oh, yes. This little piggy had none!"

***

Lisa eased the door open, glancing up and down the corridor. There was nobody there, but the screams and gunshots sounded close. What terrified her more were the ravenous moans. Her initial thought, upon hearing the carnage, was that Frank and the others were storming the prison in a rescue attempt. But now she could hear the yearning cries of the undead, she realised it was so much worse.

She held the gun in trembling hands as she scampered to the end of the corridor. With few bullets left, she knew she would have to use them wisely. But, as the screams echoed all around her, she realised they wouldn't be enough.

"What the fuck's happening? Where's your gun?"

The outburst came from the hallway to her left. Lisa crouched down and eased her head around the corner until she could see two frantic men further down the hallway.

"I don't know," one of them whimpered. "The zombies are inside. We need to get out of here!"

"You need to find a weapon. All I've got is this riot gun." The man held up a shotgun. "It's gonna do fuck all."

A squeal of agony sounded nearby, prompting the pair to snap their gaze in Lisa's direction.

"Fuck!" The man wielding the shotgun opened fire. Lisa jerked away. The rubber bullet ricocheted off the floor beside her. Not waiting for him to reload, Lisa jumped back into view and fired a shot into his chest. The shotgun clattered to the floor as the man staggered back into his companion. The remaining prisoner whimpered, lurching aside, allowing the dead man to fall.

"Hold it!" Lisa snapped, the handgun pointed at him.

"Please don't kill me." The man raised both hands, tears streaming down his face. "I don't want to be here anymore. I want to leave."

"You and me both. What's your name?"

"Dino."

"Tell me, Dino, which is the quickest way out?"

"The main entrance. That's the only way out."

"Take me."

Lisa motioned for him to turn around and walk ahead of her. With a parting glance at his fallen comrade, he obeyed. She kept the gun poised and maintained a significant distance behind him as he led the way down the hallway. The noise in the rest of the prison had subsided, with only the odd distant wail permeating the silence. If there were any zombies nearby, they weren't making any noise.

Lisa slowed down, increasing the distance between she and Dino, who had reached the end of the hallway. If there were any threats ahead, he would be in the line of fire, whether that came in the form of bullets or eager teeth. He peered around the corner, assessing the area for any danger before disappearing from sight.

"Hold up!" Lisa's heart quickened. She imagined him sprinting to the end of the corridor, or disappearing into a side room and out of sight. She dashed the last few feet to the end, at which point Dino came back into view.

"Are you crazy?" he hissed. "You're going to draw attention."

"Shut up. Start moving."

Lisa expected him to turn back down the corridor, but he remained rooted to the spot, his wide eyes looking past her. She turned, but knew what she'd see as soon as the screech echoed round the corridor.

The zombie sprinted toward her, squeaks of rubber from its trainers replacing its shrill cry. Lisa raised the gun, aware that Dino had fled in the opposite direction, but at that moment, it didn't matter.

She fired, the shot striking the zombie in the chest, but it didn't stop running.

She fired again. This time, the bullet struck above its left brow, sending it crashing into the floor. Lisa turned the corner behind her, just in time to see Dino reach the end of the corridor. He looked one way, but before he could check the other, a pair of undead inmates tackled him to the ground, out of sight.

His scream sent a chill through her body, yet she cautiously approached. She slid along the wall, conscious that more zombies could join the feast any second. Before long, the hunched backs of the two undead inmates came into view. Each ripped apart the remains in front of them, fighting over intestines and other organs. Lisa felt her stomach lurch when she saw Dino staring back at her. His wide eyes blinked. His mouth opened and closed like he was a fish out of water.

She eased around the corner and continued to slide along the wall, away from the two oblivious zombies. Once she was far enough down the corridor, she turned and dashed onward. An open gate lay ahead, with the main hall beyond.

***

Gus sighed heavily as the last tooth in Carver's mouth broke free in his pliers. He dropped the bloody molar onto the table, along with the rest of the teeth he had extracted.

"Phew, I'm goosed," he gasped, wiping the back of his hand across his brow. "It's alright for you, Carvs; you sit there and chill, eh?"

Carver bowed his head, allowing blood to spill from his mouth.

"You seem a bit deflated, son. Is something wrong?" Gus rummaged through the toolbox, checking for more implements of torture. When Carver didn't respond, he turned to face him. "Forgotten how I punish insolence? I asked you a question. Just because you're a gummy bear now doesn't mean you get to ignore me."

Carver remained silent, his head still drooped.

"Don't wanna talk anymore? Okay. I'm good with that."

He leaned forward and pried Carver's mouth open. He let out a weak cry as Gus gripped his tongue and yanked it as far out as it would go.

"Don't wanna talk anymore? That's fine by me." With a flick of his razor, he sliced the tongue from Carver's mouth and hurled it aside. "Devil's the man who says Gus Razor isn't accommodating."

He listened to the gurgling wails as he resumed rummaging through the toolbox.

"What to do next?" he muttered. "What to do?"

A powerful stench of urine drifted through the air, prompting Gus to snap his attention back to Carver.

"You've pissed yourself? Fucking hell, it's a good job there's a tin of spray in here." He pulled out the antiperspirant and squirted it in Carver's direction.

"There you go, son. Give you a bit of dignity back. Doesn't help with the wet patch, mind."

He glanced down at the man's sodden crotch.

"Although…" An evil grin creased his face as he picked up one of the remaining matches. "I could help you out there, as well."

Carver's dazed eye suddenly focused on Gus as he struck the match. The small flame became an inferno once he sprayed the deodorant over it. Carver squealed as the makeshift flamethrower engulfed his crotch.

"It feels like Christmas," Gus beamed, keeping his finger pressed down on the nozzle. The smell of scorched hair and flesh quickly filled the room. "A roaring fire. Chestnuts roasting. What more could you want?"

The fire rose up Carver's body, prompting him to scream even louder.

"Alright, I suppose it *is* getting a bit toasty in here." Gus hurled the canister aside and started booting the man's body. Carver rocked in the rigid chair, as each strike caused the flames to diminish.

"There," Gus said after the final ember faded. "You're as dry as a nun at communion."

Carver's head lolled to the side, his one remaining eye fading in and out of focus.

"Oh no. You're not going anywhere yet, sunshine." Gus reached over and slapped his face. "You think this is over? It's only just beginning. You wanted to know why they call me Gus Razor. Well… you're about to find out."

28

Frank stepped through the front doors of HMP Harrodale. Nobody was there to greet him like he had envisioned. No barricades blocked his path as he and Kev led the group into the well-lit foyer. The flickering overhead lights, coupled with the sun streaming through the door at their back, offered no shadows for their enemy to hide in. The room was empty, serving only to feed his trepidation as they slowly advanced.

"Which way?" Kev asked, maintaining his rigid stature.

"I don't know. I never came in through the main entrance." Frank nodded to the open gateway ahead of them. "But I can hazard a guess that that way leads to the rest of the prison."

"Okay, we need to get moving." Kev addressed the rest of the group. "Stay low, stay alert."

With that, they pushed on, stepping through the gate, single-file, onto the corridor beyond. That was when the first scream resounded from deep within the prison. The group stopped in their tracks.

"You were right," Kev muttered.

"Zombies," Frank groaned. "It's gotta be."

Kara whimpered behind them. "Oh my god, Abigail!"

Another scream echoed in the distance, followed by an ecstatic shriek.

"C'mon," Frank urged.

He dashed down the corridor, through another gated entryway, where they reached a flight of stairs.

"I recognise this bit," he told Kev. "That way leads to the main hall. And up here, there's a bridge that overlooks it."

"Going up might be our best bet, then," Kev replied. "It will give us an aerial advantage and be easier to assess the situation."

"Yeah, and easier for them to take potshots at us. We'll be sitting ducks."

"If there's been a zombie outbreak, I doubt there'll be many capable of shooting."

"If you say so."

Frank took the stairs two-at-a-time until he reached the top. The corridor beyond was empty, like the others. Only this one had received a makeover. The white walls were smeared red, with a bloody puddle in the centre of the corridor which ran to the next gate, as if a body had been dragged.

Frank stepped forward.

"Holy shit," Ben gasped from the rear of the procession.

"It's a bloodbath," Kara added, stifling a sob.

"Keep your heads together," Kev chided. "Remember our goal."

Frank heard Kev continue talking, but his words didn't register. He had reached the bridge overlooking the main hall and all of its gruesome contents. Whilst the sight of the huge gore-strewn space wasn't alien to him, having escaped via the same bridge a few weeks earlier, the extent of the carnage was far greater than he could have imagined.

This time, there were no dead guards, only a slew of dead inmates. None of them seemed to be intact, with various limbs, muscles, and organs scattered all over the floor. Their killers were nowhere to be seen—a minor relief, but one Frank was still unsure of. If they weren't in the hall, where *were* they?

A loud clatter sounded from one of the corridors below. He leaned over the barrier for a better look at what he thought was going to be his answer. But the figure that sprinted into view was the last he had expected.

"Lisa?" Her name floated from his lips, barely a whisper. She cleared a mass of limbs, pursued by a couple of undead prisoners who darted after her.

"Lisa!"

Frank's outburst coincided with an almighty roar from one of her pursuers and remained unheard as she darted out of sight through a doorway.

Shoving himself off the barrier, Frank sprinted across the metal walkway.

"Frank, wait!"

He ignored Kev, focused solely on catching up to Lisa before the zombies did. The metallic ring of his footfalls echoed around the hall until he reached the end, where slick, blood-spattered lino replaced the metal grates. He caught himself when his boots slipped beneath him, placing an open palm against the wall.

He glanced down the stairs ahead. Several corridors branched off at the bottom: one heading to the canteen, another to the seg, and the final one leading back to the main hall. The latter started to feel appealing. He would love nothing more than to get back outside and leave the prison of horrors behind. But first, he had to find Lisa.

Based on her direction of travel, there was only one place she could be heading, and it was a dead-end. He let out an agonised sigh, taking the corridor leading to the seg.

***

Lisa barged open a gate, finding another immediately blocking her path. It was a good job the prisoners had kept them all unlocked. If she had encountered any inaccessible gates whilst fleeing her pursuers, she would almost certainly be dead by now.

Not yet. She gripped the reassuring weight of the handgun and its three remaining bullets. If they caught up to her, she would have three chances to take them out. She swung the gate shut with an almighty clang and turned, finally taking in the area before her.

A row of cells lined one side of the passage, the doors of which were all wide. Outside one of them lay the corpse of a bearded man. His horrified eyes stared blankly at the ceiling, the only part of him that seem to be untouched. The rest of his body was a pulpy mess. Shredded fabric—the remnants of his clothes—littered the floor alongside chunks of flesh. His torso looked as if it had been folded inside out. His legs had been stripped to the bone. One trainer remained on his foot, the other lay nearby.

Lisa looked past the mutilated corpse and felt her heart sink.

The corridor ended at the final cell.

She was trapped.

"Shit!"

The first gate behind her swung open, slamming against the wall. The two prisoners bounded through, shrieking and snarling as they collided with the second, the only barrier between them and their prey.

Lisa raised the gun, but the swinging gate caught her hand, sending the gun skittering down the corridor.

She gripped the bars and pushed back.

The two men roared in anger, with one pressing against the gap, gnashing his teeth, his face inches from hers.

The gate eased open.

Lisa's arms shook with the exertion of keeping the men at bay. She needed to think of something, quick.

The shorter of the two zombies eyed her fingers wrapped around the bar. She repositioned, dodging his teeth, which slammed against the gate.

What can I do?

She scanned the corridor, looking for anything that could help her survive.

There was nothing within reach.

She fixed on the gun.

I need to make a run for it. If I can reach it, I can survive.

Her gaze drifted past the handgun as movement caught her eye. It was only subtle, and she wasn't entirely sure she had seen it. But she kept her eyes on the corpse, just in case.

It moved again.

"Shit!"

She looked away from the twitching remains, ignoring the fact they were starting to rise.

Three bullets. Three zombies. It's now or never.

The shorter zombie went for her fingers again, only this time, they left the bars entirely. Lisa whirled and sprinted down the corridor. The gate swung open, causing the undead prisoners to stumble forward and granting her valuable seconds. She stooped and grabbed the handgun, raising it just in time to blast a hole in the third zombie's head.

She hurtled over its crumpled form and turned, fixing the two remaining prisoners in her sight. They both scrambled to their feet, their incensed growls rising in perfect harmony until a bullet ended one of them.

She fired again, only this time, the bullet missed.

"Oh, fuck!"

There was nowhere to go, and as the zombie advanced, Lisa knew she only had one option. The cell to her right was small and claustrophobic, with questionable stains on the floor. But it was sanctuary, a brief reprieve from her inevitable demise. She leapt inside and swung the door closed behind her.

The zombie roared in protest, mashing its face against the viewing compartment and slamming its body against the door.

Lisa took a step back, unconsciously shuddering with each strike echoing around the small cell. She glanced around at her new surroundings, the notion of being trapped producing a debilitating effect on her limbs. She was a mouse, lost in a labyrinth, pursued by a cat. And, like the mouse, she had inevitably taken a wrong turn leading to a dead end. Now here she was, waiting for death.

Maybe it'll stop. Maybe it'll get bored and leave.

The metallic thuds continued to ring around her, and, try as she might, she could not convince herself she would survive. She watched the zombie's frantic motions on the other side of the door.

Bang.

It leaned back, raising both hands above its head.

Bang.

This time it struck the door with its shoulder.

Bang.

It mashed its face against the viewing compartment, checking its meal was still there.

Bang.

It readjusted, slamming its entire body forward.

Lisa retreated from the door, backing up towards the far wall. She didn't know why, but creating that little bit more distance from the undead corpse felt reassuring. One step further from being ripped apart. One step closer to life.

Bang.

This noise was different. Not only did it thunder down the corridor, but it also took the zombie with it. Lisa blinked, unsure why she was now staring at an empty viewing compartment. She didn't have much time to contemplate anything else. Footsteps approached, and the door swung open.

"Frank!"

He rushed into the cell, seizing her in a tight embrace.

"You were shot?" her voice came out muffled as she pressed her face into the crook of his neck, attempting to hide her tears.

"Yeah. It's just a flesh wound. Are you okay?" He leaned back, appraising her injuries.

"I'm fine."

"Did they…?"

Lisa shook her head. "I'm just beat up. He was coming for me later."

"Who?"

"Carver."

Frank snarled. "That motherfucker. I'm going to rip him to pieces."

"I think Gus already has."

"What?"

Lisa remembered the peculiarity of Gus' behaviour, and the dead look in his eyes. "He's… different, now."

"Yeah? He's going to be dead when I find him."

"I don't think you should kill him."

"Are you kidding? He fucking shot me!"

"He didn't have a choice. If he hadn't shot you, chances are you'd be dead by now; we all would."

Frank's brows knitted as he contemplated her words.

"I've seen him shoot," Lisa continued. "He doesn't miss. He hit you exactly where he wanted—"

A gunshot caught their attention.

"We need to get out of here," Frank urged. "I'm guessing you're out of bullets?"

"Yup." Lisa glanced down at the handgun still held firmly in her grip.

"Okay, take this." He handed her the shotgun, retrieving his own handgun as he moved to the door, peering out to the hallway. An enigmatic howl sounded from afar, closely followed by more gunshots—a clear sign others were still alive. For now, at least.

"C'mon."

He led the way to the end of the passage, through both gateways and towards a blood-soaked corridor. Lisa was relieved to see it was empty. Despite the shotgun cradled in her hands, the notion of fighting through a wave of undead prisoners was one she did not want to face. Fortunately, the banging and wailing seemed to be coming from a distance. That was until a figure sprinted past at the end of the hallway.

They flinched, stopping in their tracks.

Had he seen them? He was running at such speed, Lisa only caught a glimpse of him. But the bloody shirt he was wearing, and the ominous growl, told her he was no longer amongst the living.

They carried on, weapons at the ready, warily eyeing the end of the passage, waiting for the man to step back into view.

He didn't come.

They reached the end of the corridor, with options to go left or right. Lisa looked up the left passage where the bloody figure had disappeared. It was shorter than the last, with doors sporadically spaced along both walls.

She turned to the identical passage on the right. The only difference was the stairwell that stretched up to the next floor at the end of the corridor.

"Which way?"

"That way leads to the main hall." Frank motioned to the passage with the stairwell. "But this way will take us around it and back to the entrance. There'll be fewer people down here."

Lisa looked back down the left corridor. "We already know there's one person this way."

She eyed the doorways, waiting for the zombie to emerge.

"This way is quicker. Trust me."

Lisa shrugged and followed Frank down the left corridor.

They walked through the prison without incident, stepping through gateways leading into room after room, but nobody was there. All the while, the guttural roars and occasional gunshots became fainter. Hope started to outweigh her trepidation, especially once she recognised areas she had seen before. They were getting close.

Another gated entryway led to a trashed room. There was the usual spray of blood, to which she had grown accustomed, with tables and chairs scattered all around.

Then she saw the man in the far doorway. Her fear returned, but she did not allow it to take over.

The catastrophic injuries to his face and torso told her everything she needed to know. She readied her shotgun, waiting for him to attack. Then an intrusive thought formed. One that kept her trigger finger at bay. One that caused her aim to falter. They were so close to the exit—to freedom— and had been fortunate enough not to encounter any zombies until now. But if she fired the shotgun, the noise would bring every undead prisoner running. The freedom they were so close to achieving could instantly slip into fantasy.

The zombie lunged. Frank's handgun cracked, lodging a bullet into its forehead. It crumpled to the ground, allowing passage through the doorway beyond.

"That's the trigger," Frank teased, pointing out the part of the shotgun.

A screech accompanied the sound of footfalls nearby. Any of the undead that had been idling nearby were now actively searching.

"And those are zombies," Lisa retorted.

She followed Frank into the next room and felt her heart soar. The bright overhead lights were now coupled with the radiant beams from outside streaming through the open doors. Lisa instantly recognised the foyer where she and Abigail had first been introduced to the prison. It had only been a few hours, but it seemed a lot longer.

"That's how I felt when I got out of here," Frank grinned, reading the look on her face.

A distant gunshot reached their ears, followed by a scream. "Ben!"

The voice belonged to Amy, deep within the prison. Frank's smile faded. Lisa knew what he was thinking. Despite all the pain, torture, and bloodshed, their ordeal was finally over. Now, here he was, contemplating going back in. Had the prisoner without a conscience finally been reformed? If he had, his timing couldn't have been worse.

29

Gus looked up as the door to the interview room swung open. Henderson rushed in, but judging by the look on his face, it was a decision he instantly regretted. He stopped in his tracks, examining the room in horror. Or was it awe? Gus couldn't tell. But what he could tell, as Henderson's eyes settled on his, was that a flicker of fear was now present behind the guard's steely blues.

"Gus… What…?"

Gus smiled. Henderson's blathering was almost reminiscent of Carver's, back when he'd had a tongue. He recalled cutting it out, but his memory was hazy at best. He was sure the organ was nearby, but from his position on the floor, he couldn't spot it. Gus leaned back against the wall, extending his legs through the bloody sea of entrails, bone, and other remains.

"Spit it out, Henderson. While we're young."

The guard blinked, escaping the crimson allure surrounding them, and fixed his eyes on Gus once more. "The prison is under attack. We need to move."

"Wow. That's awfully kind of you. Coming back for little old me instead of saving yourself."

"Yeah. Well, some of us have scruples."

He shuffled through the gore-covered room and extended his hand to help Gus up.

"Do me a favour. Scruples," Gus sneered, knocking his hand aside. "You'd upturn a cripple from his wheelchair just to rest your legs!" He got to his feet, wiping his blood-soaked hands on his trousers.

The gunshots sounded again, much more amplified now the door stood ajar.

"Those boys certainly have some fight in them," Gus said, kicking aside a hefty organ as he made his way to the exit. "I would've thought they'd be dead by now."

"Those aren't just ours," Henderson snarled. "Your lot are attacking the prison."

Gus stopped, turning on the guard with wide eyes. "Aha! So that's why you came for me; you want me to stop them killing you. Scruples my arse."

The corridor beyond was empty, but with rapid footfalls sounding nearby, it wouldn't be that way for long.

"Well, I hate to disappoint you, Henderson," Gus continued, "but they're just as likely to kill me. You should've legged it when you had the chance. Do you have a piece?"

"No, I gave it to you!"

Gus groaned.

"Don't tell me you've lost it," Henderson snapped.

"I haven't *lost* it. I know exactly where it is. I just haven't *got* it."

"Well, this is great. How are we supposed to survive without a weapon?"

"There's a good-sized femur in there," Gus said, pointing back to the interview room. "Perfect for bashing zombie skulls. Why don't you go and fetch?"

Henderson ignored the remark and strode to the end of the corridor.

"The first floor is a bloodbath." He edged round the corner, quickly assessing the area. "Our best chance is to go up."

"Okay. After you."

Gus followed Henderson along the passageway. His low, hunched stature, sliding along the wall, was an incongruous alternative to the arrogant, self-assured guard who relished in tormenting prisoners. How times had changed. Gus shook his head, unable to hold back a sneer.

"What are you laughing at?" Henderson asked.

"You. It's funny how the tables have turned."

"What do you mean?"

"You used to walk around like you ran this place. Look at you now."

"That's rich, coming from you."

"I *did* run it," Gus countered. "The difference being you're sneaking about like a little bitch, and I'm still walking with my head held high."

"In case you didn't realise, there are zombies all over the place, and your trigger-happy pals baying for blood. We're gonna be dead if we don't get out of here quick."

"Que sera, sera," Gus muttered. He followed Henderson around a corner leading to a stairwell.

Another gunshot sounded above them, but it was the growl further down the corridor that caught Gus' attention. An undead prisoner shuffled into view, gore oozing from his mouth. He fixed the duo with a hungry stare, but only Gus seemed to notice.

"Shit," Henderson hissed, backing away from the stairs. "They're on the walkway. We have to go back."

"You do you." Gus shoved past the guard. The growl he had heard down the corridor sounded again, much louder this time, as the zombie darted after them. "I'm going up."

He heard a yearning screech as he bounded up the stairs, with the guard hot on his heels. He knew he'd be safe. If the zombie did catch up, it would take Henderson out first. But what concerned him was the distinct murmur of conversation, which became clearer as he reached the top.

Gus emerged onto the next floor, immediately catching sight of an armed group only a few feet ahead. They raised their weapons, but he darted to the side behind a large pillar.

"Don't shoot!" he called.

Next came Henderson. Gus wondered briefly whether they would heed his plea, or whether they would riddle the guard with bullets before he even caught sight of them. A second passed without gunfire, allowing Henderson to appraise the scene and leap towards the same refuge as Gus.

Finally, the zombie dashed into view. Its wild eyes and bloodthirsty grin served as a trigger to the group, who immediately opened fire. The corpse fell back down the stairs, vanishing from sight.

"Come out!" a deep, authoritative voice commanded. Gus shared a glance with Henderson and nodded.

"Don't shoot," he repeated, raising both hands as he stepped onto the walkway. "We're unarmed."

The large, bearded figure at the front held a huge rifle— The sniper that had saved Frank and Zielinski. Gus looked for them amongst the others, but he couldn't see them.

"You're the one who abducted two of our party," the sniper growled. "The one who shot Frank."

At mention of his name, Gus expected Frank to step into view. He glanced at each gun pointing at him, and the face above it, but he didn't recognise any of them.

"Where's Abigail?" a young woman demanded, stepping forward.

She was the one he had met earlier that day. The one with Miranda. Memories of his dead wife swam through his mind, leaving a trail of grief in their wake. His sorrow must have been evident.

The woman cupped her nose and mouth, emitting a horrible sob that prompted a brunette to drape her arm across her shoulders.

"What about the other one?" the bearded man demanded.

"Fucked if I know."

A sharp bang suddenly echoed around them before one of the gunmen hit the walkway.

"Ben!" the brunette shrieked, dropping to the floor beside him as another bullet ricocheted off the metal railings. Gus looked down and saw a rifleman aiming up at the party. He fired again, his aim directed at the bearded sniper, who was already lining up his shot. The prisoner's bullet whizzed past them, but the sniper's shot hit home, obliterating the man's right-hand side, sending him hurtling into the wall.

A furore of screeches and roars came from the stairway behind them, prompting Gus into action. He raced forward, shoving the sniper aside, and leaping over the downed couple. The metal clang of his footsteps was accompanied by another. Henderson ran close behind him, sprinting to the end of the walkway.

Gus felt a flicker of relief. If the group tried to shoot them, Henderson would serve as a human shield. At least for the first bullet. He didn't dare chance a look back. Instead, he focused on reaching the other end unscathed. With only the clang of a single pair of shoes behind him, Gus was sure the others weren't following. He leapt through the gateway, followed by Henderson, who slammed the gate behind him.

"Fuck me, that was close," Gus wheezed. "Are you gonna lock that or what?"

"I don't have the keys."

"You're a fucking guard. How do you not have keys?"

"Carver took them off me. He said the boys weren't happy while the doors could be locked."

"Did you lube him up as well, or did you let him go in dry?" Gus sneered. He turned away and started down the corridor.

"Fuck you, Gus," Henderson snapped, stomping after him. "You don't know what it's like."

"What? To be oppressed by a power-hungry wannabe? No, Henderson, none of us have any experience of that. Not in good old HMP Harrodale."

"Oppressed," Henderson scoffed. "When did I ever oppress *you*?"

"Of course you didn't oppress *me*. You'd be wearing your bollocks for earrings if you ever tried. But you know fine well what you did to the others."

Henderson fell silent.

"It's good to see you get your comeuppance," Gus continued. "Karma's a bitch, after all. Now shall we get going?"

Henderson looked ahead at one of the closed doors. "No—uh—you go on. I'll catch up."

Gus followed his line of sight to the governor's office. "Oh ho, you have a key to that door, though, don't you? What are you stashing in there?"

"It's nothing."

"Nothing? Then why don't we go take a peek?"

"No. I don't think so."

"Give me the key, Henderson." Gus reached out his hand, prompting the guard to recoil slightly.

"Gus, I'm warning you."

"Warning me? No, I'm fucking warning *you*!" He took the razor from his pocket and yanked open the blade. "The door. Now. Or I can slice you into tenderloins like young Carver?"

With a reluctant sigh, the guard retrieved a key from his pocket and unlocked the office. He pushed the door wide. "After you."

"On your bike," Gus scoffed. "Get in there."

He shoved the guard into the office, his eyes immediately darting to the closed door to the side of the room.

"Open it."

"Look, Gus—"

"If I have to repeat myself one more time, I'm slicing your ears off."

Henderson looked at the blade and the closed door. His head drooped dejectedly, and he marched to the side of the room.

"Fine."

He swung the door open, revealing a sink, a toilet, and a bound woman sitting atop it. She wore a filthy blouse which looked like it had been white once, long ago. Her tanned legs were bare. She kept them clenched together, but Gus could see the side of her underwear—a similar faded colour as her blouse. She watched the pair with wide eyes, an inaudible mumble escaping the tape over her mouth.

"Ooh, you naughty boy," Gus said, leaning against the door frame. "You're banging on about being all high and mighty, and here you are with your very own sex slave."

"It's not like that."

"Bollocks, you're as bad as the others. Wait—is that Doctor Miller?"

Gus leaned closer, examining the visible features of the despondent woman. "Holy shit," he muttered, turning back to the guard. "I'm guessing this is Carver's *reward*? For your loyalty?"

Faced with Henderson's continued silence, Gus looked back at the doctor. Despite her insistence he was psychotic, and being the one who had initially prescribed him Solenian, he actually liked her. She had a warm, caring nature, and he had developed a good rapport with her over the years. Seeing her in such a state—bruised, beaten, broken—was a shock.

"Has she been here from the beginning?"

"Yeah," Henderson replied. "We were doing a sweep of the prison and she'd barricaded herself in here. Carver let me have her in exchange for continued loyalty."

"You're *worse* than the creeps in here—"

A shrill screech radiated from the main hall.

"We have to go," Henderson said. "Let's untie her. We can use her as a human shield."

"Funny, that's the role I saw you playing in this little endeavour."

He stepped forward, opening his razor, which prompted Dr Miller to shuffle as far back as her restraints would allow, a terrified cry escaping the duct tape over her mouth.

"Don't worry, Doc. I'm cutting you free."

"Careful, Gus. Make sure you keep hold of her. She's a bit of a handful."

Gus turned back to hurl a retort at the guard, but stopped when a handgun appeared against Henderson's temple. The doorframe concealed its wielder, but Gus guessed it was female, judging by the small hand encasing the grip. Then she spoke, cementing his theory.

"Don't move."

30

"You're okay, you're going to be okay."

Amy kneeled beside Ben, examining his blood-soaked hand cradled against his body. It looked weirdly distorted until she realised he had lost two fingers. Only a bloody stump remained where his ring finger used to be, while his little finger dangled limply beside his palm.

Amy ignored the exchange of gunfire, focusing instead on Ben's rapid breathing.

"Take deep breaths," she urged, placing her palm against his chest. She felt Kev drop beside her.

"Shit," he hissed, raising Ben's hand into view, and then the rifle he had been carrying. The metal beside the trigger had warped where the bullet had struck. He made to hoist Ben up.

"Wait. I need a bandage," Amy said. "Or something to stop the blood."

"Donna. Give us a bandage, hurry."

Kev took the rolled-up fabric from his wife and turned back to Ben. He lifted the little finger that dangled by a thin strand of flesh.

"What are you—?" Amy's words had barely left her lips before Ben's scream overshadowed them. She clasped a hand to her mouth, as Kev yanked the severed digit and dropped it onto the walkway.

"Are you fucking crazy?" she yelled, forcing Ben's hand away.

"It was a lost cause," Kev replied coolly. "Unless you're also a surgeon, there'd be no way to reattach it. It'll be easier to dress without it."

"Leave the first aid to me!" She snatched the bandage from him and draped it around Ben's hand. A dark circle immediately formed until she wrapped it a number of times.

"Here, hold your arm up like this."

She raised his hand into the air, applying pressure to the wound. Ben hissed in pain, squirming against the metal grates.

"We need to keep the pressure on it."

She looked past him, down at the hall below, where a pair of figures darted into view. They checked the area, glancing at the dead prisoner who had shot Ben, and then at each other. Finally, their gaze snapped skyward to the bridge. Their eyes widened, each emitting a longing roar, before sprinting through a doorway and out of sight.

She looked up at Kev. "Okay, help me get him to his feet."

Together, they hoisted Ben up, supporting his arms and shoulders. Donna reached down for Ben's rifle.

"Leave it," Kev ordered. "It's knackered. He's not going to be shooting any time soon, either."

Donna nodded and stepped to the front, her rifle propped against her shoulder.

"Which way did those guys go?" Amy asked.

"That way." Kev motioned to the open gate at the end of the walkway. "We could try following them. They might know a quicker way out."

"What about Frank?"

"He left us," Kev shrugged. "I told him we needed to stick together. He's on his own."

"Wait. Where's Kara?" Amy looked around. There were only two ways she could've gone, three if she included the large drop below them, but Kara was nowhere to be seen.

"She must've gone that way." Kev pointed to the open gate once again. "Let's get him out of here."

They started ushering Ben across the bridge, but he struggled free.

"I'm fine," he said, clutching his chest. He took a step forward, but started to sway.

"No, you're not." Amy draped her arm behind his back and hoisted his injured hand around her neck. "Hold on to the railing. We need to get you out of here."

They made slow progress across the bridge, all the while listening to the encroaching sounds of the undead. Kev and Donna waited for them at the end of the walkway, each aiming their weapon in a different direction.

Amy felt the bridge vibrate beneath her feet. The rattle of footfalls sounded behind her, accompanied by a shriek from the two zombies who had appeared on the opposite side of the walkway.

"Move!"

Kev raised his rifle, firing once Amy and Ben lunged into the railings. The shot thundered around the large room, accompanied by the rapid successive shots from Donna. Both zombies collapsed in a heap, the gunshots still hanging in the air. The impending silence was stolen by more feral whines coming from the staircase at the other end of the bridge. Ben and Amy reached the gates as the first zombie appeared.

"Let's move, Donna."

Kev waited for his wife to enter the corridor with Ben and Amy before swinging the gate shut. He opened and closed it a few times, sighing under his breath.

"It's not going to lock without a key."

He didn't wait for a suggestion from the others. Instead, he propped his rifle through the bars and aimed.

"Wait," Donna said. "I've got more bullets."

She placed the machine gun next to her husband's and opened fire. Every zombie that appeared quickly fell, scattering along the bridge like pebbles on a beach. When the last zombie had fallen, Donna took a step back. They all stared through the bars, waiting to see if any more would rear their heads.

Silence ensued.

"Come on," Kev said, clapping Ben on the shoulder. "Let's get him out of here."

"Do you remember the way out?" Amy asked.

"Yeah, it's down there." Kev pointed down the corridor—not only the route of their escape, but also the source of a gunshot, which suddenly cracked from one of the rooms.

***

"Easy now, sweetheart." Henderson held his hands up beside his head. "Think about what you're doing."

"I know exactly what I'm doing," Kara growled. "Now tell me, where's Abigail?"

"Who?"

Kara jammed the barrel into Henderson's forehead. "Don't give me that shit! You know who."

Henderson looked at Gus for support, but he wasn't going to give it. He was happy to see how the scene would play out.

"You mean the dark-haired girl?"

"Yes." Kara took a step back, the handgun still trained on the confused guard.

He shot Gus a perplexed glance. "You said her name was Miranda?"

As if suddenly aware of Gus Razor's presence, Kara glanced into the bathroom. "Get out."

Gus obliged, keeping the blade behind his back. He stepped into the office. Kara stood alone, the rest of the group nowhere to be seen.

"No backup?" he asked.

"I don't need backup. Go and stand behind him."

Gus nodded. He eased the bathroom door closed and leaned back against it. Once it had clicked shut, he made his way behind Henderson, ensuring the blade in his hand remained obscured.

"Where is she?" Kara repeated.

"How the fuck should I know?" Henderson snapped. "Carver took her. I had nothing to do with it."

"You were there! You could've stopped it."

"Let me tell you something, sweetheart. You don't stop somebody like Carver. If I had, I'd be lying dead next to your little friend."

Kara recoiled, as though his venomous words had lashed her face. "Where is he?"

"Carver?"

Kara nodded.

"Carved," Gus said, taking a step toward the desk. Kara's aim followed him.

"Don't move."

"I'm just getting a drink." Gus motioned to the unopened bottle of bourbon on the desk. "Do you want one?"

A series of gunshots in the corridor caused them all to flinch. Henderson took a step forward, but Kara regained her composure in the blink of an eye.

"Get back!" she snapped, training the gun on him.

Seconds passed, with the machine gun continuing to rattle outside. Gus took a seat in the chair, observing the showdown like a spectator at a sporting event. After a final burst, the gun stopped. The corridor fell quiet, allowing silence to envelop the room once more.

"I'm getting bored with this," Henderson sighed. "What are you going to do, kill us?"

Gus twisted the cap off the bottle, revelling in the mounting tension. Kara was in over her head. He watched her through the neck of the bottle as he took a swig, her eyes darting between him and the irate guard.

"You're not a killer," Henderson continued. "Your friend wasn't a killer. Imagine what she'd think if she saw you about to gun us down in cold blood."

"She needs revenge."

"Revenge for what? We've done fuck all. In fact, *he* ripped her murderer to pieces." He jabbed a finger toward Gus. "I'd say revenge has been dished out."

Kara shook her head, uncertainty clouding her eyes. "No."

Henderson growled, his irritation on full display. Gus knew he had reached his limit. The scene was about to end, and he knew how to help it along. He fingered the bottle cap, watching the tense exchange, waiting for the perfect moment.

"No, you two helped abduct her."

Gus flicked the bottle cap across the room.

"I can't let—"

The clatter caught Kara's tongue, and she looked back, allowing Henderson to make his move. He rushed her, pushing the gun aside and grabbing her throat. Kara yelped in alarm, trying to fight back, but it was no use. She fired off a shot, which punctured the wall close to the ceiling. Henderson quickly disarmed her and wrapped his arm around her neck.

"Well, this is a turn of events, isn't it?" He grinned. "This is what happens when you're indecisive, sweetheart."

He pressed the gun against Kara's head. She stopped struggling in his grip.

"Me, I know exactly what I want." He leaned in beneath the gun and licked her earlobe, causing her to squirm. "But first, let's get out of here."

He shoved her over to the open door, just as the rest of the group appeared in the corridor.

"Get back!" Henderson snapped, jamming the gun against Kara's head. He shoved her out into the hallway, his glare fixed on the group, who retreated a few steps.

"Let's talk about this," the bearded sniper said, holding out an arm as a warning to the others.

"We're not talking about anything," Henderson snarled. "In fact, you're already too close. Why don't you all back off?"

He looked from face to face.

"Now!"

Kara flinched at the outburst, but it prompted the group to shuffle back.

"Good." Henderson glanced back into the office to look at Gus, who remained seated behind the desk. He offered a supportive thumbs-up before taking another swig from the bottle.

"Right. Now we're going to get out of here. If any of you try to follow us, she's dead. If you so much as raise your guns, she's dead. Understand?"

"This isn't going to end well," the sniper warned. "Just let her go. I promise we will not harm you."

Henderson sneered. "You clearly don't understand what's going on here, big man. *I'm* in control."

Now it was time for the bearded man to laugh. Henderson frowned, pressing the gun harder against Kara's head, prompting her to cry out.

"Control," the man muttered. "You don't know the meaning of the word. Every operation I've ever led has required control. It needs planning, strategy, and tactics. I need to be in control of every variable, and that includes our kit."

"Am I supposed to be impressed?"

"Maybe. You see, it's not just my kit I need to keep tabs on, but my oppos, too. A good leader knows how many rounds each of their oppos has discharged and how many they have remaining. Like Kara's gun there."

Henderson's eyes flicked to the handgun.

"That's a Glock 17, which, funnily enough, also holds 17 rounds. When Kara was given it, there were only ten."

Henderson shook his head as the purpose of the conversation was becoming apparent.

"Up until she left us, she'd fired nine rounds. I know, because I was going to offer her my gun once she was empty. I wasn't in the room just now, but I *did* hear a firearm discharge, which sounded a *lot* like a Glock 17. Now, I'm not a betting man. But if I was, I would put everything I hold dear on that gun being empty. Which, if that's the case, would mean you've got no leverage at all."

Henderson smirked, his eyes flitting to the sniper rifle. "I guess there's only one way to find out."

He extended the gun, aiming it at the bearded man's face, and pulled the trigger.

Bang.

31

Frank kept the gun poised towards Henderson's back, tempted to fire another if he didn't go down. He took a few more steps down the corridor, with Lisa at his back, no longer requiring a stealthy approach. Henderson's gun clicked continuously as he pulled the trigger again and again. His grip on Kara loosened enough for her to break free. She shoved him aside, causing him to stumble into the office.

"You took your time," Kev said, once Frank and Lisa had reached him. "I thought you were never going to shoot."

"I just wanted to hear more of that bullshit you were spouting," Frank retorted.

"It wasn't bullshit. I knew it was empty."

"Yeah, right." He saw Ben supported by Amy. The contrast of the blood-red hand clasped against his shoulder gave his face a sickly pallor. "What happened to him?"

"He's been shot," Amy said. "We need to get out of here."

"Yeah, in a second. I've just got one more thing to do."

Frank turned into the office where Gus Razor sat in a swivel chair, his feet crossed over the desk in front of him, a dark bottle held against his lips.

"Frankie!" he beamed. "Good to see you back on your feet, son."

"Yeah, no thanks to you."

"Ah, you know I had no choice. These pricks would've killed all of us if I didn't take a pop at ya. Your tart would be a bit worse for wear 'n' all." He nodded to Lisa, who was standing in the doorway. "She'd be looking like a punched lasagne after all the boys in here had had a turn."

Frank felt the handgun tremble in his hand. He took a breath, trying to keep his rage at bay. Gus took another swig from the bottle and rose to his feet.

"You gunned down the Tash then?" he motioned to Henderson, who had squirmed onto his back. His raggedy exhalations escaped as he struggled to breathe, his trembling chest rising and falling spasmodically.

"Yeah. I made the mistake of leaving him alive last time. I wasn't going to do it again."

"He's lying on his back, putting pressure on the wound." Gus tilted the bottle toward him. "Might survive."

"I've got one more bullet."

Henderson's eyes met his. He tried to form words, but it appeared to be at the expense of his breathing.

"Lee…" he managed, trying to raise his head.

"Don't waste your breath, Henderson," Frank muttered. "You've not got much left."

"Y'know," Gus said, placing the bottle back on the desk. "I've always wanted to slice that moustache right off his face."

Frank scoffed, shaking his head as they watched the dying guard fight for each breath. After a few seconds, Gus spoke again.

"Anyway, Frankie. Whaddya say? Shall we let bygones be bygones?"

He offered his hand.

Frank closed his eyes, a thousand thoughts racing through his mind. He nodded, finally settling on one. "Yeah."

He raised his gun.

Bang.

Gus' eyes widened. He clutched his side and fell to the ground, blood pumping through his fingers.

"An eye for an eye, Gus. You taught me that." Frank stepped over him and grabbed the bottle of bourbon off the desk. He turned to Lisa in the doorway. She shook her head, lost for words. But Frank didn't need words, he needed to get out of the prison for the last time. He stepped past her, leaving her to stare transfixed at the two dying men in the office.

"Here you are, Rambo." Frank placed the bottle in Ben's good hand. "This'll help with the pain, believe me; I know."

"Which way do we go?" Kev asked.

Frank motioned to the end of the corridor. "By the way, I'm out of bullets. How many have you got left?"

"Enough."

"Good, you can lead."

He groaned as a fresh wave of pain pulsed through his wound. He grasped his side, surprised when he felt moist fabric beneath his palm. The blood had soaked through his shirt, forming a disc the size of a saucer.

"We need to get that bandage changed," Lisa said. He looked around and saw she had caught up to him.

"Need to get out of here first. I might end up with a lot more holes in me yet."

Lisa smiled, wrapping her arm around him.

They followed the winding corridor until they reached a flight of stairs, where they walked two-by-two, descending in silence, listening for any untoward sounds. When they reached the bottom, Kev turned to Frank.

"Left here and then on to the exit?" he asked.

"That's right. You didn't need me after all."

"Control, remember?"

They followed Kev through the meandering halls, stepping around fresh puddles of blood.

"I wonder how many are still alive?" Frank said, stepping over a trail of intestines.

"Hopefully, none." Lisa kicked what seemed to be part of a liver into the corner. "I'd prefer to face zombies over rapists."

They reached the final door—one that would lead into the foyer, and to freedom beyond. But there was something different this time. The room wasn't as clear, the beams of light interrupted by passing bodies.

"Looks like you're going to get your wish," Kev said, his focus fixed on the mass of zombies ahead. He swung the rifle over his shoulder, switching to his handgun. Amy released Ben, allowing him to lean against the wall. She stepped forward, rifle raised, along with Donna, who aimed her assault rifle into the room.

"How many are in there?" Lisa whispered, trying to peer past Kev's frame in the doorway.

"We're about to find out."

Kev led the charge, his handgun the first to fire, quickly followed by the rifles. The trio entered the room. A cacophony of shrieks, roars, and gunshots surrounded them, with countless bodies hitting the floor. Lisa stood in the doorway, appraising the slaughter. Her shotgun swayed left and right as potential targets came into view, only to be brought down by one of the three weapons ahead of her.

A new noise joined the furore. Frank groaned when he saw a pair of zombies appear at the far end of the corridor, attracted to the chaos. They growled, sprinting towards the prey ahead of them.

"Lise!" Frank called. "We're going to need that shotgun here."

Lisa turned just in time to see the first zombie near. She brought the shotgun up and fired, blasting the dead man into his mutilated counterpart. The pair fell in a heap, where they were blasted again. The shot brought with it an end to the turmoil. The ringing dissipated, leaving a silence in its wake.

Amy stepped out of the foyer with Kev and Donna in tow.

"Is everyone okay?" she asked.

"Yeah." Ben shoved himself away from the wall. "Let's get out of here." He shook his head as Amy approached. "I'm okay, honest."

"Told ya, that bottle will help." Frank clapped him on the shoulder as he staggered past, the pain in his side pulsing through his torso.

"Looks like *you* need some," Lisa said, allowing Frank to pull her closer. He wrapped his arm around her shoulder and they entered the foyer together. The stream of light through the doors revealed a sea of bodies scattered all around them. They walked onwards, careful not to lose their footing on a wayward limb or a slick, bloody surface.

"Is that all of them?" Donna asked.

"Looks like it." Frank was the first to reach the double-doors, and the first to taste the hot, clean air of freedom. The area surrounding the prison was desolate, as it had been from the moment they'd arrived.

"Ugh, thank god," Lisa sighed, running her fingers through her hair. "I couldn't stand another minute in there."

"Try five years," Frank muttered. The others joined them, a look of relief etched on their faces, all except for Kara. The young woman wore a mask of sorrow, one which Frank suspected would remain for some time.

"Okay, let's move out." Kev retrieved the keys for the van and pulled open the side door. He then made his way around to the front and jumped in the driver's seat.

"You came in a prison van?" Lisa laughed. "How did you bring yourself to get back in one of those?"

"By calling shotgun."

They watched as Donna stepped inside, closely followed by Ben and Amy. Kara remained still, her blank gaze looking through the van.

"Are you coming with us?" Lisa asked.

"What's the point?" Kara didn't look up. "I've lost Abigail. I've lost everything. What else do I have to live for?"

Lisa placed a hand on her shoulder. "You're still alive. You have *everything* to live for."

Kara looked at the ground, shaking her head forlornly.

"Look. I was with Abigail, right to the end." Lisa swallowed the fresh wave of sorrow, keeping her composure. "She told me about the promise you two made."

Kara's lip trembled, her eyes flooded with tears, and she dropped to her knees as an agonised wail escaped her.

There were no zombies in sight, but that didn't mean they weren't within earshot. Frank longed to voice his concerns to Lisa, but held his tongue as she knelt beside Kara.

"I failed her," Kara sobbed.

"Of course you didn't."

"I promised not to leave her."

Lisa sighed, wrapping her arm around her. "My dad once told me that promises can only be kept if they stay within the realm of possibility. And outside of that realm, they're nothing but words."

Kara wiped her eyes, a quizzical look on her face.

"You couldn't control what happened," Lisa continued. "You stayed with her right until the moment you couldn't. Then you did everything in your power to get back to her."

"And I failed. I always keep my promises. Every time."

"I know. She told me. She also told me you promised not to die."

Kara closed her eyes, fighting back tears.

"*That* promise is still in the realm of possibility—a promise you can keep. Do you know what Abigail's biggest fear was? It wasn't what those guys were going to do to her, it was what *you* were going to do."

Kara looked up, her tear-filled eyes fixed on Lisa's.

"She was worried you thought you had broken your promise to her, and you were going to die trying to right it. She wanted you to survive. More than anything. Come with us. For *her*."

Kara clasped her head in her hands. Her breath whooshed between her fingers until she wiped away her tears. She nodded and rose to her feet.

"Yes, let's do this." Lisa followed her up and stood beside Frank. He waited for Kara to jump into the back of the van before speaking.

"So, did your old man *really* say all that 'realm of possibility' shit?"

"Oh yeah." Lisa smiled at the recollection.

"Really? What was he, some kind of philosopher?"

"No, he was a pisshead."

Frank snorted. It was not the response he had expected.

"But out of all of his drunken ramblings, that's one that stuck with me."

"I'll take your word for it." Frank tried to laugh, but a jolt from his side robbed him of his humour. "C'mon, let's get out of here."

He approached the passenger side of the van and jumped in. The door behind slammed shut, indicating Lisa was on board as well.

"Are we all in?" Kev asked.

"Yeah, let's get the hell out of Dodge. I've been here long enough."

They veered away from the prison and back onto the road leading towards the woodland.

"You didn't seem in a hurry just now," Kev said.

"That's because Lisa was trying to stop that lass from topping herself," Frank replied.

"She that bad, huh?"

"She's just lost her other half. Wouldn't you be?"

Kev nodded. "I guess."

They approached a fork in the road. The van slowed momentarily until Kev opted for the right turn.

"Wouldn't it be quicker to go left?" Frank asked, peeling his sodden shirt away from his side.

"Six and two threes," Kev said. "Besides, we need to head back to Doxley so I can get the four-by-four. This thing would be shite going cross-country."

Frank scowled. "Why would we be going cross-country?"

"*We*?" Kev glanced at him. "I wasn't under the impression you were staying with us."

"We're not. Once we get back to the army base, we'll be going our separate ways."

"Then there isn't a problem."

Frank shook his head, turning his attention to the passing woodland in an attempt to distract himself from the throbbing pain. It didn't work. The trees racing past in a blur made him nauseated. But pondering where Kev's party would be heading certainly did the trick. He wondered what kind of off-road locations they were considering. The surrounding hills would provide a good vantage point, but that would not be practical without supplies. Or did they intend to head across the moors in search of another farmhouse? He had considered it himself before they had discovered the hotel—their very own Eden.

While the hotel was large enough to house all of them, his gut told him not to reveal its location. At least not yet. He was warming to Amy and Ben, but the police officer and his wife were still an enigma. Until he was convinced of their character, he knew he had to keep quiet.

32

"Here we are!" Kev's triumphant outburst split the silence, which had hung for most of the journey. That was fine by Frank. The pain in his side had become unbearable, and he doubted his ability to hold a conversation. His hand ached from applying pressure—something which may well have had a detrimental effect, given the agony he now faced as he readjusted in his seat.

They neared the upturned prison van, and the abandoned Transit parked nearby. The headless corpse of the broad man came into view—unmoved, with a coagulated pool of blood circling his neck stump. His female counterpart, however, had moved—and continued to move as they neared.

"Yikes," Kev said.

The woman's remains were sparse. Minimal flesh clumped around her neck and face. The rest of her body was a bloody pulp, with large portions of her skeletal structure clearly visible. At the sound of the rumbling engine, she dragged her eviscerated remains along the road, her wide, eager eyes fixed on the van. She reached out longingly as they passed, a guttural, breathy protest barely escaping the remnants of her lips.

"That's all you," Frank murmured. "They weren't a threat."

"You don't approach folk with a machete, looking to shake hands."

"No. But you don't have to blow them away, either."

"I was protecting my party."

"Itchy trigger finger, more like."

Kev glanced in the side mirror as the van slowed to a stop beside the police SUV. The street was deserted. The bodies in the road remained motionless as the doors swung wide—a clear indicator they *were,* in fact, dead.

"Okay, we're in Doxley," Kev announced as he slid open the side door. "Those who want to travel in a bit more comfort, go and jump in the four-by-four." He stepped back, allowing Donna to emerge, closely followed by Amy and Ben. Lisa was the last to step out, closing the door behind her.

"The young lass staying with you?" Kev asked.

"She just wants some time alone."

"Fair enough. We'll wait 'til you're ready, then follow you to the base."

Lisa nodded and approached Frank, holding the bottle of bourbon.

"What's this?" he asked.

"Courtesy of the three-fingered bandit." She motioned to the SUV, where Ben and Amy sat behind tinted windows.

"He told me to express his thanks, but insisted you needed some as well."

She handed the bottle over.

"Fuck me, he's had a good go at it, hasn't he?" Frank sloshed the liquid inside, suppressing a laugh which he knew would feel like fire spreading through his body.

"Go on, get in," Lisa insisted. "I'm driving."

"I'm fine."

"No, you're not."

"I can drive."

"No, you can drink. Now mush!"

She bundled him back into the passenger seat and walked to the front of the van. Frank took a hefty swig of the bourbon as she climbed in beside him, replacing his blood-slicked hand against his side.

"Christ, he's tall," Lisa muttered, adjusting her seat. "Did you two have a nice little chat?"

"Oh yeah, riveting stuff. We spent the journey discussing statement-writing and handcuffing techniques." Frank rolled his eyes, taking another hit of alcohol.

"Really? Well, when you've recovered from your gunshot, maybe you can show me what you've learned."

Their sanctuary floated into Frank's mind once again. Hot water, clean bedding, miles away from anything and anyone. Just him, Lisa and…

"Is that lass still coming with us?"

"If she doesn't top herself before then, yeah."

"Are you sure that's a good idea?"

Lisa started the van, checking the mirrors, ensuring they were still alone. "Why wouldn't it be?"

"What does she bring that can help us?"

Lisa veered out onto the road, retracing the route they had taken in the lead up to them being abducted. She checked for the SUV in her side mirrors before increasing her speed.

"Another pair of eyes, for one," she said. "We can't defend that place by ourselves. It's too big. I know it's not ideal, but I think we need to be realistic. There might be others out there, worse than those bastards in the prison. It's not only zombies we need to fear."

Frank thought back to the couple who had confronted them in the street. Their conversation replayed in his head.

"We've got a community. There's just over seventy of us, with more survivors joining every day. We've got a ready supply of food, water, and electricity."

"Where?"

"Nearby."

Frank turned his attention back to the bottle, that last tantalising word swirling around his mind.

Nearby. But where? Somewhere big enough to house seventy people…

He took a long swig. The liquid burned his throat, diverting his attention from his side.

A church? A shopping centre? A supermarket?

There were endless possibilities, each more viable than the last, but he knew it would only be speculation. They'd never find out. Not after Kev had blasted them to pieces.

"What's up?" Lisa asked, as they turned onto a winding country road.

Frank chewed the pad of his thumb. He considered telling her. But suppose she wanted to go in search of this 'community.' Suppose she wanted to invite them all to Eden. Then they really *would* be running a hotel.

"Nothing."

He spat the calloused flesh out the window and settled back in his chair. He guessed they were about ten minutes away from the base—more than enough time for him to finish the bourbon.

***

"How are you holding up?" Amy reached across and squeezed Ben's thigh.

"I'm not holding anything up." He raised his wrapped hand into view with a smirk.

Amy couldn't help but smile back. His ability to make light of such a traumatic injury made him even more endearing. "You know what I mean."

"I'm alright. That booze feels like it's taken the edge off."

"It hasn't helped with the dizziness, though. You were staggering all over the place out there."

"Ah, I've always been a lightweight." Ben laughed. He reached down and slipped his hand in hers. "Thank you," he added.

"For what?"

"For everything. I don't know what I would've done without you."

Kev made an indignant cough from the driver's seat, but didn't chip in. Instead, he focused on following the prison van as they neared the army base.

"I haven't dressed it yet," Amy countered. "But remember, when I'm cleaning it, it's gonna hurt."

"It's fine. They have loads of bottles in the bar. I'll just get absolutely blotto and I won't feel a thing."

"I'm guessing a couple of alcopops will do the trick, Mr Lightweight."

"So what's the plan after we've hit the base?" Kev called from the front.

"Once Ben's patched up, we can head back," Amy replied.

"Do you still want to go to the industrial estate today?"

Amy felt her stomach sink at the prospect. After the day they'd had, all she wanted was her bed. "No, I don't think that's appropriate, Kev. We need to rest more than anything."

"What about the fuel?"

"We'll address it when we need to. The cottage still has a supply. For all we know, that could last us weeks."

Kev remained silent, his attention fixed on the road.

"Yeah, she's right," Donna said. She smiled warmly when Kev glanced across to her. "We've been through a lot today. We'll go when we need to."

"We didn't visit the garden centre either," Ben said. "I was looking forward to playing Old McDonald."

This earned a snigger from Kev, who glanced back over his shoulder. "Losing some of those green fingers hasn't put you off, then?"

Ben shook his head. "Not at all. But my dreams of being a pianist are over."

An uncomfortable laughter filled the SUV as the prison van ahead started to slow.

***

The army base loomed ahead. *Just in time*, thought Frank. He tapped the last drops out of the bottle before hurling it out of the window. He readjusted his seat, wincing as he tried to take pressure off his side.

"Where's your Polish friend?" Lisa asked, as if suddenly aware of the man's absence.

"You mean the Lone Ranger? Fuck knows. Hopefully getting ripped apart as we speak."

"What happened?"

"He decided to go solo. Didn't want to 'risk his life for two tarts who're probably already dead.'"

"Ouch. Well, that hurts."

"Not as much as he will if I ever get my hands on him again."

"Is he not at the base?" Lisa asked, turning onto the winding gravel track leading up to the building.

"I hope not, for his sake."

"Was he there when you left?"

"I don't know. He disappeared."

"Spooky."

"He'll probably turn up like the rat he is. And when he does, he can get the same treatment as Gus."

They pulled up to the front of the building in silence, with the police SUV behind them. Frank knew she disagreed with his shooting Gus, but he was never going to let the former gangland boss get away with it, either. *An eye for an eye.*

He climbed out of the passenger seat as the others congregated outside. Ben staggered into view, holding himself steady against the frame of the car.

Lightweight, Frank mused, but he was conscious of his own inebriation. The world felt buoyant, and the pain in his side, despite still being intense, felt numb. He made his way up the stone steps towards the double-doors, with Lisa beside him.

"Better not be locked," he snarled. He shoved the doors, expecting to meet resistance. Instead, he stumbled forward, almost falling flat on his face as the doors swung in. He caught himself before hitting the ground, stumbling into the lone chair in the middle of the hall.

"I think it's open," Lisa said. "C'mon, let's get that dressing changed. Where's the first-aid kit?"

"In the bar," Amy answered. She stepped past, chaperoning Ben down the hall and through the door leading into the bar area.

"So, that other guy not around?" Kev asked, looking at the upper floors.

"Doesn't look like it," said Frank.

"I'm gonna go and have a look. And make sure this place is secure while Ben's getting patched up."

"You do you."

"Donna, are you coming?"

His wife nodded and followed him towards the staircase, leaving Frank, Lisa, and a despondent Kara, who appeared in the doorway.

"So, where's this better place you've found?" she asked.

"Shh!" Lisa held a finger to her lips, in case the others were within earshot.

"Sorry."

"We're going to head there as soon as we've got Frank patched up," Lisa whispered. "C'mon."

She led them to the bar, where Amy and Ben sat opposite each other at the pool table. The first-aid kit had been upturned in the middle, with the remaining bandages, bottles, and boxes strewn over the green felt surface. Ben's hand was outstretched, allowing Amy to gingerly peel away the sodden bandage. He hissed in pain.

"Sorry," Amy murmured, her focus on the bloody stumps where his fingers had been. "I need to wash it. This is really going to hurt. Do you want to bite down on something or…?"

Ben shook his head. "Just do it."

Amy gathered a bottle of saline solution and a roll of bandages.

"C'mon then, you." Lisa clapped Frank on the back. "Get your shirt off. Let's see the damage."

Frank stepped away from the bar and allowed Lisa to lift his shirt over his head. The bandage over his side was soaked in blood, without a single trace of the previously white padding. She peeled off the tape, exposing the raw wound. It hurt like hell, but Ben's sudden agonised roar drowned out any protest Frank was making.

"Fuck!" Ben slammed his fist against the table, almost falling off his stool as Amy dabbed at the stumps.

"Nearly done." Her soothing voice was lost amongst his tortured cries. Everyone looked on as she finished wiping down the wound and quickly bandaged it. Ben's outburst became a murmur, his breathing ragged as he placed his head against the pool table.

"Pussy," Frank said, rolling his eyes at Lisa.

"You'll need to clean yours, too," Amy said, looking past Ben as she continued to wrap his hand. "If the bandage is soiled, you'll need to wash the wound before re-dressing."

"Don't worry, I'll do it." Lisa reached over the pool table and picked up the saline solution. Frank watched her, curious about her sudden enthusiasm, until the liquid met his tender flesh.

He yelped in pain, batting her hand aside, and shrieked again when she brought it straight back.

"Pussy." Lisa smirked, gently pressing the gauze pad against his side. She unrolled a stream of surgical tape and secured it before giving him his shirt back.

Frank hoisted himself onto a bar stool, not wanting the others to see his trembling legs. The bullet wound would heal over time, but until then, he knew he would have to endure the clean-and-redressing procedure regularly— which was less than he hoped Gus had to endure.

Bastard, Frank thought. He eased back into his shirt, hoping the former gangland boss was suffering just as much as him. While he didn't know how much pain he was in, or even if he was still alive, what Frank did know was that he would never set foot in that prison again.

Epilogue

Gus lay on his back, staring at the flickering fluorescent tube fixed to the ceiling. He clutched the side of his abdomen. Warm, sticky blood plastered his hand and dribbled through his fingers. Beside him, Henderson's guttural wheezing continued, like a foot pump blowing up an airbed.

Why won't he hurry up and die already?

Because he's Henderson. The persistent fucker will outlive all of us.

Oh, you're back, then?

Back? I never left, Gustav. You *were the one who disappeared.*

What?

The task was beyond your capability. So, I took over for a while.

What task?

Revenge for Miranda, of course. You don't remember?

Gus thought back to the interview room. The screaming, the pain, the blood. It was all there, but out of sync. Various seconds interwoven into minutes of incomprehensible flashback.

You took over.

I told you your resolve was weakening. All you had to do was listen to my input. To take action when I suggested. But you ignored me. Cast me aside like some lecherous parasite.

Is that not what you are?

No. I'm you, and you are me. Remember? You can't get rid of me, Gus. If you're not going to do what I say, then I'll just do it myself.

Then why give up that control? Why not take over now?

We got shot. You don't think I'm going to lie there in pain, do you?

Gus grimaced. He heaved himself onto his hands and knees and slumped back against the desk. Henderson turned from his prone position onto his back, staring with wide eyes.

"Gus…"

"Shut up, Henderson. Just die already." He squeezed his side harder, trying his best to ignore the pain.

"Get Doctor… Miller."

That's not a bad idea, Gus. She can fix us up.

Fix me *up, you mean.*

Come on. Don't be like that. We've got another chance here. Go untie the quack and she can fix us.

Gus ignored the voice. His eyes remained glued to Henderson and that stupid moustache of his, which shuddered with each trembling breath. He reached into his pocket and opened up the razor.

"Gus… what… you doing?"

He leaned forward onto his knees and shuffled closer. Henderson tried to move, but in his weakened, dying state, all he could do was watch.

"Gus. Don't—"

His words turned into a scream as Gus grabbed his top lip and sliced into it. He worked expertly, despite the debilitating pain in his side, the pooling blood beneath the blade, and Henderson's breathless screams of agony. He ran the razor across the entire lip, prising off the moustache once he reached the end.

Henderson's howls continued, quickly becoming a frantic gurgle as blood filled his mouth. The absence of his top lip gave him a permanent grin, exposing all his yellowed teeth. Gus lifted the moustache up to the light. It almost looked like a furry slug, or even a leech.

Another parasite to join you. He shoved the lip into his pocket and placed the blade against Henderson's throat.

Yes. It's time. Kill him. Open his throat. Let his blood flow.

Gus applied gradual pressure to the blade until it sliced into Henderson's flesh. He pushed it deeper, feeling the tissue rip beneath it. Then, with a flick of his wrist, he opened the guard's throat, bringing with it a geyser of blood.

Yes! We did it. He's finally dead!

Gus ignored the voice and shuffled toward the door concealing the doctor.

Thank you, Gus. I can see this being the start of a beautiful partnership. What's next for us?

"We get patched up. We look for any survivors in the prison. Then we prepare for war."

Yes! Those bastards are going to regret the day they infiltrated our prison. Which one are we going after?

"All of them."

A LETTER FROM THE AUTHOR

Dear Reader,

Thank you so much for purchasing the latest instalment of *The Virus* series. I sincerely hope you enjoyed reading it. I have to admit, some of these scenes pushed me beyond my usual boundaries. However, I feel they were imperative for developing the characters, which will hopefully become evident in the coming novels.

The success of *The Virus* caught me by surprise, and I was overwhelmed with all of the positive feedback. However, embarking on a series creates new challenges. Statistically, it's even harder to get reviews for subsequent instalments—books two, three, and so on. Every review I receive is a massive help in getting the series noticed. Amazon prioritises books with lots of interest as 'recommended reading', so every little helps. If you would be kind enough to leave a review, I would be absolutely thrilled! Even a line or two with a rating will go a long way.

Without a *Host*, *The Virus* can't spread, so thank you again for reading!

Damien Lee

They didn't think things could get worse, but they weren't
ready for…

THE MUTATION

The past few days have taken their toll on Frank, but R&R
is not an option. Eden isn't quite the utopia he'd expected.
When they come under attack from zombies and humans
alike, difficult decisions must be made.

With the horrific events still fresh in their mind, Amy and
Ben finally feel safe in their secluded cottage. But that's
when things start to go wrong. The undead are getting
faster. They're smarter. They're mutating.

To make matters worse, something else lurks in the
shadows; something far worse than any zombie.

THE MUTATION: Book Three in the Virus series
is out now!

Printed in Great Britain
by Amazon

22231787R00208